FROM THE GRAVE

ALSO BY DAVID HOUSEWRIGHT

Featuring Holland Taylor

Featuring Rushmore McKenzie

Other Novels

FROM THE GRAVE

David Housewright

MINOTAUR BOOKS
NEW YORK

First published in the United States by Minotaur Books, an imprint of St. Martin's Publishing Group

www.minotaurbooks.com

Library of Congress Cataloging-in-Publication Data

Names: Housewright, David, 1955– author.
Title: From the grave / David Housewright.
Description: First edition. | New York : Minotaur Books, 2020. |
    Series: Twin cities P.I. Mac McKenzie novels ; 17 |
Identifiers: LCCN 2019051875 | ISBN 9781250212177 (hardcover) |
    ISBN 9781250212184 (ebook)
Subjects: GSAFD: Mystery fiction.
Classification: LCC PS3558.O8668 F76 2020 | DDC 813/.54—dc23
LC record available at https://lccn.loc.gov/2019051875

Our books may be purchased in bulk for promotional, educational, or business use. Please contact your local bookseller or the Macmillan Corporate and Premium Sales Department at 1-800-221-7945, extension 5442, or by email at MacmillanSpecialMarkets@macmillan.com.

First Edition: May 2020

10 9 8 7 6 5 4 3 2 1

FOR
RENÉE MARIE VALOIS

ACKNOWLEDGMENTS

The author wishes to acknowledge his debt to Hannah Braaten, India Cooper, Kayla Janas, Keith Kahla, Alison J. Picard, and Renée Valois.

And to my dear friend, Her Honor Judge Tammi Fredrickson. Godspeed.

FROM THE GRAVE

ONE

The young woman who identified herself as a psychic medium moved with almost absentminded confidence among the fifty people who had paid forty dollars each for a seat in the community center lecture hall with the hope that she might help them connect with a dead mother or father, uncle or aunt, a dead child—but no promises.

She was tall and slender with shoulder-length hair, high cheekbones, and amber-tinted eyes; if you met her at a party or in a club you would say, "You should be a model." Both beautiful and dashing. Even her name had a kind of au courant vibe—Hannah Braaten. At least that's what Shelby Dunston was thinking when the woman slowly strolled up the aisle toward where she was sitting.

Shelby braced herself. She had come with the hope of connecting with her grandfather, but now she wasn't sure if she wanted to. What would he tell her after all these years? "Sorry I died on your sixteenth birthday? Sorry that now whenever June eleventh rolls around your mother and father and aunts and uncles and cousins get sad and mournful?"

Hannah halted two rows from where Shelby was sitting, looked directly into her eyes, and smiled.

Okay, this is why I came, Shelby told herself.

Only Hannah turned her head and looked off toward the people sitting on her left.

"There's someone stepping forward," Hannah said. "A woman—oh, this one is a talker. She's talking a hundred words a minute—Yes, I hear you. Yes . . . please slow down. Okay, okay."

Hannah glanced to her right and then to her left.

"Alice?" Hannah asked.

No one responded.

"I'm sorry," Hannah said. "Alison."

A woman in her early sixties, Shelby decided, was sitting half a row away. She cautiously raised her hand.

"The woman who came forward, she's your mother," Hannah said.

The older woman shook her head as if she didn't want to believe it.

"People called her Chrissy," Hannah said. "But it wasn't short for Christine or Christina. Her real name was Chrysanthemum."

The woman clasped her hand over her mouth; tears appeared in her eyes as if someone had turned on a faucet.

Hannah clutched the right side of her chest.

"Okay, I feel that," she said. "Chrissy, I feel that. Alison, your mother died of lung cancer, didn't she?"

Alison nodded, her hand still covering her mouth.

"She wants you to know—your mother wants you to know, that she's sorry. She used to always have a cigarette in her hand. She used to wave it around when she talked, and she talked a lot, didn't she?"

Alison nodded some more.

"*Chrissy says she never went more than five minutes without a cigarette. She's making me smell it. C'mon, Chrissy, don't do that . . . She says she's sorry. She said that everyone smoked back then and that she didn't know any better. She's sorry that she left you and your sisters so young. She says—Chrissy, wait, too fast . . . She says you have to stop blaming yourself. She says—Alison, did you win a writing contest with an essay on the dangers of cigarette smoking?*"

Alison nodded her head. She removed her hand from her mouth and spoke softly. Shelby could barely hear her.

"*In the eighth grade,*" *Alison said.* "*The winners read their essays live on WCCO radio.*"

"*Chrissy wants you to know that she was very proud of you, not only for the essay but for the woman you've become,*" *Hannah said.* "*She wants you to know that you can't blame yourself for not trying harder to make your mother quit smoking and that she's sorry she didn't pay closer attention to your essay. But you have to remember that she was the parent and you were the child. She was responsible for you, but you weren't responsible for her. You would tell her, 'Don't smoke anymore, Mama,' and she'd say, 'Yeah, yeah,' and keep doing it anyway. That's her mistake, not yours. She says—oh, you have a daughter that's named after a flower, too. Poppy. You named your daughter Poppy.*"

Alison nodded her head vigorously.

"*Chrissy said that the poppy was her favorite flower.*"

"*I know,*" *Alison said.*

"*That's why you named her Poppy.*"

Alison nodded again.

"*Chrissy says thank you. And she says—wait—okay—she knows that Poppy is pregnant again. Things didn't go well the last time.*"

"*She miscarried,*" *Alison said.*

"Chrissy says not to worry about a thing. She says it'll go perfectly this time. Expect another baby girl. She says she's been watching over Poppy and—and she's been watching over you and your two sisters and your two daughters and your four nieces and nephews all these years and she's going to keep at it."

"I've often felt like she was with me," Alison said.

"She always will be, too."

Alison bent forward in her seat and began weeping. The woman sitting closest wrapped her arms around her; Shelby didn't know if they'd come together or not.

Hannah retreated back down the aisle and began moving up the next.

Shelby shifted in her chair, tucking her long legs beneath her the way she does. She was surrounded by multiple strings of Christmas lights, and they gave her a playful appearance, although she wasn't happy at all.

"Why are you telling me this?" I asked.

"So you know that she's legitimate," she said. "So you know that Hannah Braaten is the real thing, that she's not a phony."

"I don't know that."

"She knew Chrissy's name and that it was short for Chrysanthemum and that she died of lung cancer. She knew Alison's name and that she wrote the antismoking essay. She knew about Alison's daughter, the number of her sisters and her daughters, and the number of her nieces and nephews."

Nina Truhler was sitting next to me on the sofa in the Dunstons' living room, her legs tucked beneath her just like Shelby's. That's where the resemblance ended, however. They could swap their size four/six dresses, and had on rare occasions, yet while Shelby had shoulder-length wheat-colored hair and eyes the color of green pastures, Nina had short black hair and the most startling silver-blue eyes I had ever seen.

She leaned forward, retrieved a long-stemmed wineglass from the coffee table, and said, "Facebook," before taking a sip.

"I know you don't believe in an afterlife," Shelby said.

"I do believe in an afterlife," Nina said. "At least I want to. I want there to be a heaven because if there's a heaven than there's a hell and people like Putin and al-Assad and Kim Jong-un and the president will get what's coming to them. I just don't believe in ghosts."

"How can you not believe in ghosts? Your jazz club is haunted."

"Rickie's is not haunted, and I wish people would stop saying that."

"Your own daughter—"

"Erica was pranking me." Nina turned toward me. "That's what the kids call it, pranking?"

"Yes," I said.

"Erica was pranking me. She was pranking all of us. It was her going-away gift before she went off to Tulane University."

"I don't even know exactly what a psychic medium is," I said.

"A medium can talk to the dead," Shelby said. "A psychic can tell you what's going to happen a week from Thursday. A psychic medium can do both."

"If that were true, wouldn't they all be making millions of dollars betting basketball games in Vegas?"

"It's more personal than that."

"Besides," I said, "why would you care if I believe this woman—what's her name?"

"Hannah Braaten."

"What do you care if I believe that this woman is legitimate?"

Shelby cast a worried glance at her husband.

Robert Dunston was the best cop I had ever known—much better than I was. We started together at the St. Paul Police Department nearly twenty-five years ago. I retired to accept a reward on a rather ambitious embezzler—$3,128,584.50 before taxes—that a financial wizard named H. B. Sutton had more than doubled for me over the years. The plan was to give my father, who raised me alone after my mother died, a comfy retirement. Unfortunately, he passed six months later, leaving me both rich and bored. Meanwhile, Bobby stayed with the SPPD, eventually moving up to commander in the Major Crimes Division, mostly running the Homicide Unit. Still, Bobby didn't look like a cop while dressed in his Minnesota Wild hoodie and sipping a Grain Belt beer. He looked like a guy watching a movie that he already knew the ending to.

"Oh, it gets better," he said.

Hannah Braaten continued to move up the aisle.

"There are a lot of people who want to talk," she said.

A son who died of a drug overdose told his parents that they shouldn't blame themselves, that it was all on him. "I'm the one who messed up."

A man who suffered a sudden cardiac death while playing hockey with his brother admitted that he should have taken better care of himself and that his passing was no reason for his brother to give up the game.

"Who's Cornelius?" Hannah asked.

A young man in the front row stood up.

"I have your grandfather here," she said. "He says he's sorry you got stuck with his name; it wasn't his idea that your

father name you that. He says he hopes the money he left you in his will made up for it."

The young man smiled broadly and said, "A little."

"Your grandfather, he also says that when he passed he was in the hospital and you couldn't get there in time to see him off. He says he knows that you feel terrible about it. He says if he knew you were going to feel so bad he would have hung on a little bit longer, but your grandmother was calling him, so he had to go. Please know, Cornelius, that there's no reason for you to feel guilty. It doesn't matter to your grandfather. You were his first grandchild, and he loved you best of all, but you're not to repeat that to your sisters and cousins. He says you and he will get together in about sixty years and play dominos and watch baseball and everything will be wonderful."

Cornelius started sobbing uncontrollably as the woman next to him attempted to comfort him by rubbing his back.

"She was very specific," Shelby said. "She didn't ask if the letter S meant anything to anyone or if someone had a grandfather who recently passed or anything leading like that. She knew exactly who was talking to her and for whom the message was meant."

"Okay," I said.

"Just so you know."

"Okay."

Hannah moved to the front of the small lecture hall again and started drifting to her left. She passed a young, serious-looking woman who was jotting notes on a pad fixed to a clipboard. She grinned slightly and shook her head like a professor might to a student in a lecture hall who was keen on recording every word the instructor said without considering what they meant.

"A woman—oh, she is so very pretty," Hannah said. "She wants—Ryan, are you here?"

In the back of the room a man stood. Shelby placed him in his late thirties. He looked like he had worked out every day of his life.

"My name is Ryan," he said.

"Your mother died when you were twelve years old."

"Yes," Ryan said.

"Her name was Judith," Hannah said.

"Yes."

"People called her Judy."

"Yes."

"She wants you to know—wait. There's someone pushing past her. Someone—he won't tell me his name. He, he, he won't—he doesn't, he doesn't have positive energy, it's all black. He was kinda mean. Cruel even. Narcissistic. He cared only about himself. Yes, I mean you. Who do you think—he's pushing the woman away. He wants—he keeps repeating numbers. One one eight eight zero zero four one. I don't know what that means. He keeps repeating them. One one eight eight zero zero four one. Does anyone know . . . ?"

"That's me," Ryan said.

"You?"

"I'm one one eight eight zero zero four one."

"I don't know what that means. Oh."

Hannah brought her hand to her head.

"Oh God, that hurts," she said. "Something about his head." She brought her other hand to her head, holding it as if she were afraid it would fall off. "He hurt his head. I don't know how. He's hiding things. He's hiding . . . What? What is it?"

Ryan slid along the row until he was standing in the aisle. One slow step at a time he approached the psychic medium.

"Stop," Hannah said. "Stop it. Oh, that hurts, my head hurts so much . . . He's showing me something. He's showing— it's money. He's showing me money. A lot of money. Bags filled with money. Canvas bags with leather straps and a name on the bag . . . He won't let me see the name. He's hiding . . . Stop hurting me. He's repeating the number again. One one eight eight zero zero four one."

"I'm here," Ryan said. "Tell him that I'm here."

"He says the money is safe. He says it's all for you, it's all yours."

"Where is it? Where did he hide the money?"

"He won't, he won't—he won't let me see. He won't . . . My head hurts so badly. I need to stop this."

"No, please," Ryan said. "Tell me where he hid the money first."

"The woman—Judy—she's trying to get past him, but he won't let her. He's showing me a brick. I don't know. Stubborn as a brick. I don't know. She's telling him to stop hurting you, that he's hurt you enough already but—the man, the man, he's not, he's not . . . A name. Now he's repeating a name. Oh, it hurts."

When he was talking about his mother, Ryan seemed like an average-looking guy, Shelby decided. A little more fit than most. Now he seemed almost crazed. As he approached Hannah, most of the people left their seats to move away from him. Hannah didn't seem to notice how close he got until he shouted at her.

"Where's the money?"

Hannah's hands came off her head, and she stared at Ryan as if she had never seen him before.

"*McKenzie*," she said. "He keeps repeating the name McKenzie."

"Wait, what?" I said.

"Who's McKenzie?" Hannah asked. "No, no . . ."

She was staring directly into Ryan's eyes when she brought her hands together and then flung them outward as if she were attempting to shove a cloud away.

"No," Hannah said again. "I'm shutting this down."

"Where's the money?" Ryan asked.

"I need you to leave. I need you to leave right now."

Ryan grabbed the woman by her shoulders and shook her. "Where's the goddamned money? If you think you can keep it for yourself . . ."

Most of her audience backed away or stood perfectly still. Shelby rushed forward.

"Leave her alone!" she shouted.

"That's my girl," Bobby said.

Before Shelby could reach them, however, a couple of guys, possibly prompted by Shelby's shouts, stepped in.

"What do you think you're doing?" one of them asked.

Ryan's response was to release Hannah, pivot toward the man, and shove him hard enough that he fell backward against the auditorium seats. The second man froze and, no doubt, began reevaluating his life choices. Shelby kept moving.

"Are you crazy?" she shouted.

Ryan looked at her as if he might be wondering the same thing.

He spun back toward Hannah, who was backing away from him.

"I'm sorry," Ryan said. "I—I don't know what I was thinking."

He turned and walked swiftly to the exit.

Shelby reached Hannah and wrapped her arms around the younger woman.

"Are you okay?" she asked.

Hannah accepted her comfort, yet only for a few moments.

"That happens sometimes." Hannah eased herself out of Shelby's arms and spoke to the crowd. "The dead are pretty much the way they are in life. Nice people are nice. Terrible people are terrible. They have nothing positive to say until they go to the other side and take responsibility for their actions, and sometimes it takes a long time for them to get clear of all that, depending on the extent of their sins. I believe we're made to feel everything that we made others feel. That's why some people won't go to the other side. They're afraid they'll be judged and punished, that they'll be held accountable. Some of them don't even know they're dead. But he knew . . ." Hannah's hand went to her head. "He knew. I'm sorry, but I think we need to call it quits for the evening."

People began filing out of the auditorium. No one asked for a refund; no one seemed disappointed that they didn't get their money's worth.

Shelby remained behind. She waited until they were quite alone except for the young woman still writing feverishly on her clipboard.

"Hannah," she said, "why did the dead man chant Mc-Kenzie's name?"

"I really can't say. Most people in our profession follow a code of ethics about the information we disclose . . ."

"You don't understand. I'm pretty sure I know McKenzie. I know him very well."

Hannah stared at the woman for a few beats as if trying to judge her honesty. The woman with the clipboard stopped writing.

"What's his profession?" Hannah asked.

"I have no idea what to call him now, but McKenzie used to be a police officer like my husband."

Hannah grabbed Shelby's wrist and squeezed hard.

"He's in danger," she said. "If you are really his friend, you must tell him, he's in danger."

"Why? What kind of danger?"

"The man, the dead man, he wanted Ryan to kill McKenzie. He said that he would tell Ryan where he hid the money, but only if he killed McKenzie first."

TWO

Nina took another sip of wine, then leaned forward and set the glass on the table. After she straightened up she looked at me and said, "It's always something with you, isn't it?"

"Me? How is this about me?"

"The dead man singled you out by name," Shelby said.

"There are plenty of people with the name McKenzie; most of them spell it differently. Bobby, remember the gypsy Ian brought to hockey a couple of weeks ago? He claimed that we were descendants from the same clan in Scotland until he found out I spelled my name M-C and he spelled his M-A-C."

"How many of *them* were police officers?" Shelby asked.

"I'm guessing a lot."

I glanced at Bobby for confirmation. He gave me what I referred to as his ignorance-apathy shrug, the one that said, "I don't know and I don't care." And I thought, He's left us again. At any given moment only half of Bobby's brain was fixed on the here and now. The other half was working a case. I was convinced he was thinking of Ruth Nowak, who was listed as a missing person, but who we all knew was dead. You don't wander away from your comfortable Crocus Hill home into an icy Minnesota winter night without your coat, without even your purse. 'Course, Bobby couldn't prove that she'd been murdered. Yet. Not without a body. Not without other physical evidence. But he knew. He also knew that her husband, Robert, who had proven himself to be very adept at giving teary-eyed interviews to the local TV news stations, was probably the one who killed her.

Shelby ignored her spouse. She lowered her eyes and spoke in the voice that she used when she warned her pretty teenage daughters about men. I had met her in college, met her, in fact, just a few minutes before Bobby had, and loved her every way it was possible to love a woman without actually touching her ever since. I knew when she was serious.

"McKenzie, last night I heard a dead man put a price on your head," she told me.

"A ghost," Nina said.

"Whatever. I would think, I would wish, that you'd be a little concerned. Do you think I'm making this up? Do you think that I'm pranking you?"

"No," I said.

She glared at Bobby. "Do you?" she asked.

"Hmm? No, but . . ."

"But what?"

"Honey, we've had this discussion before. I'm a law enforcement professional. I deal in facts. Facts you can see and hear and touch; facts that can be proven by science. Facts that you can take to court. What you're telling us, these are not facts, and even if they were, what do you expect me to do about them?"

"You, nothing." Shelby pointed at me. "But you . . ."

"What?" I asked.

"Don't you care that a dead man is threatening your life?"

"Okay, a couple of things. Thing one: I don't know that he's threatening my life. Thing two: What's he going to do? Hide my car keys? Drag chains across the floor of our condo?"

"Hardwood floors," Nina said. "He had better not leave a mark."

"You're missing the point," Shelby said. "It doesn't matter if you believe it. What matters is if Ryan believes it, or someone else that the dead man might contact."

Bobby waved his beer in his wife's direction. "There are a lot of nutjobs out there," he said.

"Excuse me?" Shelby said.

"I'm agreeing with you, honey. McKenzie, you should be careful."

Nina laughed. "I've been telling him that for years," she said. "Does he listen?"

"You guys are making fun of me," Shelby said. "I asked you to come over tonight so I could help you, so I could warn you, and you're making fun of me."

"We are not," I told her.

"What was the name of the embezzler that you collared?" Bobby asked.

"Thomas Teachwell. Last I heard he was alive and well and living in a cabin on Lower Red Lake, the same cabin where I caught him. He moved there after doing eight and two-thirds at Oak Park Heights."

"It needs to be someone who's dead," Shelby said.

"That doesn't mean I killed him, does it?"

"No, I guess not. Just someone you made angry."

Both Bobby and Nina laughed at the same time.

"That's a long list," Bobby said.

"Are you kidding?" Nina said. "Half the time he makes me angry."

"I'm at, like, eighty percent," Bobby said.

Shelby folded her arms across her chest and glared.

"Now you're making me angry," she said.

Something about the way her green eyes sparkled took me back to that day in college, to the party that we had all attended.

Dammit, Bobby, my inner voice said. *How different would life be if I had been the one who spilled that drink on her dress instead of you?*

"I'm sorry," I said aloud. I meant it, too. "You've always been my very good friend."

We all sat like that for a few moments, everyone staring at everyone else, until Shelby herself broke the silence.

"My mom wanted me to thank you again for the gift you gave her on her seventieth," she said. "She said it was the best birthday present anyone has ever given her."

"She's very welcome," I said.

"I have to admit, that was pretty clever," Bobby said.

"What gift?" Nina asked.

"My mother-in-law loves to go to the casino in Hinckley and play the nickel slots," Bobby said. "It's her chief form of entertainment. So, McKenzie gave her a hundred dollars' worth of nickels."

"It came in rolls packed in a box," Shelby said. "It looked like a big brick."

"It weighed twenty-two-point-five pounds, which doesn't sound heavy until you carry it for her," Bobby said.

Nina gave me a nudge. "You've never given me a brick of nickels," she said.

"I gave you a baby grand piano."

She dismissed me with a wave of her hand and a noise that sounded like the word "pooh."

"Really?" I said.

"All I can say—Christmas is coming. I expect you to step up."

It was cold when Nina and I left the Dunston house, the house where Bobby grew up. He bought it from his parents when they retired. It's also where I practically grew up after my mother died when I was in the sixth grade. I didn't have a family except for my father after that, and the Dunstons had all but adopted me. Or maybe I had adopted them.

The temperature had dipped to twenty degrees, which was about average for 10:00 P.M. in the Cities during the first week of December. There was no snow on the ground, though, and usually we'd have at least a foot by now. Some people were actually concerned that we might not have a white Christmas. I wasn't one of them. It was Minnesota, for God's sake. Snow was coming. It was always coming.

We climbed into my Mustang GT, which Nina had given to me on my birthday, thank you very much, and I started it up.

"Where to?" I asked.

"We could go back to the condo, set a fire in the fireplace, turn off the lights and get cozy on the sofa . . ."

"Hmm."

"And wait for the Ghost of Christmas Past to appear."

"A viable option."

"Or we can go to Rickie's and catch Davina and the Vagabonds playing their last set."

"They always sell out. Can we get a seat?"

"I know the manager."

Fifteen minutes later, we strolled through the front entrance of the club on Cathedral Hill in St. Paul that Nina had named after her daughter, Erica. Jenness Crawford met us at the door.

"Hey, boss," she said.

Nina held up her hands as if she were surrendering. "Don't worry," she said. "I'm not here to check up on you. We just dropped by to grab a drink and listen to Davina."

Jenness knew Nina's penchant for managing the club every minute of every day, which she'd done since she opened its doors twenty years ago, and said, "I don't believe you."

Nina hugged her manager's shoulder and glanced around. Rickie's was divided into two sections, a casual bar on the ground floor with a small stage for happy hour entertainment and a full restaurant and performance hall upstairs. The bar was crowded for a Wednesday evening, and the customers seemed to be in a festive mood. Perhaps the Christmas decorations had something to do with it. Our condominium had only a few, but Rickie's was loaded with them.

"How are things going, anyway?" she asked.

"See?" Jenness said. "I told you."

"Seriously, everything good?"

"We had another incident in the basement."

Nina stepped away and glared at her manager as if that were the very last thing she had wanted to hear.

"You asked," Jenness said.

"Let me guess, someone turned off the lights again."

Jenness held up two fingers. "Twice," she said.

"It's a problem with the wiring."

"Yes, ma'am."

"Rickie's is not haunted."

"No, ma'am."

Nina spun toward me.

"Do you have anything to say?" she asked.

"Not a word," I told her.

Nina went to the bar. She returned with a Rekorderlig, a hard cider imported from Sweden that she had become addicted to during our last trip to Europe, and a Summit Extra Pale Ale for me, and led the way up the red-carpeted staircase to the performance space upstairs. We found a tall table against the wall in the back of the room with fair sight lines and good sound and settled in.

Davina and the Vagabonds was a terrific blues band that combined Memphis soul with New Orleans charm. They channeled everyone from Fats to Louis to Aretha. Their best tunes, though, were the ones that Davina Sowers wrote herself— "Black Cloud," "Sugar Moon," "Bee Sting," "Sunshine," "Red Shoes." And no Christmas songs; thank you, Davina! As much as I enjoyed their sound, though, I couldn't shake Shelby's story out of my head. My mind began to wander.

Is there really a dead guy trying to buy a hit on you? my inner voice asked.

Stop it, I told myself. Listen to the music.

Bags of money—why is that familiar?

Where would you keep your money if you were a ghost?

A secret room inside a haunted house?

Sure.

How 'bout a haunted jazz joint?

During the pause between numbers Nina said, "Are you thinking about what that psychic medium said? That's kind of nuts, don't you think?"

"Yeah."

Still, while Davina and her band were cutting loose on "Shake that Thing," I slipped a pen from my pocket and started doodling on a napkin. Nina noticed and said nothing. She knew it was something that I did when I couldn't stand up and pace.

It was while Davina sang *I've got a feeling something ain't right, I don't know what to do,* that I wrote out the numbers one one eight eight zero zero four one.

The dead man was chanting these numbers, my inner voice told me. *And Ryan said it was him, that he was one one eight eight zero zero four one. What did that mean? Was this his Social Security number?*

No, a Social has nine digits, I reminded myself.

A passport?

A U.S. passport also has nine numbers.

A cell phone?

That's ten.

I kept running the pen over the numbers one at a time, doubling their size. I was starting on the second zero when I stopped and stared. The way the numbers appeared on the napkin, **1 1 8 8 0** 0 4 1, prompted me to add a dash so that it read **1 1 8 8 0**—0 4 1.

"Damn," I said.

Nina leaned in.

"Shhh," she said. "What?"

I lowered my voice to a whisper and said, "Every inmate sentenced to a federal prison is assigned a five-digit identification number plus a three-digit suffix. A register number, they call it. Anyway, the suffix is the code number of the district where the inmate was processed into the federal correctional system. There are a hundred districts. Well, ninety-eight, to be precise. The code for the District of Minnesota is zero four one."

"You think this Ryan guy that Shelby told us about was a federal prisoner?"

"Let's find out."

Rickie's had very good Wi-Fi, and it was easy for me to pull out my smartphone, access a search engine, and call up the website for the Federal Bureau of Prisons. The website included a Find an Inmate app that allowed anyone armed with the right names or codes to locate the whereabouts of any inmate incarcerated in a federal prison since 1982. It took me a minute because the screen was small, the keyboard was smaller, and I was all thumbs, yet I managed to type in the number and hit SEARCH.

About fifteen seconds later, I was told that Ryan Hayes, a thirty-nine-year-old white male, had been transferred a dozen years ago to the Federal Correctional Institution in Sandstone, Minnesota, a low-security prison for male offenders located about a hundred miles northeast of the Twin Cities, where he served the remainder of his sentence. The "Release Date" field indicated that he had been discharged from Bureau of Prisons custody last May.

Davina and her boys were swinging on "St. James Infirmary," one of my favorite tunes, when I leaned back in my chair, closed my eyes, and said, "That's an unexpected coincidence."

"What?" Nina asked.

Nina must have read the screen of my smartphone to get her answer, because a few moments later she leaned in close again and whispered in my ear, "Do you know this man, this Ryan Hayes?"

"We've never met," I said. "But I had dealings with his father, Leland Hayes. I'm the one who shot him in the head."

THREE

I knew it was me. Knew it the moment I squeezed the trigger. I didn't say anything, though, until ballistics confirmed it. When it did, I said, "I'm sorry." My colleagues wouldn't hear of it. It was a good shoot. A righteous shoot. Everything by the book. We even had dashcam video to confirm that the suspect had fired first. "You saved lives," I was told and put on administrative leave, which is what always happens when a police officer shoots a suspect. It was while on leave that I came *this*close to retiring from the St. Paul Police Department. Bobby and a few other officers talked me out of it. "You didn't do anything wrong," they said. Yet it felt wrong.

I explained it to Nina when we returned to the high-rise condominium that we shared in downtown Minneapolis.

The armored truck pulled into the asphalt parking lot directly behind the old Midway National Bank located on the southeast corner of Snelling and University. I say "old" because it was torn down years ago. You need to remember, this was long before they put in the Green Line, the high-speed train that runs down the center of University Avenue from downtown St. Paul to downtown Minneapolis; long before they built Allianz Field, where Minnesota United plays soccer. Still, even then it was probably the busiest intersection in St. Paul. There was a shopping center and a liquor store, an office building, several restaurants, fast-food joints and a couple of bars, a used-book store and the cars, buses, and pedestrians all that attracted. It was no wonder that the truck crew didn't notice the battered red two-door Pontiac Fiero idling nearby or the two men sitting inside it.

I never learned if the truck was delivering money to or taking money from the bank, only that somehow the back of the truck was opened and a guard grabbed two canvas sacks filled with cash. That's when one of the men jumped out of the Fiero wearing a black ski mask and white coveralls. He had a gun in his hand that he pressed against the guard's spine.

Words were exchanged along the lines of "Do what I tell you or I'll blow your brains out" and "Don't do anything stupid" and "It's not your money."

The guard dropped the sacks and his hands went up. The gunman forced him to his knees and snatched the cash bags off the ground.

At the same time, the driver moved the Fiero out of its parking space and stopped next to the truck. The car's trunk was opened and the gunman began tossing sacks of money inside it.

There were plenty of witnesses, some of them actually standing inside the bank and watching through the glass doors, yet no one moved to intervene. Again, all this took place before smartphones had become indispensible, something that everyone carried everywhere they went, and years before Myspace was invented, much less YouTube, Facebook, and Instagram. No one was shooting video that they hoped would go viral. I did learn later that one guy ran to a pay phone to call the police—remember pay phones? Anyway, he needn't have bothered, because the driver, who was safely tucked inside the cab of the armored truck, knew what was happening and sent out a call for assistance.

It came, as coincidence would have it, in the person of Officer Robert Dunston.

Bobby was working out of the Western District back in those days and was actually patrolling University near Hamline Avenue, about a half mile away, when the alert was issued.

He arrived on the scene with lights flashing but no siren. Because he came silently, the armed robbers were taken by surprise.

The gunman froze, staring as the patrol car approached.

The driver shouted at him.

The gunman tossed the last bag of cash into the trunk and slammed it shut. As he moved toward the passenger door, though, the driver stomped on the accelerator and the Fiero lurched forward without him.

The guard was now on his feet and trying to escape to the far side of the armored truck. His route took him directly in front of the small Pontiac. The driver didn't care. In his haste, he clipped the guard's legs and sent him tumbling across the pavement.

Bobby angled his cruiser to intercept the car. He halted, hopped out, and brought his Glock to bear across the roof of the patrol car, the car between the Fiero and the parking lot exit.

The driver of the Fiero turned sharply away and headed toward the exit on the far side of the parking lot.

The gunman began sprinting after it while shouting, "Don't leave me, don't leave me."

Bobby was smarter than everyone else even back then. He aimed his service weapon at the fleeing vehicle yet did not fire. There were far too many pedestrians in the area; there was far too great a risk that he might shoot an innocent civilian by mistake.

Instead of firing on the Fiero, Bobby trained the Glock on the gunman and ordered him to halt.

I don't think the gunman even considered shooting it out with Bobby, because I was informed later that he immediately tossed his weapon on the ground and raised his hands without being told to.

Bobby approached just the way that we were trained at the academy. He ordered the suspect to one knee, then to the second knee, told him to put his hands palm down on the ground in front of him, slide his legs back until he was lying facedown in the parking lot, and cross his ankles. He grabbed one hand, holstered his firearm, pressed his knee against the suspect's back, wound the cuffs around the suspect's wrist, swept his back looking for a weapon, ordered the suspect to give him his other hand, cuffed the second wrist, and swept the rest of the suspect's body for a weapon.

Unfortunately, all this took precious minutes. Midway National Bank was located close to the freeway. By the time Bobby was able to, first, call for assistance and, second, describe the fleeing Fiero complete with license plate number, God knew where it was. 'Course, it was only a second later that a half-dozen other patrol cars arrived at the scene.

Bobby pulled the black ski mask off the suspect and discovered that he had busted a seventeen-year-old high school dropout named Ryan Hayes and that Ryan was terrified out of his mind. He began weeping and shaking while Bobby read him his rights from a laminated card.

Bobby asked him who his partner was.

"My father," Ryan said.

"What's his name?"

"Leland Hayes."

"Where does he live?"

Ryan told him.

"The red Fiero, is that his car?"

It was.

Bobby decided right then and there that they were the dumbest criminals alive. But then, most of the criminals we met on the job were dumb. That's why they were criminals.

Sometime during all of this, the FBI was contacted. As far as they're concerned, robbing an armored truck is the same as robbing a bank—they like to make a federal case out of it.

The manhunt for Leland Hayes began in earnest. Again, this was a long time ago. There weren't as many traffic cams back then that they could access, so that didn't help the Feds find the Fiero. Units were dispatched to Leland's home and to his place of business—or at least his last place of business. He had been unemployed for months. He wasn't anywhere they looked.

It was while the Feds were working up a profile, learning everything they could about the man, that I came into the story.

I was working out of the Phalen Village Storefront in the Eastern District when the BOLO went out to the state, county, and local cops. What was it, my second year in uniform? I was cruising the mean streets of what they now call the Payne-Phalen neighborhood but back then was simply known as the East Side, miles and miles from the Midway Bank. I remembered thinking at the time how much I would love to catch the fugitives, if for no other reason than the pure joy of it. Especially if they were driving a Fiero. I had driven one once. It had a 140-horsepower V-6 engine with all the pickup of a vacuum cleaner. It was a very light car, and once you got it up to speed, it tended to float; it was like driving a kite. What's more, it ran hot and was prone to oil leaks. A Fiero would literally catch on fire. GM had stopped making them a decade before the heist, and yet this was the vehicle a couple of armed robbers chose for a getaway car. Amazing.

Hours passed, though, and no such luck. It was getting near the end of my shift. I was heading north on Arcade, which was also Highway 61. My plan was to drive up to Larpenteur, turn around, and come back down. That's when I saw it—a red Fiero.

I didn't do anything until I was about six car lengths back and could read the license plate. The number fit the BOLO. I called it in. While I was explaining the situation to dispatch, the suspect driving the Fiero started accelerating. Why he didn't see me sooner I couldn't say.

I hit both my lights and siren and started chasing.

"Four forty in pursuit of red Fiero north on Arcade passing Ivy Avenue East," I told dispatch.

"Four forty copy. Additional squads are being routed to your location."

So it went. I wasn't concerned with losing him; he was driving a frickin' Fiero. Yet I was very concerned that the suspect would slam into another car at high speed as we headed up Arcade.

We crossed Larpenteur, so technically we were in Maplewood, but I kept chasing. No one seemed to mind, later.

The Fiero abruptly turned off of Arcade onto a narrow road—Phalen Drive. I have no idea what the suspect was thinking. Phalen Drive ran between the Phalen Golf Course and Phalen Regional Park. There was no way to get off it until it reached Wheelock Parkway. I thought maybe he intended to stop and try to escape on foot, only there was nowhere *to run except onto the golf course or into Lake Phalen. I was about six car lengths off his rear bumper, too. It wasn't like I wouldn't be able to see where he was going, wouldn't be able to follow.*

Dispatch informed me that units had set up a roadblock at the intersection with Wheelock Parkway.

"Four forty, we'll be there in about twenty seconds," I said.

Except when the suspect saw what was in front of him, he hit the brakes and turned the Fiero sideways. Again, I had no idea what he was thinking. Was he going to try to drive across the lake? You know, they used to make cars that did that, amphibious cars. Maybe they still do.

The Fiero stalled, though. Or he turned it off. All I know is that the suspect hopped out and started shooting at the officers in front of him. I also turned my vehicle sideways, so that when I slipped out of the driver's side door the car was between me and the suspect.

Bullets were flying; I don't know how many rounds were fired.

I went into a Weaver stance, just as I had been taught at the academy, holding the nine-millimeter Glock with both hands, my right hand pushing out, my left pulling in, my shooting elbow slightly bent, my support elbow bent straight down, my feet in a boxing stance. I took a deep breath, released half, squeezed the trigger, and watched Leland Hayes's head explode.

The saddest part of all this—I didn't feel it, neither good nor bad nor indifferent. Not at the time. Later, I would experience some long, sleepless nights, but at the time all I could think was "Nice shot, McKenzie." Do you believe that? I didn't say anything, though. I think I was half hoping that someone else would take credit for it.

Anyway, time passed. The kid, Ryan, was tried as an adult

in federal court, charged with one count of interference with commerce by robbery. He pleaded no contest. His public defender argued at his sentencing that Ryan was forced to participate in the robbery by his father and presented a boatload of evidence proving that Leland was the worst kind of sonuvabitch who had abused and bullied his son ever since Ryan's mother died when he was just a little kid.

Only Leland wasn't there to be punished, so the judge put it all on Ryan. He said that this was a serious and alarming crime "because the armed robbers had targeted an armored truck guarded by armed guards, indicating a callous disregard for life." Plus, the guard who had been hit by the Fiero had suffered a broken leg, a broken pelvis, and a fractured skull, and although he was expected to recover, "the victim can't do the job he did before," the judge said. "This is a life-changing event for everyone involved."

Also, the judge reminded the court that the federal authorities had been unable to locate the money that had been stolen—$654,321, an easy number to remember. It hadn't been in the Fiero or Leland's house or buried in his backyard. The FBI tried mightily to track his movements during the three hours between the time he stole the money and the time I shot him, but they came up empty. They checked his credit cards to see if he had stopped to buy gas somewhere; they looked at his personal checking account. Nothing. They interviewed all the people that knew Leland, talked to his neighbors. No luck there, either. They simply couldn't find all that cash. Somehow Ryan was blamed for that, too.

"Armed robberies are cruel," the judge said. "They terrorize our businesses and our citizens, and must be met with significant sentences. This dangerous offender has sown violence and greed, and will now reap the full penalty for his criminal conduct."

Usually, the sentence would have run about ten years. The judge decided to make an example of Ryan and gave him twenty-five years and one month to be served at Big Sandy, the high-security penitentiary in Inez, Kentucky.

And I went back to the police.

Nina stared at me with such tenderness that I nearly started to cry.

"It's okay," I said. "I'm fine. It's—you know—it's just part of my life now. I've seen so many things, done so many—I don't even think about it anymore."

Nina didn't believe me.

She wrapped her arms around me and held me close.

"You and Bobby," she said.

Bobby? my inner voice said. *Like the vast majority of cops, that lucky sonuvabitch has never shot anybody. I doubt he's even unholstered his weapon more than a half-dozen times.*

"It's the life we chose," I said aloud.

"I'd remind you that you quit that life, but you didn't really, did you?"

"I like helping people with their problems. It got to be a habit with me."

"I know."

"Live well. Be useful."

"I know."

Nina took my hand and led me toward the master bedroom.

"Let's go to bed," she said.

But then she's always been kind.

Nina's kindness wasn't enough to get me through the night, however. Sometime before dawn I began to dream about Leland Hayes. Actually, it wasn't so much a dream as a reenactment. All the details were the same except that when I shot him this time, Leland did not fall. Instead, he turned and asked me what I thought I was doing.

"My job," I told him.

Your job, your job, your job . . .

Leland wasn't the only one to chant those words back at me. He was joined by a chorus of more than a half-dozen other men that I've killed over the years. Have there really been that many?

Your job, your job, your job . . .

I had never had this particular dream before, but I've had others like it. My psychologist friend Jillian DeMarais told me that I was displaying symptoms of PTSD and I should seek professional help, only not from her. We had dated at one time, and she hadn't cared for what was going on in my head back then, much less now. I never did see anyone, though. I mean, the dreams and other symptoms weren't *that* bad.

Your job, your job, your job . . .

"All of you," I shouted back. "You hurt people. You killed people."

What did you do?

"I made the world a better place."

They laughed and laughed until I woke up in darkness. I was shivering. It didn't last long, though, neither the darkness nor the shivering. The rising sun soon sent slivers of light through the gaps in our bedroom drapes, and that was enough to warm me.

FOUR

Later that morning I was sitting in front of my computer in the office area. Our condo didn't have rooms so much as areas— dining area, TV area, music area where Nina's Steinway stood. The entire north wall was made of tinted floor-to-ceiling glass with a dramatic view of the Mississippi River where it tumbled down St. Anthony Falls. The south featured floor-to-ceiling bookcases that turned at the east wall and followed it to a large brick fireplace. To the left of the fireplace was a door that led to a guest bedroom with its own full bath that Erica used whenever she was in town. Against the west wall and elevated three steps above the living area was the kitchen area. Beyond that was a master bedroom.

Nina stepped out of the bedroom and moved to the kitchen area, where she poured herself a cup of coffee from the French press that I had assembled. She was wearing a silky red night-gown that accentuated her curves and sparked my imagination.

"I like your outfit," I said.

"Really? Last night you couldn't wait for me to take it off." Nina moved to a stuffed chair facing my desk and sat with her legs tucked beneath her. She sipped her coffee and said, "What are you doing?"

"Just a little research."

"Such as?"

"I discovered that Ryan Hayes served eighty-seven percent of his sentence before he was released for good behavior. That's about average for federal prisoners. By exhibiting 'exemplary compliance with institutional disciplinary regulations' they can get up to fifty-four days per year knocked off their sentences. It didn't hurt that Ryan also earned his GED and some college credits while behind bars. Anyway, he served only twenty-one years, eight months, and ten days of his twenty-five-year sentence. What a break, huh?"

"Lucky him. What else?"

"The money, the $654,321, has never been found. You know *City Pages*, calls itself an alternative newspaper when actually it's all about promoting the Twin Cities club scene?"

"What about it?"

"It ran a story six years ago titled 'Lost Treasures of the Twin Cities.' The money taken in the armored truck heist was rated number six. Do you know what was number one? The gold bullion hidden by the bank robber Frank 'Jelly' Nash in 1933."

"That you found."

"That *you* found," I insisted.

"You found it. I only told you where to look." Nina took another sip of her coffee. "I can't believe how little money we made from that deal."

"I blame the IRS and the United States Treasury Department."

"Plus everyone else who was in on it."

"Jelly's Gold did gather a crowd. Anyway, according to *City Pages*, the money is still out there; they believe Ryan Leland knows where it is and intends to claim it."

"If that were true, he wouldn't have gone to a psychic medium."

I watched as Nina sipped some more coffee. Somehow she made the process seem sexy. But then I did mention the silky red gown, right?

"So what's your plan?" Nina asked.

"Plan? I don't have a plan. Why would I?"

"I was thinking about Leland Hayes putting a hit on you from the grave."

"I thought you didn't believe in any of that stuff."

"I think it's a load of hooey."

I smiled at the noun. Nina rarely cursed, and when she did you'd best pay attention. Instead, she employed a number of euphemisms that always sounded more colorful.

"Well, then?" I said.

"Shelby might be right. It doesn't matter what I believe or even what you believe. What matters is what Ryan Hayes believes, and apparently he believes that this whatshername, Hannah Braaten, he believes she knows where the money is or she can find out. That's why he reacted the way he did. Grabbing her, shaking her, saying if she thinks she can keep it for herself . . ."

"You want me to look into it?"

"I most certainly do not, but I figure you're going to anyway. That's why you're up early doing the research, isn't it?"

"Just curious," I said.

"Uh-huh."

I gestured at the computer screen.

"Hannah has a website," I said. "If the media reports and quotes from satisfied customers are to be believed, she is a very gifted young lady."

Nina left her chair and came around the desk so that she could get a good look at what I was gazing at. What she saw was a pic of Hannah Braaten sitting on a huge rock overlooking Lake Superior and appearing all windswept.

"I'll say she's gifted," Nina said. "Look at those eyes and cheekbones."

"Your eyes are prettier."

Nina pressed her cheek against my hair. "Thank you," she said. "I need to get dressed and head down to the club."

I called after her as she moved away.

"Need any help with buttons and zippers?" I asked. "Hooks and clasps?"

Nina grinned and gestured with her head for me to come along.

Ninety minutes later, Nina was heading for the door.

"Are you going to drop by later?" she asked.

"Who's in the Big Room tonight?"

"Debbie Duncan."

"I love Debbie."

"That's always been a prerequisite when we book acts. Who do you love, who can you flirt with?"

"Unfair. I didn't flirt with Davina."

"That's because her husband is one of the Vagabonds and he would have hit you with his trumpet."

"That is so accurate I don't even know where to begin."

Nina was chuckling when she stepped through the doorway.

"Let me know how the ghostbusting goes," she said.

I poured another cup of coffee, sat behind my computer, and perused Hannah Braaten's website some more. According to her origin story, "It wasn't until Hannah was fifteen and working as a model . . ."

She really was a model, my inner voice said. *From the pics on her website, I believe it.*

". . . that she began to realize that she could communicate with the spirits of those who have passed to the other side. Before that, she had suppressed her gifts, telling herself that the spirits she saw around her every day were products of an overactive teenage imagination. Once she fully understood that she could perform almost like a human telephone to talk with those who have passed on, however, she sought out professionals to help her develop and hone her gifts.

"Hannah put herself through an intense two-year training program during which she immersed herself in psychic classes. Afterward, like a great musician or athlete, she continued to train for ten years with professionals she trusted before she felt comfortable enough to share her gifts as a psychic medium and ghostbuster . . ."

They actually use the term "ghostbuster"? Huh.

". . . with the public. Today, she continues to study and expand her gifts even as she uses them to help others."

I searched more of the site. There were plenty of testimonials that spoke of Hannah's "insightful, sensitive, and thought-provoking readings" and how she was "right on target on so many levels." What it didn't have was a way to contact her directly. She had an email address for the media, an email contact form for her fans, and a PO Box number for people who still used snail mail, but no phone numbers or home address.

Maybe she can feel that you're trying to contact her, my inner voice said. *Maybe she'll call you.*

I took a couple of long sips of coffee before I decided that wasn't going to happen.

While Hannah's contact information was limited, I discovered that she did provide a calendar listing of all of her public appearances.

One was scheduled during the lunch hour that day at the Deephaven Room in the Minnetonka Community Education

Center in Excelsior, where Hannah was going to present an introductory class that would teach students to trust their instincts. It was called "Trust Your Instincts."

According to the class description, "Every one of us is intuitive. We have all experienced a feeling, a gut instinct, a sense of déjà vu, or a dream foretelling a future event. Hannah will answer questions about everything intuition-related and present exercises that will help you strengthen and fine-tune your intuitive abilities, as well as conduct gallery-style readings on spontaneously chosen audience members."

I glanced at my watch, which, in addition to telling time, counted the steps I took, the miles I walked, the calories I burned, and the beats of my heart. Right then my heart rate was higher than usual, but I blamed Nina. When I took a deep breath I could still taste the scent of her.

Excelsior is about twenty miles west of the Twin Cities. If you hurry, you should get to the community center at right about the time Hannah's class is breaking up.

Except Hannah's class went long. I found myself pacing the corridor outside the Deephaven Room while waiting for it to end. There were chairs in the corridor, and a handsome older woman was sitting in one of them near the door. She was wearing cheaters while reading her smartphone. Every once in a while she'd glance up at me and sigh as if she knew exactly who I was and why I was there.

The Minnetonka Community Education Center was one of those all-things-to-all-people institutions, which explained why its holiday decorations were all secular in nature; they wished their clients a Happy Holiday but not a Merry Christmas.

The center provided adult fitness and recreation classes, CPR and first aid training, an enrichment program that included art, computer, dance, financial, gardening, health, and cooking courses, music and driver's education, day care, and a preschool that included a playground where kids could play on equipment that was guaranteed safe by various insurance companies. It even hosted a LEGO League and a dodgeball tournament. Yet except for me and the woman, it seemed empty.

Finally, the door to the Deephaven Room opened to the sound of applause. The woman put away her phone and glasses and stood, draping her big bag over her shoulder.

People began filing out of the room. Some moved like they were afraid their illegally parked cars would be tagged and towed. Others lingered as if they had just enjoyed a particularly satisfying meal.

The woman remained near the door until Hannah Braaten appeared. I recognized her immediately from her photographs. Even if I hadn't she would have stood out, and not just because of her height. The woman moved quickly to her side, attaching herself to Hannah the way a bodyguard might as the younger woman greeted fans, shook the hand of anyone who wanted to shake hers, and paused for a few selfies. Seeing them standing side by side I noticed the resemblance. Mother and daughter didn't share the same height, figure, or eye or hair color, but those cheekbones . . .

I tried to stay out of the way until the corridor cleared, yet Hannah seemed to notice me anyway, glancing several times in my direction. At one point she stopped and stared for a good five beats. I wondered if the older woman had told her that I had been waiting.

A few minutes later, a couple of community center employees began preparing the Deephaven Room for whatever came next. Except for them and the older woman, Hannah and I were alone.

Hannah moved to my side. She was one of the few women I've met personally that was taller than I was, and I found myself looking up into her amber-tinted eyes.

She smiled and pressed her thumb and index finger tightly together.

"Bzzzzzzzzz," she said, then reached out and pinched my ear.

What the hell? my inner voice said.

I jumped backward. My hand went to my ear. The pinch hadn't hurt, but still . . .

Who does that?

"Bzzzzzzzzz," Hannah said.

She reached to pinch me again, only I deflected her hand.

Then it occurred to me that I knew exactly who does that, or at least who *did* that when I was growing up, and it caused me to stare.

"You're afraid of bees, a big guy like you," Hannah said. She added a "Tsk, tsk," just the way that Agatha Mosley had.

"I was stung when I was a kid," I said.

"I know, Rushmore."

You haven't told her your name.

"You were stung sixteen times after you thumped one of Mr. Mosley's hives with a football. Mr. Mosley was a bee-keeper and he told you to be careful, only you weren't. I say Mr. Mosley because Agatha says that's what you called him every day of his life."

What is going on?

"Agatha wants you to know that she's proud of you," Hannah said. "Proud of the man you've become. Proud of the way you help people."

I repeated the name like a prayer. "Agatha."

"She knows you're skeptical. She says that's one of the things she's always loved about you. Every time the Jarheads told you something in that we're-the-adult-you're-the-child tone of voice they used, you would ask why, and when they said 'Because, we said so,' you'd ask why again."

When she was annoyed at them, "Jarheads" was what Agatha called Mr. Mosley and my father, lifelong friends who had fought together with the First Marines at the Chosin Reservoir in Korea when they were practically children.

I glanced all around me and saw no one.

"Agatha is here?" I asked.

"Yes, but she can't stay. She says not to worry, though. Someone is always watching over you. You have so many guardian angels."

"Angels?"

"Agatha's gone now," Hannah said. "She hung up."

"Hung up?"

"That's how I think of it when someone from the other side breaks the connection, like they've hung up the phone."

"I'm very confused right now, and I don't like being confused."

"So you're pretty much like everyone else, Rushmore."

"Most people call me McKenzie."

"But not Agatha."

"No, never Agatha."

"Should we sit down?"

Hannah gestured at a few chairs grouped together along the wall. We sat. Hannah reached out and patted my knee. The older woman moved down the corridor a few yards to give us the semblance of privacy and fished her smartphone from her bag, but not her reading glasses.

"How can I help you?" Hannah asked.

"A good friend of mine was at a reading that you performed a couple of nights ago during which my name was mentioned. She said that a dead man threatened my life."

"'Spirit' is a more accurate term, although I use the word 'dead' all the time, too. We don't actually die, McKenzie. We pass on to a different plane."

"In any case, I found the news very disconcerting."

"I imagine you would. Don't be afraid, though. The dead hold no sway in this world."

"Ms. Braaten—"

"Hannah."

"Hannah, I don't know how any of this works. My entire database comes from a single episode of a TV show I watched once where some kid told a Hollywood celebrity that his mother loved him."

"What would you like to know?"

"According to my friend, you can talk to the dead—to spirits, excuse me."

"That's true."

"How?"

"It depends. Some of us receive messages telepathically. Messages are sent in the form of words or pictures from the spirit's mind to the psychic's mind. If they want the psychic to say the word 'coffee,' for example, they might show them a picture of a Starbucks, which is pretty confusing, if you ask me. With others, messages are sent through emotions and feelings. Spirits can make mediums feel depressed when they want to convey a message of sadness, or they can make their chests feel tight if they want to convey that someone had a heart attack."

Can he make you feel the pain of being shot in the head? my inner voice asked.

"The problem is deciphering the message, in presenting an accurate translation to the sitter," Hannah said.

"The sitter?" I asked.

"The individual for whom I'm giving the reading. There are plenty of charlatans who bring suspicion and discredit to the craft, of course. As for myself, I believe the greatest damage is done by honest and conscientious psychic mediums who make mistakes, who misread messages; who provide confusing readings or give the sitter information they don't want to receive. Intuition is not entirely different from singing karaoke, McKenzie. Some people are very good at it. Some are not. Yet we all believe in our own voices, don't we? I try to be very careful in that regard.

"Fortunately, along with those abilities, I can also see and hear spirits the way everyone else can see and hear someone they meet on the street. I can actually talk to them, carry on a conversation when they let me. Sometimes it gets complicated if the spirit isn't a very good communicator. Often I can hear them but it's as if they're mumbling, or it's like the volume is turned way down low. I can't always make out what they're saying, so I try to be cautious about what I pass on to the sitter."

"The dead man who spoke to you the other day—you had no difficulty in reading him."

"He was very clear in what he wanted done."

"But you didn't tell Ryan."

"Most of us follow a code of ethics about what we tell people. We try not to give bad readings; we try to ensure that the information given is positive even if the sitter is currently experiencing negativity in their life. A son wants to reconcile with the spirit of his mother, and she says she wishes the son had never been born? Why would I pass that on, make the son miserable? True story—a man who was diagnosed with cancer went to a psychic medium he knew personally, who was his friend, and asked if he would be all right. She told him the truth. She shouldn't have. It served no useful purpose and probably terrified the sitter. As it was, the man didn't speak to her again from that moment until the day he died. And what if she had been wrong? You can't lie, but sometimes it's better to withhold the truth."

"Including the fact that your father wants you to kill a man?"

"That, I have to admit, was a new experience," Hannah said.

"It's a first for me, too."

"I can't read minds, McKenzie, no matter what some people might think. I know why you're here, though. I knew you would be coming."

"Did Agatha tell you?"

"No, Shelby Dunston called. She'd said you'd show up eventually. She said you wouldn't be able to resist."

I don't know why I thought that was funny, yet I laughed just the same.

"We exchanged numbers after the reading," Hannah said. "Shelby was convinced that you were the McKenzie the spirit named."

"Circumstantial evidence suggests that she might have been right."

"What evidence?"

I explained.

Hannah rested a hand on my knee. "His name was Leland Hayes?" she asked.

"Yes."

"You killed him?"

"Yes."

"I'm sorry for you, McKenzie."

"Sorry?"

"It must be a terrible burden to carry, killing a man."

I was surprised by her sincerity, and the way I found myself gazing into her eyes probably revealed that. There was something about this woman . . .

"Sometimes it is," I said.

"The other man was his son, you say. His name was Ryan Hayes?"

"You didn't know that? The people who come to your readings, you don't know who they are?"

"I know the names of the sitters who come to me for private readings, of course. But group readings, gallery readings, no, I don't know who they are."

"They must make reservations, right? When they buy tickets."

"And leave their names so I can Google them, read their Facebook accounts, you mean? I don't do that."

"Never?"

"I've been called a fake before, McKenzie, and much worse than that. Many times in fact. Often to my face. I used to resent it. Now I try to shrug it off."

"I was being rude. I apologize."

"What do you want of me, McKenzie?"

"My girlfriend thinks this is all a load of hooey—"

"Nina Truhler?"

That caught me by surprise, and my expression must have shown it.

"Shelby told me," the young woman said. "Sometimes people talk to me like I'm a priest or an old friend that they haven't seen for years and years. They tell me things they would never tell even their closest friends."

"Truthfully, Ms. Braaten—"

"Hannah, please."

"Hannah, truthfully, I'm not sure what I think of all of this. It goes pretty hard against what I've been taught growing up."

"That there's no such thing as ghosts?"

"Something like that. I came here for two reasons. The first is to find out if I should be worried. It occurred to me, to me and Nina, since her name was brought up, that what we believe doesn't matter. It's what Ryan Hayes believes that counts, and he might believe that I'm standing between him and a lot of money."

"I didn't tell him what his father wanted him to do."

"The other reason, he might also believe that you know where the money is hidden. He might come back to get that information from you. If he does, I want you to feel free to call me. I might be able to help."

"Is that the truth?"

"Excuse me?"

"Are you sure that you don't want the money for yourself?"

I paused before I answered, partly because I was annoyed by the question. On the other hand, I had questioned Hannah's integrity. Why shouldn't she doubt mine?

"Pretty sure," I said.

"Shelby called you an adventurer."

"Did she?"

"She said you might try to recover the money just for the fun of it."

"No," I said. "Not this time."

"Is that because of what happened to Leland Hayes?"

I stood and looked down into her amber-tinted eyes. I decided I was right before—Nina's eyes were prettier.

"My offer still stands," I said. "If you need help with Leland's son, call me."

"Agatha said you were a good man."

"It's nice to be well thought of."

"I won't be calling you, though," Hannah said.

"No?"

"There are ethics in our profession about what we can share, like I said. I've already told Shelby Dunston, and now you, way more than I should have. My excuse with Shelby was that I was a little panicked at the time and that it had been a public reading, so the rules of confidentiality that we follow were already a little bent. With you—we're in kind of a gray area. Although I did tell Shelby to warn you, didn't I?"

"You did."

Hannah shrugged as if to tell me that she had no intention of making the same mistake twice. I glanced down the corridor at the older woman.

"Excuse me," I said. "Ma'am?"

The woman turned to face me.

"Am I right in assuming that you are Hannah's mother?"

The woman glanced at Hannah and back at me before nodding slightly.

I walked toward her. Hannah stood up behind me.

"Am I also right in assuming that you've been listening carefully to every word we've said?" I asked.

Again she shot a glance at Hannah before nodding.

I reached into the inside pocket of my brown leather coat and retrieved a wallet. Inside the wallet was an off-white business card printed with my name and cell phone number.

"My experience," I said, "mothers don't care nearly as much about professional ethics as they do about the safety of their children."

I offered the card to the woman. She took it without looking at her daughter.

"If she's in danger because of this Hayes guy, you call," I said.

"Mother," Hannah said.

The woman ignored her daughter and dropped the card into her bag.

"Thank you," she said. She offered her hand and I shook it. "I'm Esti Braaten."

"Esti?"

"My parents were planning to name me Esther after my grandmother. At the last moment, though, they decided they wanted a more modern name, so they called me Esti, instead. E–S–T–I."

"A pleasure, Esti," I said.

I turned to leave. Hannah stopped me.

"There's a man standing behind you," she said. "A tall man. African American . . ."

Mr. Mosley? my inner voice asked.

"He says . . . no, no, wait, wait, don't go." Hannah sighed. "He hung up."

"Who was he?"

"He didn't give me his name."

"What did he say?"

"Semper fi. I don't know what that means."

"It's short for *semper fidelis*, 'always faithful' in Latin. It's the motto of the United States Marine Corps."

FIVE

I thanked both women for their time and moved toward the exit of the community center. Hannah and Esti followed me outside, staying far enough behind that someone conducting surveillance in the parking lot wouldn't think that we were together, yet close enough that I could hold open the door for them without looking creepy.

I turned left and walked toward the Mustang. I could see my breath, but twenty-nine degrees in Minnesota wasn't cold enough to bother with gloves and a hat. Hell, the girls on the Nicollet Mall were probably still wearing their summer skirts.

My car was parked in the far back row of the lot. The Braaten women, however, had managed a spot in the front row near the entrance. Hannah was driving a white BMW X5 Sports Activity Vehicle, what the Germans call an SUV, and I thought being a psychic medium must pay pretty damn well, a $60,000 car.

I had just reached my own vehicle when the X5 drove past me on its way to the exit. A half beat later, another SUV, this one a black Chevy Tahoe, also passed me, going much faster than it should have in a parking lot. I watched as it took a hard right onto Vine Hill Road and accelerated, staying close to the rear bumper of Hannah's X5, and I thought, Really?

I hopped into the Mustang, fired it up, and began following the two vehicles, staying far enough back not to rattle the driver of the Tahoe. I wasn't convinced yet that he was actually following Hannah. Still . . . What was the name of Hannah's seminar? *Trust Your Instincts?*

We went south on Vine Hill Road, speeding past Old Excelsior Boulevard, until we reached Minnesota Highway 7. The X5 drove east with the Tahoe close behind. I accelerated into the intersection to avoid being trapped by the traffic signal, quickly decreased my speed so as not to alert the Tahoe, and continued following them.

Hannah was driving five miles above the speed limit. The Tahoe kept pace, remaining only a couple of car lengths behind her, which meant either the driver wasn't actually tailing Hannah and I was just being my usual paranoid self or he wasn't very good at it. I stayed well behind the Tahoe and in the next lane over.

My Mustang was equipped with all of the latest technology, so it didn't take much effort to activate my hands-free cell phone and place a call. A couple of moments later it was answered.

"Special Agent Brian Wilson."

"Hi, Harry," I said, which was Brian's nickname, bestowed on him because of his uncanny resemblance to the character actor Harry Dean Stanton.

"Hey, McKenzie, what's going on, man?"

"I'm tailing a Chevy Tahoe that's following a BMW X5 east on Highway 7."

"Here I thought you had tickets to the Wild that you were willing to share."

"Next Monday, I promise."

"Do I really want to know what's going on?"

"It does involve the commission of a federal crime, so . . ."

By then we had passed County 101 and were fast approaching Williston Road in Minnetonka. I had three things to watch—the Tahoe, the X5, and the traffic ahead of both of them. Highway intersections with traffic lights, exit and entrance ramps, construction sites, and suddenly congested traffic all triggered choke points that would eventually force me to either close the distance between my Mustang and the vehicles I was following or risk losing them.

"What federal crime?" Harry asked.

"Interference with commerce by robbery."

"Where?"

"Since the bank doesn't actually exist anymore, the question should really be when."

"All right—when?"

"Twenty-two years ago."

We blew past Williston and headed toward the busy I-494 interchange. I closed the distance, moving to a couple of car lengths directly behind the Tahoe. I was hoping that the driver was too concerned with what was in front of him to worry about what was behind.

"Twenty-two years ago?" Harry repeated.

"Uh-huh."

"There's a legal term, what is it now? Oh, yeah. It's called the statute of limitations."

"Sounds familiar."

"For bank robbery, it's five years."

"Actually, it was an armored truck robbery."

"Nonetheless."

The X5 slowed and then the Tahoe slowed and then I slowed, until we all entered the cloverleaf and one by one maneuvered onto the ramp that led to I-494 north. The X5 accelerated until it was going five miles above the posted speed limit again; apparently that was one of Hannah's driving habits. The Tahoe kept pace, again staying only a couple of car lengths behind her. I dropped back and gave them plenty of room.

"Anyway," I said, "the miscreants involved all paid the price decades ago, so that's not an issue."

"I'm afraid to ask—what is the issue?"

"It's kind of a long story."

"Take your time," Harry said. "It's not like I have anything better to do. I mean, besides supporting and defending the Constitution of the United States against all enemies foreign and domestic."

I started to explain. By the time I reached the part where Hannah was telling Shelby that I was in danger, our little caravan was fast approaching the I-394 interchange. Again I closed the distance between my Mustang and the Tahoe, again hoping that a driver who was tailing someone else wouldn't be too concerned about being tailed himself. The three of us took the gentle curve that led from 494 to 394 and headed east toward Minneapolis.

"I didn't know Shelby was into all that paranormal stuff," Harry said. "Last I heard she was taking classes to become certified as a scuba diver."

"The girl has eclectic interests."

"Remember when she helped map that huge cave in southeastern Minnesota? That would have scared the hell out of me, and I carry a gun."

There were a lot of places where we could have left 394, and all of them made me nervous—Plymouth Road, Hopkins Crossroad, Louisiana Avenue, and Highways 169 and 100—yet we kept heading east toward the Cities. I continued telling my story.

"I didn't know about Leland Hayes," Harry said.

"It's not something you talk about, is it?"

"We've been friends a long time."

"I didn't even tell Nina until last night."

The traffic where 394 met Interstate 94 on the edge of downtown Minneapolis was aggravating even during the best of times and positively brutal during rush hour, which now started at about 3:00 P.M. I was forced to attach myself to the Tahoe's bumper as we negotiated our way through the bottleneck, around the never-ending construction sites, and past the intersection with I-35W.

"You're telling me all of this because—why exactly?" Harry asked.

"Don't you want to recover the $654,321?"

"The money that a ghost—"

"Spirit."

"That a spirit is allegedly offering to pay his ex-con son if he shoots you?"

"What do you mean, allegedly?"

"We in the FBI tend to be careful when throwing around accusations of criminal behavior, even at ghosts. So what exactly do you want from me, McKenzie?"

"I'd thought you might contact the Bureau of Prisons and find out where Ryan Hayes is living these days. Oh, and if he's driving a Chevy Tahoe with Minnesota plates." I recited the number that I had already memorized.

"Ahh, no."

"It's a simple request, Harry."

Our three-car caravan followed 94 east across the Mississippi River into St. Paul. Both the X5 and the Tahoe stayed in the far right lane, however, which meant I had to stay there, too, or risk cutting myself off from all of the exits that we were fast approaching. I felt better about it when a Hyundai Sonata managed to squeeze between me and the Tahoe, but only until I realized he was driving as if it were Sunday and he *wanted* to be late for church. I passed him right away to make sure I wouldn't lose the Tahoe and again hoped the driver didn't notice.

"Is Ryan Hayes a wanted criminal?" Harry asked.

"Not that I'm aware of."

"Are you a member of the federal law enforcement community, or any law enforcement community, for that matter, engaged in an ongoing criminal investigation?"

"Not exactly."

"Well, then?"

"Do you know how much I pay in taxes, Harry?"

"As little as possible, like everyone else."

Hannah finally left the freeway system, maneuvering her X5 up the exit ramp toward Cretin-Vandalia. The Tahoe stayed close behind her. I followed the Tahoe and wondered which way they would turn. I found out when I reached the top of the ramp—right on Cretin Avenue. The traffic light went to yellow just before I reached it. I accelerated, passing through the intersection as it turned red. Instead of looking forward at the Tahoe, I glanced in my rearview mirror looking for a cop.

"What do you expect me to do?" Harry asked. "Knock on the door of the special agent in charge and say, 'Excuse me, ma'am, but I'd like to open an investigation into a dead bank robber who's threatening a friend of mine from the grave?' I like this job, McKenzie. I like working in Minnesota. Besides, you don't really believe any of this shit, do you?"

"How did Hannah know about Agatha and Mr. Mosley?" I asked.

"Mr. Mosley was murdered, wasn't he? You tracked down his killer, didn't you?"

"That was six and a half years ago."

"It made the papers, though, didn't it?"

"Not the part about how I was stung sixteen times."

"McKenzie, give me twelve hours and I can find out everything I need to know about anyone in the country. You could do it, too, but it would take you longer because you don't have my resources. C'mon."

"You sound like Nina."

"I can live with that."

I was now a few car lengths behind the Tahoe. Cretin started as a busy two-lane avenue that quickly became an even busier one-lane street as it passed the University of St. Thomas. It also had a number of traffic lights in fairly close proximity to each other. I knew it was a matter of time before I was stopped by one. It was like the old folk song "Sixteen Tons," about a man with one fist of iron and the other of steel—*If the right one don't a-get you, the left one will.* In this case, I managed to stay with the Tahoe through three lights before I was halted at Grand Avenue by a fourth—that and a vehicle filled with college kids from St. Thomas that discouraged me from attempting to break yet another traffic ordinance. Fortunately, Cretin ran straight and level, so I could track the black SUV as it receded into the distance while I waited out the light. I caught a break when it was also halted by a traffic light, this one at St. Clair Avenue, although I could no longer see the X5.

"You're a great disappointment to me, Harry," I said. "I might have to rethink those Wild tickets next week."

"Yeah, well, call anytime, McKenzie. I haven't had this much fun since the last time they shut down the federal government."

Once the light changed, I maneuvered around the college kids and accelerated at a speed that invited arrest. I closed half of the distance between me and the Tahoe before the light on St. Clair changed. The Tahoe sped forward and turned right.

Only I wasn't close enough to determine exactly where he turned; there were three side streets between St. Clair and Jefferson Avenue, the next busy intersection. I turned onto the first, Berkeley Avenue.

I was now in the heart of a high-income residential neighborhood, Macalester-Groveland or Highland Park, I didn't know exactly which one, only that it possessed an eclectic selection of expensive homes. It also seemed to be Christmas Central; nearly every home had some kind of oversized decoration out front. I was more interested in the cars lining the narrow street, though. I slowed to get a good look at them as I drove past and found nothing that interested me.

I kept going until the street came to an end at Mount Curve Boulevard, where I caught another break. All of the side streets halted there; there were no through streets between St. Clair and Jefferson.

I hung a left and drove half a block before I found what I was searching for, a white BMW X5 SAV parked at the top of a short driveway next to an English Tudor–style house with a steeply pitched roof, tall narrow windows, a ground floor built of red bricks, and a top floor of white timber. The black Chevy Tahoe was parked directly in front of the house, the driver still behind the wheel.

I made a point of not looking at him as I drove slowly for another half block before pulling over and turning off the engine.

A car has plenty of mirrors, and I angled mine so that I could use them to watch the Tahoe, the driver, and the house, without turning around in my seat. I could have parked the Mustang on the other side of the street, of course, and watched them straight on through the front windshield, but I was less likely to attract the attention of the driver I was following if he could only see the back of my headrest.

I waited for a solid twenty minutes for the driver to exit the

Tahoe while my inner voice wondered, *Is that Ryan Hayes? Why did he follow Hannah? Are Hannah and her mother in danger? What are you going to do about it?*

That's when the front door of the house was opened and Esti Braaten stepped outside. She was wearing a blue Eddie Bauer down jacket that she held close with her left hand as she moved quickly down the cobblestone sidewalk to where the Tahoe was parked on the street. She leaned down so she could talk to the driver through the passenger window.

She sure doesn't look frightened, does she?

Esti and the driver chatted for less than three minutes by my watch before Esti turned around and moved back up the sidewalk to her house. The driver started up the Tahoe and drove off before she had a chance to open the door and disappear inside. I ducked down so the driver wouldn't see me, giving it a long ten count before peeking up to make sure he was gone.

A couple of scenarios buzzed through my head to explain all of this. I didn't like any of them, though. The driver could have met Hannah at the community center and requested a private reading; Hannah had an opening in her schedule and invited him to follow her and Esti home but later changed her mind. That might work. Or he could have been a bodyguard hired to escort Hannah to and from the event and parked on the street until he was dismissed by his employers. Except, if that were true, he would have been in the BMW with them, would have escorted them from the center to the Beamer, would have been hovering nearby when I accosted Hannah in the corridor, would have searched the house before he allowed them to enter. Wouldn't he?

Unless he sucked at his job.

I started up the Mustang, moved along Mount Curve Boulevard to Stanford Avenue, hung a left and followed it to Cretin

Avenue. I pointed the Mustang north. As I drove, I considered how I was going to learn the name of the owner of the Chevy Tahoe. Back in the day, I would have been able to contact the Minnesota Department of Motor Vehicles, fill out a form, pay a few bucks, and voilà, I'd be rewarded with the owner's name, address, and phone number. If I was in a hurry, I'd contact one of my law enforcement pals and ask for a favor.

Only that was before a particularly fetching Twin Cities morning news anchor filed a lawsuit when she discovered that her license information had been accessed more than 3,800 times during a ten-year period. That was before a former member of the Department of Natural Resources pleaded guilty to a criminal charge of misconduct by a public employee after he was accused of illegally searching the database about 19,000 times over five years. Most of the people he looked up were women and included police officers, celebrities, and politicians.

As a result, you are no longer allowed to run the license plate of someone else's vehicle in Minnesota unless you have a damn good reason that can be put into writing. Which raised the question my inner voice asked: *Who do we know who's willing to commit a criminal act for you on short notice?*

Apparently not Harry. I knew better than to ask Bobby, too. Instead, I accessed the cell phone in my car. I made a call. A few moments later, a man answered, identifying himself with the name of the building that he was hired to protect.

"Is this Smith or Jones?" I asked.

"Jones. McKenzie? What's going on, man? Anything exciting?"

Smith and Jones—I could never tell them apart without reading their name tags—worked the security desk in the building where Nina's and my condominium was located. They had both made it clear when we moved in nineteen months ago that they had checked me out—acting under building management's orders, of course; it was SOP for all new tenants—and they knew who I was and what I did.

"The job can get so boring," they told me, and said that anything I could do to add spice to their days would be appreciated.

So, on occasion, I'd ask them to help me out. In exchange, I would "find" things lying around the building, like a case of Irish whiskey or Minnesota Twins tickets, that I would turn in to the lost and found because security personnel weren't allowed to accept gratuities from the tenants.

"No, nothing exciting," I said.

"Too bad." Jones sounded disappointed.

"Although . . ."

"Hmm?"

"I've noticed a vehicle hanging around the building that I don't think belongs to one of the tenants. I'm sure it's nothing."

"Vehicle?"

"Black Chevy Tahoe, Minnesota plates." I recited the number again.

"No kidding? We'll get right on that. You know, we're always looking out for the residents."

"All this time I thought your job was to protect the building."

"The building comes first, of course."

"Just a name and address for now, and you know, don't take chances, don't put yourself at risk."

"Never."

"Christmas is coming," I said. "Anything you guys want Santa to bring you?"

Fifteen minutes later, I parked my Mustang in the garage built below the building, took the elevator up to the ground floor, and approached the security desk. There was a tiny artificial

Christmas tree on the desk, and along with their dark blue suits and crisp white shirts, the guards wore red and green ties.

"Hey, guys," I said.

"McKenzie," Smith said. "We were just thinking of you."

"Oh?"

"Someone pushed this through the mail slot."

Smith handed me a sealed white number 10 envelope with my name written across it.

"Huh," I said and put it in my pocket. "So, have you heard? Southside Johnny and the Asbury Jukes are coming to the Dakota Jazz Club here in Minneapolis."

"I used to listen to them when I was a kid living on the East Coast," Jones said.

"Really? That is a coincidence, cuz I just heard that there's a table for four reserved and paid for under the name Jonas Smith. If you should run into someone named Jonas Smith, you might want to tell him."

"We'll do that."

"Oh, and don't mention this to Ms. Truhler. She might not understand, what with the Dakota being a competitor and all."

"Not a word."

I took the elevator to the seventh floor, got off, and started walking down the corridor. Up ahead, a man exited the condominium next to mine and turned toward me. He paused when he saw who I was.

Frank Fogelberg was a retired, twice-divorced stock trader, and he didn't like me one bit. He complained bitterly because I have, on occasion, cranked the volume on my speakers all the way to eleven. He was right, of course; I was out of line. I apologized. Unfortunately, that wasn't good enough. Instead, he brought me before the building's tenant association and complained about being forced to listen to "that music," the music in question being various forms of jazz. The association took my side, however. Not because it liked me but because it hated Fogelberg. Half of its members had fallen under his wrath at one time or another. He had actually accused a woman on the third floor of criminal negligence for having the audacity to bring brownies containing gluten to a potluck.

"Good evening," I said as we approached each other.

Fogelberg refused to reply or even look at me as we passed.

"A pleasure chatting with you, Frank," I said. "Let's do it again real soon."

He kept walking until, apparently, he thought of an appropriate reply.

"McKenzie," he said, "I haven't forgotten you."

Well, okay, then.

A couple of minutes later, I was inside the condominium. I put a reusable pod into the K-Cup machine, reusable because it allowed me to brew my own blends instead of relying on the pods of tasteless coffee you get in the grocery stores and also because I'm on the environment's side. While I waited, I tore open the envelope and found a sheet of paper with a name and address written in longhand.

Karl Anderson, my inner voice read to me. *How many Karl Andersons can there be in Minnesota?*

After my coffee was brewed and poured, I took the mug to my computer and Googled the name to find out. Turned out that there were about a hundred and sixty, but only one with a Mendota Heights street address. It took all of twenty seconds to find a match.

"Huh," I said, probably for the twentieth time that day.

Apparently, Karl J. Anderson was "an award-winning private investigator, confidential, discreet, licensed, bonded, insured, call for a free consultation."

According to the website, Anderson ran a full-service detective agency with twenty-five years of experience out of St. Paul that offered to assist clients involved in business law, criminal law, and personal injury law. Hell, he could do just about anything including surveillance, due diligence investigations, employee theft and financial fraud investigations, report retrieval and evaluation, subpoenas and court order service, and accident scene photography and video documentation as well as accident reconstruction.

The website didn't mention that he provided close protection services. *That doesn't mean he won't,* my inner voice said.

What made me pause, though, was the part where Anderson claimed he offered comprehensive criminal and civil witness background research, thorough background investigations, and expert social media research and analysis.

I told the computer to play some Gershwin. Instead of his better-known works like *Rhapsody in Blue,* the virtual assistant surprised me by broadcasting *Concerto in F* through the speakers placed strategically in every nook and cranny in the condominium. Knowing Fogelberg wasn't around to hear, I told the computer to increase the volume as I began to pace, because that's what I do when I'm in a state of confusion, I pace.

I had finished my coffee and the computer was playing the *Second Rhapsody* when Nina walked through the door.

"Hey," I said. "I didn't expect to see you until late."

Nina took off her coat and dropped it and her bag on a chair near my desk. She told the virtual assistant to lower the volume as she approached me.

"Are you trying to annoy Frank again?" she asked.

"Never."

"You're going to think I'm wanton."

"In what way?"

"You know what we did last night? And this morning? All day long I've been thinking how much I want to do it some more."

"You're the girl of my dreams, you know that, right?"

We crossed the living room area and met in the middle for a hug and a kiss.

"Aren't you going to at least buy me dinner first?" I asked.

"Later."

We kissed some more.

"I noticed you were pacing," Nina said. "What's on your mind?"

"I've been thinking—why would a psychic medium require the services of a private investigator?"

"I know why I would. Are we talking about Hannah?"

"We are."

"She's involved with a PI?"

"I don't know if involved is the correct word. Or even that he's working for her. But Hannah, or at least her mother, knew him well enough to invite him to their home. Nice house, by the way. You'd like it."

"A couple of thoughts come to mind," Nina said.

"Yeah, I can imagine. Harry's on your side, by the way."

"I've always liked Harry."

"Here's the thing, what's got me pacing—as unlikely as it sounds, all of this makes perfect sense if Hannah is telling the truth about Leland and Ryan Hayes and the missing money. If she's not, what's the point? You need to remember, she didn't come to me with all of this nonsense. It was revealed at a group reading that Shelby just happened to attend. Hannah couldn't have known that Shelby and I were friends, could she? Even if she did and this is all part of some elaborate plot, what's her endgame?"

Nina removed her shoes, took my hand, and led me toward the bedroom.

"I don't know," she said. "Why don't we sleep on it?"

SIX

Nina snuggled up close to me, her arm thrown over my chest, her head resting against my shoulder.

"Your cuddling skills have improved immensely," she said.

"Practice makes perfect."

"I nearly didn't come home."

"I'm glad you did."

"I almost didn't come home because—should I tell you what I'm afraid of?"

"I didn't know you were afraid of anything."

"A couple of things," Nina said. "Mostly I'm afraid of becoming my mother. I told you about my mother."

"Bits and pieces."

"My mother was a whore. For a long time I thought she was a sex addict. Except addicts try to hide their disorder, don't they? They lie about their behavior; they do their thing at times and in places where there isn't anyone around to see. They don't want the people they care about, who care about them, to know that they're hooked. Isn't that so?

"Only Mom didn't care who knew. She even brought partners home with her. To our home. One day my father found her in bed with a man, she didn't even know his name. Mom told him to pull up a chair and watch. Dad didn't care for that. She told him that if he didn't like it, he should leave. So he left. Left me in the care of a woman who neglected me, who often spent nights and weekends away, at least when she wasn't entertaining guests in the room next to mine. I was fourteen years old going on thirty. I never saw Dad again. I don't think he actually divorced my mom, because he kept sending her money, enough to keep a roof over our heads, enough to keep me in a good school, enough to help me get through college without any debt. As for the rest of my family, my grandparents and aunts and uncles, apparently their disgust for my mother extended to me as well. Naturally, the first chance I got, I ran off to marry a man who abused and demeaned me every single day. 'Course, you know all about that."

"Bits and pieces," I said.

"If it weren't for Erica, I don't know what would have become of me. Her birth shocked me into a kind of sanity. From that moment on, I took charge of my life, disowned my mother and the rest of the family, divorced my husband, moved to a different city, built Rickie's, and lived in such a way that no one would dare call me the names they called Mom. I gave Erica the life that she deserved. And what did she do? She enrolled at a university that's located twelve hundred miles away; she tried to get as far away from me as she could."

"How often does she call?" I asked.

"What do you mean?"

"How often does she call you, this wayward daughter of yours? Every day?"

"No. Maybe three, four times a week?"

"Plus texts. Plus Facebook postings. I'm not entirely sure why Erica picked Tulane over the other schools that accepted her. Maybe she did it for the scholarship money they offered so she wouldn't have to put too much of a burden on her mother. Or because it was ranked in the top fifty among national universities. Or because she simply liked New Orleans. As for going away to college, if I had to guess, I'd say she did it for the same reason most kids go away to college, because she needed to figure out who she was, and remaining home under the watchful eye of her mother wasn't going to help. It certainly wasn't to escape her mother, who is absolutely nothing like her grandmother. I mean, the girl comes home and it's you and her for at least a full day, hugging and kissing and talking and shopping and taking selfies and acting like best friends who haven't seen each other for a dozen years, so let's not hear any more of this 'my daughter doesn't love me' crap because that's what it is."

"You don't know that," Nina said. "I mean the part about not being like my mother."

"Why are we having this conversation, anyway?"

"My runaway libido has given me cause for concern."

I started to chuckle.

"You think that's funny?" Nina asked.

"I just had an image of you chasing your libido down the street and me chasing after."

"I don't know why I talk to you."

"Nina, how often have you left work in the middle of the day because you wanted to have sex with me?"

"I don't know."

"Fortunately, I've been keeping track. Not often enough."

"Stop it."

"I think this is a first."

"I guess."

"Trust me," I said. "I'll let you know if it becomes a bad habit."

"It's just that sometimes, McKenzie—all this talk of psychic mediums, Shelby wanting to talk to her grandfather, all those other people wanting to connect with dead relatives, it reminds me . . . My mother died a couple of years before I met you. She asked to see me before she passed. I didn't go. I was too busy. I wasn't, but that's the excuse I used. Add that to everything else . . . Sometimes I become afraid."

"Of what exactly?"

"It's hard to say."

"Hard to say because you don't know or because you don't want to speak the words out loud?"

Nina hesitated before she said, "My father abandoned me. He left my mother, I get that, but he also abandoned me. Then I abandoned her and later my husband."

"Are you afraid that I'll do the same thing? That Erica will do the same thing? She won't, you know. Neither will I."

"You're in love with Shelby Dunston."

"What does that have to do with anything?"

"You made her daughters your heirs."

"Yes, I did, right after I came into my money. I also named their father my executor. A couple of years ago, I gave him a copy of a revised will that added Erica to the list. The three of them will share equally."

Nina raised herself up with an elbow and looked into my eyes. "You never told me that," she said.

"Yes, I did. Didn't I?"

"No."

"Oh. Well, I wrote Erica into my will. I hope you don't mind."

Nina settled back against me after kissing my cheek. The fact that her warm body was so close made the conversation easier. If we had been standing on opposite sides of the room, I'm not sure how it would have gone.

"That doesn't change the fact that you're in love with Shelby," Nina said.

"Shelby's the childhood crush that I never quite got over and probably never will. She and Bobby both understand that. You, on the other hand—you are the woman of my dreams. And my life. I'm pretty sure I've told you that many times. Plus, you're right here." I pulled her close to prove it. "I am not letting you go. Ever. Is there anything else you want to talk about?"

"Nothing comes to mind."

"How many times have I asked you to marry me, anyway?"

"Just the three."

"What have you always answered?"

"Why ruin a good thing, something like that."

"The last time?"

"It was at the Louvre in Paris. You went down on one knee in the same room where they keep the *Mona Lisa*."

"After you said why ruin a good thing, what did I say?"

"You said the next time I'd have to ask you."

"Are you asking?"

Nina remained silent. She remained silent for a long time. When she finally did speak, she said, "We should get something to eat."

We were wearing robes, mostly for convention's sake, sitting on stools at the island in the kitchen area and eating a Denver omelet that I put together in about ten minutes. Nina said I was a great cook. I said if she gave me another thirty minutes I would really impress her. She looked at her watch, paused, and said, "Starting now." I said, "Are we talking about the same thing?" She said, "Your phone is ringing." I said, "Don't change the subject."

My phone *was* ringing, though. I had left it on my desk in the office area and went to retrieve it.

"This is McKenzie," I said, which is how I usually answer my phone.

"Mr. McKenzie, this is Smith down in security."

"Smith." I looked at my own watch. "I thought you and Jones were done at five."

"The bosses have decided to alter the shift patterns, don't ask me why. Jones and I caught the two-to-midnight shift."

"That sucks."

"My wife agrees with you. On the other hand, we now only work four days a week. Anyway, Mr. McKenzie, there's a woman down here who wants to speak with you."

I was watching Nina when I said, "You can't possibly imagine how bad your timing is."

"Her ID says her name is Kayla Janas."

"I don't know a Kayla Janas."

"She claims to be a psychic medium."

SEVEN

"I don't want her in my house," Nina said.

She waved a hand in front of herself as if to say look at this.

"Okay," I said.

"Also, you can't just get dressed and go down there. You need to take a shower first."

"Why?"

"Because you smell like me."

"I like the scent. I want to bottle it and use it as cologne."

"Shower. Please."

I did, thinking at the time that Nina was being modest, that she didn't want Kayla Janas or anyone else, for that matter, to suspect what we've been doing for the past hour.

But if Kayla really was a psychic, wouldn't she know anyway? my inner voice asked.

The ten minutes that I said it would take for me to get downstairs became twenty. Kayla Janas didn't seem to mind. She was sitting in one of the four stuffed red chairs gathered around a low round table in front of the security desk, her hands resting on the arms of the chair, her eyes closed. She appeared positively serene.

Smith had pointed her out to me after I emerged from the elevator, although it wasn't necessary. It was the lobby of a condominium, not a hotel. There were only the three of us; I had no idea where Jones had gone off to.

I approached soundlessly across the carpet. When I reached Kayla's side, she said, "McKenzie. Your name is Rushmore McKenzie, of course, but nearly everyone calls you McKenzie."

Kayla opened her eyes and smiled. She reminded me for a moment of one of the few nuns at St. Mark's Elementary School who actually liked me, if the nun had been about twenty years old.

"And you are?" I asked.

The woman rose from the chair. Her long winter coat fell open to reveal a soft blue sweater, dark blue jeans, and knee-length high-heel boots. She was half a foot shorter than I was even with the heels and possessed a kind of a girl-next-door ambiance. Most people would have said that she was pretty, but I had just spent the day with Hannah Braaten and Nina Truhler, and my judgment was compromised.

She took my hand in both of hers. "I'm Kayla Janas," she said. "I am so very pleased to meet you."

"Ms. Janas," I said.

She gestured at the red chairs. "Please, sit with me."

We sat and stared at each other for a few beats.

"You seem nervous," Kayla said.

"I always get jumpy around women, especially when I don't know who they are or what they want."

"I don't believe that. I think it's because the security guard told you that I was a psychic medium. Do you know what a psychic medium is?"

I repeated what Shelby had told me. "A medium can talk to the dead. A psychic can tell you what's going to happen a week from Thursday. A psychic medium can do both."

"A somewhat abrupt definition, yet accurate, I suppose. I see that you took a shower before coming to join me."

"Is that your psychic abilities speaking, or have you noticed that my hair is slightly damp and I smell vaguely of body wash?"

"You don't believe in psychics, do you?"

"Time and experience have taught me to keep an open mind. What can I do for you, Ms. Janas?"

"Kayla, please."

"Kayla."

"I *am* a psychic medium. I can communicate with the dead. I understand if you don't believe me. Most people don't. Among those that do, there is a large contingent that is convinced I'm going against the Bible, that I'm an instrument of Satan. I tell you this so you'll understand that I am prepared to accept whatever reaction you have to my words, although I sincerely hope that you will take them seriously."

"What is it you've come here to say?"

"This is going to sound absurd."

"Try me," I said.

"Your life is in danger."

"In what way?"

"A man wants to kill you."

"Okay."

Kayla stared at me for a few beats as if she couldn't believe how calmly I was taking the news.

"A man called yesterday," Kayla said. "He told me that he had a bad reading with another psychic medium and that he wanted me to read him as soon as possible. He seemed so distraught that I agreed to meet him today. I left him just over an hour ago."

"What's his name?"

"I—I can't tell you."

"Your professional ethics allow you to tell me that I'm in danger but not to identify the man I am in danger from?"

"People in my profession view a visit to a psychic or a medium as the same as a visit to a doctor. Confidentiality must be maintained. I felt morally obligated to come here, yet at the same time—ethically—I wish there was someone I could call, someone who could give me permission or at least clarification. I'm kind of new at this."

"Perhaps I can help."

"How?" Kayla asked.

"Let's see if we're both on the same page. The man who came to you for the reading, his name was Ryan Hayes. His father was Leland Hayes. They robbed an armored truck twenty-two years ago. The son went to prison for most of that time. The father was killed. The money was never recovered."

"I didn't know those details."

"It was Ryan Hayes who came to see you, though, wasn't it?"

"His father came through during the reading," Kayla said. "He had a very dark, dark energy. He was cruel and he was angry and he seemed—he seemed put out, like he didn't want to be there, like he didn't want to talk to Ryan, which seemed odd to me. The whole thing seemed odd. I've learned through experience, if someone from the other side doesn't want to come through, well, then, they don't. Only he was there, like he was waiting for Ryan to speak to him instead of the other way around. Finally, Ryan asked me to ask the father—"

"Leland," I said.

"Yes. Ryan asked me to ask Leland if it was true."

"If what was true?" I asked.

"I was made to understand that Leland had hidden a great deal of money before he died—I don't know how much—and that he would tell Ryan where it was if he would . . . if he would kill you."

"Leland told you this?"

"No. Ryan told me to ask Leland if all of that was true. Leland laughed at Ryan. He called him names, names that some men call women. At the same time he chanted yes, yes, yes, that's exactly what he wanted. I shouldn't have repeated it to Ryan. It just spilled out before I had the presence of mind to edit the information. I'm very sorry."

"It's okay."

Kayla leaned toward me. "He was sincere, McKenzie," she said. "The dead man."

"I believe you."

"Afterward, Ryan became very quiet. The dead man, though, Leland, suddenly he had a great deal to say, like it was about time Ryan wised up, stuff like that, only I didn't repeat most of it. I decided I had done enough damage. Anyway, after a few minutes, Ryan got up to leave."

"He didn't ask Leland where the money was?"

"No, and then—and then I messed up again."

"How?"

"I asked Ryan if he already knew where the money was hidden, I don't even know why."

"What did he say?"

"He said—he said eff the money."

"Eff?"

"You know—eff."

"Okay."

"Are you sure that Leland didn't provide any hints?"

"I'm sure."

"Could you see anything with your second sight, whatever you call it—anything that might reveal the location?"

Kayla leaned back in her chair.

"No," she said. Her voice suggested that she was both surprised and frustrated that I had even asked.

"Then you're no help to me," I said.

"Something I did see, pictures of the man's head. It was . . . shattered."

"Yeah, I know."

Kayla stood and began buttoning her long coat.

"I'm sorry to have troubled you," she said.

I stood, too.

"No, I'm the one who needs to apologize," I said. "You're very kind to come here to help a complete stranger. I know it was difficult for you, and I am grateful. If I seem rude, it's because you're not the first person to tell me this story, and quite honestly, it's starting to get old."

"The name of the other person who told you, so that we're both on the same page . . ."

"Hannah Braaten."

"I know her," Kayla said. "I know of her; we've never met. Mr. Hayes, Ryan Hayes, told me that she was the psychic that he first went to see. He's convinced that Hannah is trying to find the money and keep it for herself."

"I don't know Ryan Hayes," I said. "I don't know what's in his head. I don't know if he thinks the money belongs to him after all these years, that somehow he earned it. But I don't think he's going to let it go. If he attempts to contact you again, tries to force you to tell him where his old man hid the loot, call me. Perhaps I can help."

"You would do that? Come to the aid of a complete stranger?"

"Why not? You did."

Kayla pulled her long black gloves from her pockets. Before putting them on, she offered me her bare hand, and I took it.

"There are a lot of good people looking out for you," she said. "Now I understand why. Good night, McKenzie."

Kayla turned and walked toward the exit. I called after her.

"You don't know my cell number," I said.

"Yes, I do."

"How?"

"The same way I knew where you lived."

A moment later, Kayla was gone.

I turned toward the security desk. Jones had returned, and he and Smith were now seated behind it.

"If this is what the night shift is going to be like . . ." Smith said.

"I like it already," Jones added.

I found Nina lying on the sofa in front of the fireplace. She was wearing her red silk nightgown that seemed to come alive in the firelight and reading a novel by PJ Tracy. How she could manage to make out the words I couldn't say, but then that's what everyone did before Nikola Tesla and Thomas Edison came along, wasn't it, read by candlelight or firelight.

"How was she?" Nina said.

"Pleasant enough. She seemed genuinely concerned about my welfare."

"Did she read you? Put you in contact with Agatha or someone else?"

"No."

"What did she tell you?" Nina asked.

"The same thing that Hannah told me."

"Do you think they're in cahoots?"

"I like that word, cahoots. Honestly, Nina, I don't know what to think."

"Have you noticed that female psychics all seem to have interesting names? Hannah Braaten. Kayla Janas. Allison DuBois. Char Margolis. Tracy Farquhar. Rosemary Altea. There's a woman who lives in Edina named Echo Bodine."

"Doing a little research of your own, are you?"

"They're all attractive, too."

"Would you want to have your future told by the Three Witches in *Macbeth*?"

"It smacks of marketing to me," Nina said.

"Or sexism. How often have you and Erica and Shelby and Victoria and Katie railed against society for judging women by their appearance?"

"Apparently not enough."

"I wonder if unattractive mediums are like Cassandra . . ."

"Another interesting name."

"They can accurately predict the future yet are cursed by the gods so that no one will believe them."

"If the gods are anything like loan officers, you might be onto something."

"Have I told you how much I like your nightgown?" I asked.

"Yep."

"So, any plans for the immediate future?"

"I'm going to finish reading my book. You?"

I reluctantly threw a thumb over my shoulder toward the office area and my computer. "I thought I'd look up Kayla," I said.

"She has a nice website. Very clean, very elegant. Not nearly as many pictures of herself as Hannah has."

"Okay. You, ahh . . . You should turn on a light. This can't be good for your eyes."

"You're probably right."

I spun around and headed for my desk while Nina flicked on a lamp.

So much for sexual addiction, my inner voice said. *At least hers.*

I went to Kayla's website and was greeted by a quote:

Hi, my name is Kayla Janas. Welcome to my website.

I belong to a different generation of psychic mediums, one that is determined to break away from the 'weird and wonderful' stereotypes personified by Madame Acarti in *Blithe Spirit* without embracing the unnecessary suspense and drama that's required to make "great TV." I pride myself on my ability to bring clarity and closure to people and to help them find honest answers to the questions that nag their lives.

Dissin' the TV mediums, my inner voice said. *Good for you, Kayla.*

Along with the quote, her home screen provided links for FAQs, readings and events, a newsletter, testimonials, and contact information. What impressed me most, though, was what she didn't provide—a history of her life, a photo gallery, videos of her TV interviews, a blog, a press kit with media contact information, or a shopping page where visitors could purchase her books, video courses, or tarot and oracle cards, or make reservations for a seven-day spiritual odyssey aboard a luxury cruise ship.

Clearly the young lady doesn't understand marketing, my inner voice said.

Perhaps she doesn't care about that sort of thing, I told myself.

Perhaps she's new at this and doesn't get it yet.

Perhaps—hell, what do I know?

I wondered briefly if there was such a thing as ghost cops, someone I could call to have Leland Hayes arrested for conspiracy to commit murder.

I actually Googled the words "ghost cops" and was greeted by a YouTube cartoon plus a list of video games plus information about a 1990s TV series that lasted one episode before it was canceled. I tried "ghostbusters" and was directed to a couple million results devoted to the films that shared the same name. Next I tried "psychic medium ghostbusters" and was introduced to all kinds of websites, including one starring Echo Bodine. Just for fun, I started counting websites of psychic mediums, stopping when I reached an even fifty.

"You know . . ." I said.

Nina answered me from across the room. "What?"

"This is crazy."

"Yes, it is."

"On the other hand, I've had two separate and independent sources confirm that a dead man is trying to have me killed. Isn't that enough for a newspaper to print it on the front page?"

"The *National Enquirer*, maybe. One of those grocery store gossip magazines."

"I figure I can do one of two things."

"Such as?"

"Nothing. Just wait and see if Ryan Hayes comes looking for me."

"There's a thought."

"Or I can go looking for him."

"Do I get a vote?"

"Sure."

"Go to bed."

"Will you be joining me?"

"In a couple of chapters."

Dammit!

EIGHT

Our building had a modern fitness center on the second floor with all of the machines you'd find in a pay-by-the-month workout facility, yet I blew it off for a somewhat worn and battered gym in an area of St. Paul they used to call Frogtown before political correctness became the watchword. 'Course, Gracie's Gym had changed its name, too, becoming Gracie's Power Academy when it began offering martial arts training for women. I liked to drop in a few times a month to remind myself how to take a punch. Dave Gracie told me I needed to train more than that, because at my age the time I was putting in was only enough to give me a false sense of security. To prove it, he swept my leg just like the Cobra Kai did to Daniel in *The Karate Kid*. Unlike Mr. Miyagi, he didn't help me up, either.

What a way to start a day, my inner voice told me.

I changed clothes but didn't shower, telling myself that I'd take care of it when I returned to the condominium. If you had seen the antiquated showers at Gracie's you probably would have done the same thing. I was still a little sweaty, though, and when I stepped into the parking lot, the cool December air chilled my body like an ice cube. I quickly moved to the Mustang, fired it up, and waited for the heater to thaw me out.

There was a black SUV parked on the street adjacent to the lot. I had paid no attention to it until I noticed its rear lights going from red to white to red again. That told me the driver had started the car and shifted from park past reverse and into a forward gear. Except the vehicle didn't drive off. It remained in its parking spot for a few beats until the driver reversed his movements, going from a forward gear past reverse and into park again.

I probably would have ignored all of that, too, except that I recognized the SUV as a Chevy Tahoe with the same license plates as the vehicle I had followed the day before, the one driven by Karl J. Anderson, the award-winning private investigator.

My first thought: Why is he following me?

My second: No way he knew I was going to be at Gracie's, which meant he picked me up at the condo and tailed me here, and I hadn't noticed!

What a putz, my inner voice said. *Gracie was right, you do need to train more.*

My third thought: Shouldn't I be frightened? What if Anderson had heard about Leland's offer? What's stopping him from knocking me off, going to the nearest psychic medium, contacting Hayes, and demanding that he pay up?

Can they do that, just dial up anyone who's dead? Cuz if they can, there are a lot of people I'd like to have a word with. Louis Armstrong. Shakespeare. My mom. Robert Leroy Johnson—I'd ask him about selling his soul to the devil to become the most important bluesman of all time; how did that work out?

The Mustang had heated up nicely, but I still hadn't put it in gear.

Maybe you should have a word with Anderson, my inner voice suggested.

What would that accomplish, I wondered, except to let Anderson know that he had been made? He's a professional; he would never give up his client. He'd either break off the tail or pretend to break it off. He could come back with a four-man surveillance team tomorrow; I'd never know if he was behind me. Or he could tag the Mustang with a GPS transmitter. Hell, maybe he already had.

You know who you should talk to.

Yeah, I do.

I put the Mustang into gear and drove out of the parking lot. I pressed my cell phone to my ear as I passed Anderson's Tahoe to plant the suggestion that I had taken my time leaving Gracie's because I was making a call and not because I knew he was there.

A mile and a half later, I was on I-94 and heading west toward Minneapolis. Anderson had kept a respectful distance, so I couldn't see his face when I took the Cretin-Vandalia exit and drove south. I was sure that he was alarmed, though.

He stayed with me until I turned right on Berkeley Avenue. Anderson continued driving straight. That didn't surprise me. Making that final turn would have revealed his presence. Besides, he must have known where I was going.

I took a left on Mount Curve Boulevard and parked in front of Hannah Braaten's house in nearly the exact spot Anderson had parked in the day before. A few minutes later I was standing outside Hannah's front door. I rang the bell and waited. The temperature had dropped to about twenty-two degrees, and my bare hands were in my pockets. I hopped around a little bit so Anderson wouldn't notice I was studying the street. I saw the nose of his Tahoe peeking around the corner where Stanford Avenue met Mount Curve.

The door was pulled open and Esti Braaten appeared.

"Mr. McKenzie?" She sounded surprised to see me.

"Ms. Braaten," I said. "May I speak with your daughter?"

She hesitated.

"It's important," I added.

Esti opened the door and I slipped inside. She led me down a short, narrow foyer and into a living room that looked as if people actually lived there.

"Excuse the mess," Esti said. "We weren't expecting company."

She picked up a sweater that was not unlike the one she was wearing and a copy of *Enchanted Living Magazine* with a cover photograph of a beautiful woman—not Hannah—dressed in silver armor and grasping a sword. Esti glanced around for a place to set them and ended up dropping both pretty much where they had been in the first place.

"I'm sorry to intrude," I said. I glanced around. There wasn't a Christmas decoration in sight.

"What do you want?"

Hannah must have heard our voices.

"Mom, who is it?" she called from another room.

A moment later, she appeared beneath the arch that separated the living room from the dining room. She was wearing a gray form-fitting T-shirt that proclaimed her allegiance to the Minnesota Lynx women's basketball team and gray sweatpants. There was moisture around her collar and under her armpits that suggested she had indeed been sweating.

"McKenzie," she said. "How did you know where I live?"

"I'm psychic."

"Now that's a joke I've never heard before."

"I apologize for the intrusion, but a couple of interesting things have happened since we met yesterday," I said.

"Such as?"

"A psychic medium contacted me, one of your competitors, I assume—"

"We don't compete," Hannah said. "Most of us get along quite well."

"In any case, Ryan Hayes went looking for a second opinion. His father came through during the reading with the same offer as before—my head in exchange for a boatload of cash."

Hannah seemed jolted by my story.

"Are you serious?" she asked.

"Yes."

"When did this happen?"

"Last night."

"I don't know what to say. The psychic, did she actually tell Ryan that his father . . . that his father wanted you dead?"

"You make it sound like the Colonel's eleven herbs and spices. Was it supposed to be a secret?"

"It's just—she shouldn't have given a reading like that."

How do you know it's a she? my inner voice wanted to know.

"I agree," I said aloud.

"Sometimes we speak without thinking," Hannah said in support of the colleague. "We're translating, after all, not . . . Well."

"The psychic did apologize to me."

"I'm sorry, too, McKenzie, but all this has nothing to do with me. Quite frankly, I resent you showing up like this, uninvited. I've worked hard to keep my private life private going back to my modeling days. I will not tolerate personal intrusions."

"I appreciate that."

"Do you?"

"Yes. One more thing before I leave, though—the other interesting thing that happened, that's still happening. Suddenly, I'm being followed."

Hannah's smile went away. "By whom?" she asked.

"A private investigator named Karl J. Anderson. You wouldn't happen to know a private investigator named Karl J. Anderson, would you?"

Hannah gave me nothing in return for the name. Esti wasn't as good a liar. She flinched just enough to verify that she knew the man. 'Course, I had already seen them talking, so . . .

"No, I don't know him," Hannah said.

"Why would we?" Esti asked.

"He thinks I hired him to research my sitters," Hannah said. "Isn't that right, McKenzie? You suggested before that I—all right, all right. Like I said, you're not the first to accuse me."

"We don't know any private investigators," Esti said.

I decided not to call them liars to their faces. What would that accomplish?

"Just checking," I said. "All things considered, you can imagine why I might be concerned."

"Yet you don't seem concerned," Hannah said.

Just another day in the life . . .

"Just out of curiosity," I said. "Is it possible for you to call up anyone during a reading?"

"Are you asking if I can contact Leland Hayes for you?"

"Yes."

"Probably not. There almost always needs to be some sort of personal connection between the sitter and the spirit. Even so, you can't control who comes through, who wants to deliver a message. Sometimes a sitter will ask to speak to a specific individual, but the individual won't come to the phone, if you'll accept that poor analogy."

"Okay."

"I once attempted to reach the spirit of Harry Houdini during a Halloween event held at the University Club in St. Paul. Unfortunately, he was a no-show."

Hannah was smiling when she said that as if she had enjoyed the experience.

"Maybe Ryan Hayes hired this man, this private investigator," Esti said.

"There's one way to find out," I said. "Let's go ask him."

"Ask him?"

"He's parked outside." I bowed my head at both women. "Ladies." Then I headed for the door.

Mother and daughter glanced at each other, passing a telepathic message the way that some close relatives do, and followed me.

I opened the front door and stepped out onto the stoop. I was wearing my leather jacket, so the cold didn't bother me right away. It hit the Braatens hard, though, and they wrapped their arms around themselves for protection. Still, they trailed behind me down the steps to the sidewalk.

The Chevy Tahoe was parked on Stanford, its nose pointed at Mount Curve Boulevard. I walked toward it. Hannah and Esti followed behind. We took only a dozen steps or so before the SUV moved onto the boulevard, hung a left, and drove away.

"That was rude," I said.

"Was that him?" Hannah asked.

Who lies like this besides small children and politicians? my inner voice asked.

"That was him," I said.

"I don't understand any of this."

In that moment I wondered: *Could Hannah be telling the truth?*

I turned toward Esti. She continued to shiver against the December cold.

Would a mother keep secrets from her daughter? I flashed on

Shelby Dunston and her relationship with Victoria and Katie. *Of course she would.*

"You guys should go back into the house," I said. "I'll let you know if any other interesting things happen."

I returned to the condominium before 11:00 A.M. Detective Anderson did not follow me—as far as I knew.

I parked in my designated spot in the underground garage and pulled a hand-cranked flashlight from the glove compartment. It gave me a dim light, which is where the hand-cranking part came in. I pulled a lever out of the base that looked like the handle on a fishing reel and wound it about fifty times until the flashlight produced an intense beam. Afterward, I slipped out of the Mustang and began inspecting its wheel wells, bumpers, and undercarriage. It took a few minutes before I found it, a small black magnetized metal box attached to the rear axle. I didn't bother to open the box; I knew what was inside.

My first thought was to drop the GPS transmitter into the trash, yet where was the fun in that? Instead, I wandered through the garage until I found Frank Fogelberg's silver Lexus GS. I attached the transmitter to his rear axle, wondering at the time if Fogelberg ever went anywhere interesting and whether Anderson would approve.

I had wanted to ask Smith and Jones to keep a lookout for Anderson's Chevy Tahoe, but they hadn't begun their shift yet, and I didn't have the same kind of rapport with their morning counterparts. I'd catch them later, I decided, and took the elevator to the seventh floor.

The condominium was empty, of course. Nina had left for Rickie's long before, as was her habit.

I had a secret room hidden behind a bookcase between the fireplace and the south wall of the condo. I say secret even though I've shown it to just about everyone who's ever been in the place. I do like my gadgets, and you have to admit, this one was pretty cool. It was a major reason why I let Nina talk me into moving there from St. Paul.

To access the room, you needed to nudge the corner of the bookcase just so until you heard a click and then swing it outward to reveal an eight-by-ten carpeted chamber. I tripped a sensor when I entered, and an overhead light flicked on to reveal a safe filled with $50,000 in tens and twenties, credit cards, a driver's license and passport with my photograph but someone else's name, and a gun cabinet with six weapons, four of them registered. It also contained my hockey sticks and equipment bag. I brought them out of the room and set them near my desk.

Friday night was hockey night. For twenty-six weeks out of the year, I played pickup with an army of friends and acquaintances at the Charles M. Schulz–Highland Arena in St. Paul. We started at 10:00 P.M., played to 11:15, and retired to a neighborhood bar to talk it over. I usually arrived home just in time to greet Nina after she closed Rickie's, and since we were both often too jazzed to sleep, there was no end to the mischief we would engage in. Once we actually waxed our hardwood floors.

It was true that I loved Shelby Dunston and always have. Yet I wasn't *in* love with her, something that both she and Bobby understood if no one else. I didn't see her everywhere I went or hear her laugh in other people's laughs or sense her presence when I stood near someone else. I didn't feel euphoric or weak in the knees when she was near, I had no compulsion to share my thoughts or feelings with her, and I didn't need her warm embrace to get me through the day, didn't need to touch her physically and emotionally like I did with Nina. I rarely put her happiness above mine.

On the other hand, Nina had a very deep and personal relationship with her jazz club. I doubted she ever went more than a few hours without thinking about it. I knew from personal experience that she never went more than a few days at a time without feeling the urge to connect with it either in person or through calls, texts, and emails with her people, which made vacations seem less vacationlike.

It was something I had accepted a long time ago because truthfully, I didn't have a choice in the matter. You simply could not separate one from the other, and having learned a few more bits and pieces of Nina's background, I had a better understanding of why that was so. It was like Scarlett O'Hara and Tara, her plantation in *Gone with the Wind*—Rickie's was what gave Nina strength.

So exactly who had the commitment issues in this relationship, I wanted to know.

I was thinking about that while I retaped my hockey sticks and watched the afternoon debates on ESPN. Around 3:00 P.M., I wandered down to the lobby to chat with the boys about Anderson's Chevy Tahoe. I emerged from the elevator, turned toward the desk, and halted.

Detective Jean Shipman was leaning against the desk and chatting with both Smith and Jones. Shipman worked Homicide in the St. Paul Police Department's Major Crimes Division. She was "young, beautiful, and smart as hell"—at least that's how Bobby once described her to me. She had been Bobby's partner before they made him a commander, and she remained his cohort of choice on those occasions when he stepped away from his role as a practicing bureaucrat and actually did some investigating.

There was another detective with her, one I didn't know, and a uniform from the Minneapolis Police Department. The uniform was a formality. The cops in St. Paul and Minneapolis might labor in separate jurisdictions, yet they are more than willing to help each other out, happy to search for a suspect or a car, check out an address, gather intel and report back to the other agency. Only that didn't mean a detective was welcome to cross the river and flash her badge anytime she damn well pleased. She first had to notify the Minneapolis Police Department and, if the case was hot, arrange for one of its officers to accompany her.

Shipman saw me standing there. The expression on her face suggested that she was as shocked to see me as I was to see her.

"McKenzie," she said. "What are you doing here?"

"I live here."

She glanced at Smith as if she were seeking confirmation.

"He lives in the condominium next to Frank Fogelberg," he said.

"Please tell me you're not involved in any of this," Shipman said.

"Involved in any of what?" I asked. "What's going on?"

"It's Mr. Fogelberg," Jones said. "He was shot to death in St. Paul a couple of hours ago."

NINE

I almost didn't tell her. I came *this*close to shrugging my shoulders, saying, 'I'm sorry to hear that," and walking away. I couldn't do it, though. My genetic makeup, my upbringing, my training as a cop, my inner voice, whatever you want to call it, simply wouldn't allow me to do that. So, even though it opened me up to much-deserved ridicule, derision, contempt, and accusations of criminal behavior, I said, "Jeannie, we need to talk."

Shipman hated it when I called her by her first name, hated me, truth be told. Yet something in my demeanor must have softened her heart, because she stroked my shoulder and in a soft voice said, "I need my partner to sit in on the conversation."

I ushered the detectives to my condominium where we sat on stools around the island in the kitchen area. I had offered them drinks. Shipman's partner was named Mason Gafford, and he had worked in the Family and Sexual Violence Unit of Major

Crimes before being recruited into Homicide by Commander Dunston a couple of months ago. He seemed inclined to accept my offer, yet refused when Shipman refused. As for myself, I felt the desperate need for a slug of bourbon or two or ten, but decided it would be better to remain sober.

You should probably call G. K., too, my inner voice said. Only I ignored its advice. Genevieve K. Bonalay was my attorney and my friend, but I didn't think I needed either at the moment. After all, I didn't do anything wrong. Did I?

Shipman asked about Frank Fogelberg, and I told her and Gafford everything that I knew, including his attempts to have me evicted or at least fined, which was not in my best interests, believe me. I knew they would have found out anyway, though, because despite my personal misgivings, Shipman was very good at her job.

Afterward, I told them about the GPS tracker I found on my car and attached to Fogelberg's Lexus earlier that morning.

Gafford stepped away from the island and made a call. Shipman looked at me as if she felt sorry for me.

"What were you thinking?" she asked.

"I was thinking how clever I was."

A few minutes later, the detective returned.

"It was still there," he said. "The crime scene guys thanked me. They said they hadn't even thought to look."

"The box will have my prints on it," I said. "I didn't open it, though. Maybe there'll be something inside that you can use."

"Maybe," Shipman said.

"Can you tell me exactly what happened?" I asked.

"Fogelberg pulled up to a traffic light. A car pulled next to him. When the light changed to green, the driver fired at least nine rounds into him and drove off."

"Traffic cams?"

"We know how to run an investigation, McKenzie."

"Yeah. Yeah, you do."

"Other members of the unit are probably looking at footage even as we speak. I was the lucky one sent to contact the next of kin."

"Only there isn't any. At least none that I know of."

Poor dumb sad sonuvabitch, my inner voice said. *Maybe that's why Frank was always so surly. He was alone in the world.*

I flashed on Nina and Shelby and Bobby and their children and the dozen other people that I called friend and who called me friend in return. It didn't make me feel any better, though.

You shouldn't have done it. You shouldn't have attached the transmitter to Frank's car.

"God, I am so sorry," I said aloud.

"Tell us what you know," Shipman said.

I did. I expected snickering when I got to the part where I mentioned the psychic mediums and outright laughter when I told them about Leland Hayes threatening me from the grave. Yet whatever they were thinking, both Shipman and her partner remained professional, taking down most of the information in their notebooks with the occasional question and no comments. 'Course, that might have been because Commander Dunston's wife was involved.

"The PI, Karl J. Anderson," Gafford said. "You never actually spoke to him, did you?"

"No, and I only saw him from a distance. I identified him by his Chevy Tahoe."

"Who ran his plates for you?"

"I'd rather not say."

"We have ways of making you talk." Gafford was trying to keep it light, speaking with what he thought was a Russian accent. I wasn't feeling it, though.

"It's all on me whatever happens," I said.

"I appreciate the martyr routine," Shipman said. "But you know, McKenzie, there's a very real possibility that this has nothing to do with you."

"From your lips to God's ear."

"Whoever tagged your car—let's assume it was Anderson for now—has to know the difference between a black Ford Mustang GT and a silver Lexus GS."

"The killer might not have been the one who tagged my car, just the person who thought he was following the GPS signal."

"Even so, his accomplice would have told him what to look for, don't you think? I mean, c'mon."

"I don't know, Jeannie. I appreciate that you're trying to make me feel better about this, though."

"Is that what I'm doing? I need you to come down to the Griffin Building with me."

"Okay."

"And it's Detective Shipman to you."

That's the girl I know and love.

The James S. Griffin Building, headquarters of the St. Paul Police Department, was located northeast of downtown. It was part of the Ramsey County–St. Paul Criminal Justice Campus that included the Ramsey County Law Enforcement Center and the Adult Detention Center, which made things very convenient for the cops. If they didn't like the answers I gave them, they could easily slap on the cuffs and escort me across the parking lot.

They didn't like the answers. Not because they were wrong or deceitful but because they sounded ridiculous.

Deputy Chief Roger Hodapp, who was Bobby's immediate supervisor, tapped a pen on the table in the conference room where I was being questioned.

"Let me get this straight, McKenzie," he said. "You're suggesting that the murder of Mr. Fogelberg was a case of mistaken identity. You're suggesting that you were the actual target because a man who's been dead for twenty-two years announced through a psychic medium that he would pay $654,321 that he stole from an armored truck to whoever killed you—"

"As far as I know, the offer was made only to his son—"

"And that a person or persons unknown tagged your car in order to follow you, but, being a man who loves practical jokes, you put the GPS transmitter on Fogelberg's car instead?"

"Yes, sir."

Hodapp looked at Bobby. "Do you know why I love my job so much?" he asked. "It's because I get to delegate."

"Considering my relationship with McKenzie—"

"Hell, we all have a relationship with McKenzie." Hodapp turned back to me. "I was the sergeant you called when you pulled the pin to take the price on Teachwell, remember?"

"Yes, sir," I said.

"Back when we were both working out of Central."

"I remember."

"Do you also remember what I told you?"

"You told me that you always knew I was a dumb ass."

"Nothing has changed." Hodapp glanced back at Bobby. "'Kay?"

"You're the boss."

"You know, when we called this meeting, I thought we were going to discuss Ruth Nowak."

"I'm working the case."

"Personally?"

"Yes."

"Send me an eBrief."

"I will."

Hodapp patted Bobby's arm, stood, and headed for the door. He paused when he reached it.

"Despite everything, I've always liked you, McKenzie," he said. "In your own clumsy way you've been useful to us in the past."

Clumsy?

"You've been smart about what you've given the media, too," Hodapp added.

Which was nothing if you could possibly help it.

"Stay smart."

"It was a pleasure seeing you again, Chief," I said.

The deputy chief walked out of the conference room. Shipman closed the door behind him and resumed her seat.

"That went well," I said.

"You think?" Bobby said.

"I don't have a personal relationship with McKenzie," Shipman said. "I'd be happy to take lead."

Bobby knew the animosity that existed between us, though, and proved it by looking up at the ceiling and rolling his eyes.

Shipman's partner decided to keep it professional.

"We examined the GPS transmitter attached to the rear axle of Fogelberg's Lexus," Gafford said. "Pretty standard. You can get one just like it for fifty bucks from Amazon or Best Buy. We were able to use traffic cams to track the car after the hit—it was a red, five-year-old Toyota Avalon, by the way. It was reported stolen Monday night. A woman left it running in the parking lot of a Holiday Stationstore in Vadnais Heights because it was cold Monday night, all of twenty-eight degrees, while she went inside to buy a lottery ticket. When she came out, it was gone."

"Lucky her," Shipman said.

Wait, Monday night? my inner voice asked.

"Anyway, we tracked the Avalon to Railroad Island in the

Payne-Phalen neighborhood before we ran out of cameras," the partner said. "I sent a unit over there, and they found the car parked near the intersection of Beaumont Street East and Burr Street North, less than a mile from where we're sitting right now. The car was impounded; forensics is going over it. Also, we're doing a canvass of the neighborhood, asking concerned citizens if they've seen anything. I have nothing to report yet."

"Where did the Toyota come from?" Bobby asked.

"We don't know," Gafford said. "We followed the traffic cams backward. The system picked it up five minutes before the shooting where Riverside Avenue meets I-94 in Minneapolis."

"What about Fogelberg's car?"

"The system picked it up at the same location."

About two miles from the building where Frank lived—used to live.

"Mason, I want you to take lead on the investigation," Bobby said.

"Yes, sir."

"Spoilsport," Shipman said.

"Talk to the psychics," Bobby said. "I can't believe I'm saying this. Talk to the psychics and see if you can confirm McKenzie's story."

"What about the PI and Ryan Hayes?"

"I agree with Jean, you'd think Anderson would know the difference between a black Mustang and a silver Lexus, but see if he has an alibi for the time of the shooting. Hayes, too. And people, I think I can speak for the deputy chief—we don't want to see any leaks. This is the kind of story the media just loves, psychic frickin' mediums involved in a murder investigation. So keep it to yourselves. I mean it."

"I have a thought," I said.

"McKenzie," Bobby said, "are you still here? Get out."

"Bobby—"

"You are no longer a police officer. You are not a part of this investigation. If you involve yourself, I will have your ass for hindering."

"Statute 609.5, subdivision 1." Shipman was smiling when she said it. "Ninety days or a thousand-dollar fine or both."

"That's a narrow-minded attitude," I said.

"We've had this conversation before," Bobby added.

"All right," I said. "Have it your way."

I left the conference table and moved toward the door.

Gafford stopped me. "Mr. McKenzie," he said, "what thought?"

"You said the Toyota was stolen Monday night."

"That's right."

"The psychic medium told—" I nearly said "Bobby Dunston's wife, Shelby," but caught myself in time. "The psychic medium who announced that Leland Hayes wanted me dead didn't do her reading until Tuesday night."

Jeannie Shipman had driven me to the Griffin Building in her vehicle, so I had to call a Lyft to take me home. The driver was concerned about our soft winter. I told him, "When we get ten feet of snow and the temperature drops to twenty degrees below zero with a minus sixty-seven wind chill, I want you to remember this conversation."

It was pushing 7:00 P.M. when I arrived at my building. I went directly to the security desk. Smith and Jones were desperate for information about Fogelberg, and I gave them as much as I had.

"Do me a favor," I said. "Check the footage on your security cameras starting a couple of hours before Fogelberg left the building. See if you can catch a glimpse of a red Toyota Avalon."

I was hoping that the car followed Fogelberg directly from the building, which would mean the GPS transmitter wasn't necessarily involved, which would mean I wasn't necessarily involved. I so desperately wanted to shed any responsibility for Fogelberg's death. It just made me feel so low.

"What if we find it?" Jones asked.

"Inform Commander Robert Dunston of the St. Paul Police Department with my compliments."

I returned to the condominium and nearly tripped on my hockey equipment. I questioned whether or not I should play tonight. Somehow it seemed disrespectful to Fogelberg; the idea that I was responsible for putting him in harm's way weighed heavily on me. I wondered if Bobby would play and decided that he would if he could. With me it was all about the game and the camaraderie and the hanging out. For him it was a brief respite from the world he lived in.

I sat at my desk, started my computer, and read my emails. They didn't tell me anything that I didn't already know.

After a few minutes, I began to pace, moving in a circle from the office area to the living room area to the dining area to the kitchen area. I told the computer to play random songs from my playlist, and it started with "River of Tears" by Madeleine Peyroux. I made it switch to "Cotton Tail" by Ella Fitzgerald and then to "Gypsy Woman" by Muddy Waters and finally "Laughing at Life" by Susannah McCorkle before I shut it down entirely. Music suddenly held no appeal for me.

"Assume you were the intended target," I said aloud. "Who has reason to kill you?"

That's a long list, my inner voice reminded me.

"Recently. Who has reason to kill you recently?"

I created a file in my head.

Ryan Hayes.

Karl Anderson.

Hannah.

Hannah's mom.

Kayla Janas.

"Why?"

For the money, why else?

Except, I told myself, if Hannah and Kayla wanted Leland's $654,321, would they have warned me about it?

Seems unlikely.

Okay—Ryan, Anderson, and Hannah's mom.

Hannah's mom; that also seems like a reach.

She's in cahoots with Anderson.

We don't know that.

She waited twenty minutes after he arrived before she came out of her house to speak with him. Outside in the cold, not inside where it was warm. Why?

She didn't want Hannah to know about it. Probably Hannah was taking a shower or a nap or something.

Again, why?

Esti hired Anderson to keep Hannah safe at her readings.

Without telling her?

It's possible.

Why did Anderson follow you?

He doesn't know that you're a good guy. As far as he's concerned, you're just another asshole.

If he tagged my Mustang, would he admit it to the police?

Would you?

PIs need to follow certain rules or risk being brought up before the Private Detective Services Board and having their ticket pulled. One of the rules—cooperate with the police.

Yeah, speaking from personal experience we know how much people love to obey the rules.

"I should talk to him," I said aloud.

Yeah, but will he talk to you?

If he's clean . . .

That leaves Ryan Hayes.

Assuming Hannah and Kayla didn't tell anyone else about Leland's offer.

They said they didn't.

"This is crazy." I shouted at the empty room. "This is one hundred percent Looney Tunes. I don't believe any of it. Dead men do not talk from the grave. They certainly don't arrange assassinations."

Hannah Braaten and Kayla Janas believe differently.

Do they? Do they really? They're entertainers, after all. Actors. They make their living convincing the audience to believe what it already wants to believe. That doesn't mean they believe it themselves. Does the actress Gal Gadot actually think she's Wonder Woman? I mean, I believe it. But does she? I bet she doesn't.

Ryan Hayes believes.

Does he? Or does he simply want to believe?

Isn't that the same thing?

"Dammit."

Besides, it doesn't matter if the psychic mediums are telling the truth or if all this is part of some sort of elaborate scam. Frank Fogelberg is dead, and that's as real as it gets.

"Were the bullets meant for me?"

Which brings us back to where we started.

I lay down on the sofa in front of the unlit fireplace and contemplated what I should do next that wouldn't get me in big trouble with Bobby and his homicide detectives. Nothing came to mind, so I considered what I could do next that would only get me into a little trouble with Bobby and his homicide detectives.

That's when the phone rang. The caller ID claimed it was a phone number in St. Paul. I swiped right.

"This is McKenzie," I said.

"Mr. McKenzie, this is Kayla. Kayla Janas. May I—I was just speaking to a couple of detectives from the St. Paul Police Department about—about a shooting and they asked about you and what I told you and Ryan Hayes and—Mr. McKenzie, is this on me, what happened?"

"Of course not."

"May I speak to you? I mean, may I see you? Can you meet me somewhere? There's a café near where I live . . ."

I gave it a couple of beats and answered, "Sure."

TEN

I had never been to the French Meadow Bakery and Café on Grand Avenue in St. Paul. I figured it to be little more than a grandiose coffeehouse catering mostly to the students that attended Macalester College just a couple of blocks up the road. Yet it served full breakfast, lunch, and dinner menus, gourmet desserts, and, more importantly, beer, wine, and cocktails in fairly elegant surroundings. It was also tastefully decorated for Christmas, and I felt a little embarrassed that I was wearing a sweatshirt beneath my brown leather jacket and a nine-millimeter SIG Sauer on my hip.

Kayla was sitting at a small table not far from the door. She was dressed in the same kind of clothes she'd worn the first time I met her, tight jeans, knee-high boots, and a sweater, only this time the sweater was red. Again I was impressed by how young she appeared.

She smiled when I stepped across the threshold as if she were glad to see me. I couldn't imagine why. As I approached she glanced to her right. I followed her eyes while pretending not to, because I didn't want the man sitting at the corner of the bar and watching us to know that I had made him.

"Ms. Janas," I said.

"Kayla, please."

I draped my jacket across the back of a chair and sat across from her.

"The reason you're named Rushmore—your parents took a vacation to the Badlands of South Dakota," Kayla said. "You were conceived in a motor lodge very near the Mount Rushmore monument."

Okay, not exactly a secret. Still . . .

"It could have been worse," I said. "It could have been Deadwood."

A waiter materialized next to the table and asked if I would like something from the bar. Kayla had jolted me with her pronouncement, and making choices suddenly seemed difficult for me. Fortunately, there was a table tent in the center of the table advertising something called a Jamaican Moscow Mule. I pointed at it and said, "I'll have one of those."

The waiter disappeared.

"You seem to know a lot about me," I said.

"Only what people tell me," Kayla said.

"What people?"

"The ones looking out for you."

"There are people looking out for me?"

"Quite a few, actually. McKenzie, the man who was killed, the one that the St. Paul police asked me about—am I responsible for what happened to him?"

"I wouldn't think so."

"If I hadn't told Ryan Hayes what his father wanted . . ."

"We don't know for sure that Ryan is involved. This could all be one big coincidence."

"Do you believe that?"

No, my inner voice said.

"Things happen all the time that seem connected but aren't," I said aloud. "That's why we have a word for it."

"I try to do the right thing, only I'm not always sure what the right thing is, what I should do."

"You mean like the rest of us?"

"It's different with me, though, because of my—I call it a gift now, but I haven't always," Kayla said. "Growing up . . . I started talking to dead people when I was four. My parents—my family thought I had imaginary friends and that I would grow out of it, only they weren't imaginary, they were my grandfather, who died when I was three, and my uncle, who died before I was born. They'd give me messages that I would deliver to my family. I told my mom about a savings account that had somehow gone unnoticed when my uncle's estate was settled. My uncle, my mom's brother, wanted her to buy something nice for herself for her birthday with the money. My family checked, and sure enough, there was a savings account in my uncle's name at the bank. Instead of thanking me, though, they took me to see a therapist to help me deal with my issues. They took me to see a minister, for God's sake.

"Did I tell you that I'm from a small town in the northwest corner of Minnesota? Did I tell you that the members of my family are all Christian fundamentalists? That they refuse to accept that I can talk to the spirits of the dead but are more than happy to believe that I'm possessed by the devil? It didn't take long before I learned to hide my gift, to fight against it. I did not want to go to hell, McKenzie.

"Only sometimes the voices would get so loud and the messages were so compelling that I had to deliver them, even if it was just to make the voices stop. Once, when I was in high school, I gave a classmate a message from her mother, who died two weeks earlier from cancer. I was overheard and brought to the principal's office. I was suspended from school for a week for telling lies. My parents forced me to spend the entire week living on bread and water in my bedroom. Well, not bread and water, but . . . On the other hand, my classmate was very grateful to me. What I told her helped her a lot. We're still good friends; we talk all the time. You don't want to hear any of this."

"Yes, I do," I said.

"You don't believe a word I'm saying."

By then the waiter had reappeared with the Jamaican Moscow Mule I had ordered. I took a sip.

What the hell is in this thing? my inner voice wanted to know.

I read the table tent—fresh muddled lime, organic vodka, Jamaican ginger beer, fresh mint. I nudged the drink away.

That'll teach you to read the small print.

"Kayla," I said, "I'm trying to understand. Three days ago, as far as I was concerned, physics and mediums and ghosts and messages from the dead were the stuff of horror movies like *The Dead Zone* and *The Sixth Sense* and *The Conjuring*."

"Don't forget *Hamlet*."

"*Hamlet*? That's right. The king comes back from the dead and orders his son to wreak vengeance upon his uncle Claudius for killing him, seizing his throne, and marrying his wife, Gertrude, who was also Hamlet's mother."

Jesus, you're living a Shakespeare play.

"My point is," I said aloud, "I was never asked to believe it was real until now."

"I understand, McKenzie. Believe me. I asked my family to believe it was real. You know, they still send me Bibles. I have about thirty of them."

"What happened?"

"What usually happens when you go against your family's beliefs? You're asked to leave the family until you agree to live your life exactly the way they want you to. I don't suppose it's any different than coming out that you're gay. Or a liberal Democrat. It's hard. I love my family. But hiding who I am, that's harder."

"When did you decide to come out?"

"What do you mean?" Kayla asked.

"When did you start doing readings?"

"Oh. When my money started running out. I'm a student, McKenzie. I'm studying sociology at Macalester. I have a half-ride scholarship and a low-interest student loan, but that only goes so far, and this is a pretty expensive school. I'm not getting help from my family, so to make some extra money, I've been doing readings, just a couple a week. My roommate and a few friends have been encouraging me. They all think I should do this for a living. Only I haven't had the training. I've taken a few classes, but like I said, I'm a full-time student. I really don't have the time or the money. Maybe after I graduate . . .

"For now—I'm still learning my craft, so I'm trying to stay low-key. I don't do ambush readings. I don't go up to people on the street and tell them I have a message from their dead uncle even if their dead uncle wants me to deliver a message. I'm not sure anyone does that except for the mediums on TV.

"I try to be as honest as I can, as professional as I can," Kayla said. "This thing with Ryan Hayes, though . . . I shouldn't have told him what I did. Now a man is dead and I'm not sure why. The police officers that talked to me weren't very forthcoming. One of them, the woman—"

"Jean Shipman?"

"Do you know her?"

"Yes."

"She's kind of mean."

"Yes."

"Or was that an act, like in the movies? Good cop, bad cop?"

"No, she can be mean."

"Honestly, McKenzie, I'm frightened that somehow I'm to blame for all of this."

"You can't fault yourself for what people do with the information you give them."

"I keep telling myself that."

"Besides, if anyone is to blame, it's me."

"You?" Kayla asked.

"For involving myself in all of this. There's a lot to be said for staying home and reading a good book."

Kayla took a sip of the drink in front of her. She was underage, so I didn't think it was alcoholic—probably a colorless soft drink with a twist of lime, which must have cost her at least a Lincoln in a joint like that. I decided to pick up the tab, having been a poor college kid myself at one time.

"Tell me something," I said. "Have you told anyone else about Leland Hayes and Ryan and the money?"

"No. Well . . ."

"Well?"

"I told a few friends."

"The friends that are encouraging you to make use of your gifts?"

"Yes."

"Does that include the man sitting at the bar?"

Kayla's head twisted toward the bar and back at me so quickly I was amazed she didn't suffer whiplash.

"I spotted him the moment I walked through the door," I said.

"You have gifts, too."

"Does he know the topic of our conversation?"

Kayla nodded.

"Wave him over," I said.

She did.

I called him a man and technically he was, but seeing him up close I decided that he couldn't have been much older than Kayla.

"I'm McKenzie."

I offered my hand and he shook it. His grip wasn't particularly firm, but he was watching Kayla at the time, so . . .

"Join us," I said.

He waited until Kayla nodded her head before pulling a chair from an empty table and sliding it in front of ours.

"And you are?" I asked.

"Kyle Kershey." He spoke his name as if he didn't expect me to believe him.

"You kids know each other well?"

Kershey actually blushed at the question.

"We met on campus," Kayla said.

"You're going to Macalester, too?"

"I'm a junior," Kershey said.

"What are you studying?"

"Anthropology."

"Good luck with that."

"No, no, no." Kershey told me that I would be surprised at the job opportunities and listed a dozen.

I *was* surprised, too, especially when he mentioned foreign service officer and social media analyst in the same breath. I told him that I had always thought of anthropologists as the guys who dug up old bones.

He said anthropology was the science of human beings regardless of when they lived.

I flashed on Leland Hayes.

"How 'bout twenty-two years ago?" I asked.

"Now we're talking ancient history," the kid said.

If only, my inner voice said.

"This thing with Leland and Ryan Hayes and all that money—is this a topic of conversation between you and your friends?" I asked.

"Not a topic," Kershey said. "Kayla told us what happened and that she went to meet with you, to warn you. She was afraid that she broke the rules that psychics are supposed to follow."

And then broke the rules some more while she discussed breaking the rules.

"When the cops showed up at the dorm, we talked about that, too," he added.

"Whose idea was it that she and I should meet here?" I asked. "Instead of talking on the phone?"

"I prefer to speak to people in person," Kayla said.

"So you can read them?"

She nodded.

"Here's the thing," I said. "Your girlfriend . . ."

Kershey blushed again, but I guessed the term was accurate, because Kayla reached across the table and took his hand.

"I'm guessing you're here to protect her," I said. "Neither of you know me, and you want to make sure your girlfriend is okay. Think wingman on a blind date, right?"

"Yes."

"Only you're not doing Kayla any favors sitting on the other side of the room. How are you going to keep me from reaching 'cross the table and grabbing your girl by the throat?"

"McKenzie," Kayla said.

"Instead, you want to be sitting next to her. Your presence alone might discourage me from doing something foolish."

"She wanted to speak to you in private," Kershey said.

"Fine. You sit here until I arrive, introduce yourself, and excuse yourself to the bar. My knowing that you're near might also keep me from doing something foolish. I tell you this because"—I gestured at Kayla—"if you're going to do readings of people you don't know, you need to be careful. Do I have to tell you that?"

Kayla continued to hold Kershey's hand while she reached across the table with her other hand and grabbed mine. I smiled and shook her hand free before it became creepy and stood up. I reached into my pocket, grabbed a twenty, and dropped it on the table.

"On me," I said.

"McKenzie, no," Kayla said.

I grabbed my coat off the back of the chair.

"Keep in touch," I said. "Let me know if you run into Ryan Hayes again."

"I will," Kayla said.

"Take care, you guys."

"See you later," Kershey said.

I turned and headed for the door, telling myself that "See you later" was such a Minnesotan thing to say. At the same time, it made me flash on everything else Kershey had told me, especially the part about how anthropologists analyze social media. It reminded me that Karl Anderson's website claimed that he provided expert social media research and analysis.

I wonder if that's the same thing, my inner voice said.

My Mustang was parked on Grand Avenue. I put on my gloves against the ten-degree temperature as I walked to it, climbed inside, started the engine, and eased it into the traffic. I passed several other parked cars as I accelerated. One of them was started, moved onto Grand, and began following me. A sudden shiver rippled through me that had nothing to do with the cold.

I drove east along the border of the Macalester campus

toward Snelling Avenue, telling myself that I was just being paranoid. Even so, as I slowed to a stop because of the traffic light, I unzipped my leather jacket so I would have easy access to the SIG.

I watched carefully to see if the driver attempted to move parallel to me—like the driver who had killed Frank Fogelberg. He didn't. Instead, his turn signal told me that he intended to follow me south on Snelling, and when the light changed, that's exactly what he did, staying three cars lengths behind me.

My cell phone began playing Louis Armstrong's opening cadenza to "West End Blues." I refused to answer, letting the call roll over to voice mail while I concentrated on the vehicle behind me. I couldn't identify it in the dark, although I was pretty sure that it wasn't Anderson's Chevy Tahoe.

When we reached St. Clair, I hung a sharp right. The trailing vehicle kept going straight. That didn't exactly set my mind at ease, however. I continued along St. Clair until I hit South Vernon Street and hung another right, this time without signaling. Vernon took me into an area of St. Paul we called Tangletown because the streets had no rhyme or reason to them. It was as if they were laid out by a particularly creative child playing with an Etch A Sketch. I drove them carefully. If someone was still following me, I would have known it.

Unless they tagged your car again.

I returned to the garage beneath my building and searched the Mustang with my hand-cranked flashlight. This time I didn't find anything, and believe me, I looked real hard.

I didn't think to listen to my voice mail until I was alone in the condominium. I accessed it even before I took off my jacket. The message was from Esti Braaten; I remembered that I had given her a card with my phone number.

"Mr. McKenzie, my daughter and I have just suffered through a very unpleasant police interrogation."

In the background, I heard Hannah's voice say, "Really, Mom? Interrogation?"

"We would like to discuss the matter with you as soon as possible. Would it be convenient for you to meet us at eleven tomorrow morning at the Twin Cities Psychic and Healing Festival? Hannah will be giving a lecture at ten and won't be available until after that. You can find us at her booth near the wall on your right when you enter."

"Why not?" I said aloud, although there was no one to hear me.

I dropped the cell back into my inside jacket pocket and glanced down at the hockey bag and sticks still resting next to the desk.

Ahh, what the hell, my inner voice said.

I picked up my equipment and headed for the door.

ELEVEN

The Twin Cities Psychic and Healing Festival was held in a hotel in a suburb just south of Minneapolis not far from the airport. I was surprised by its size—the festival's, not the hotel. A twelve-dollar ticket bought me access to well over fifty vendors operating out of booths in an enormous ballroom, plying a dizzying array of products designed to improve my health and/or soothe my soul, including jewelry, crystals, pendulums, essential oils, diffusers, candles, incense, aromatherapy products, makeup, organic skincare products, and self-improvement courses.

They also offered me holistic means of improving my health; guidance and spiritual healing through meditations, lessons, affirmations, and spiritual coaching; products to provide me with cellular detoxification; an aura reading designed to give me insight into my personality traits, relationships, career choices, true life purpose, and areas of personal growth; cranial sacral therapy, whatever the hell that was; and a reflexology session whereby a woman, using gentle pressure with her thumb and fingers on the reflex-pressure-point areas of my feet and hands, would reduce my stress, induce deep relaxation, improve circulation, boost energy levels, and rebalance all my major health systems.

You should do that last one, my inner voice told me, but I ignored it.

I discovered a Crystal Master who used "sound healing modalities, light, and all elements of the universe" to bring peace and light to everyone she encountered at a rate of $75 for a twenty-five-minute session and $140 for fifty minutes.

Another woman claimed to be able to channel the highest spiritual guidance and healing possible to bring clients powerful, practical healing and comfort for $110.

Still another promised to help individuals seek guidance from their Light Entourage, which included their Higher Selves, Guides, Angels, and even at times their passed-on loved ones, all for a ridiculously low price of $33 for twenty-five minutes.

A psychic who went by one name, like Madonna, offered to help me achieve a greater sense of inner freedom and self-worthiness, peace, and personal power through a combination of Energy Healing, Pranic Crystal Healing, Intuitive Scanning, Personalized Meditations, and Customized Affirmations, as well as EFT tapping.

A Reiki Master provided Norse Runes readings.

A Brazilian shaman offered readings with Avalon cards, Peruvian coca leaves, and Afro-Brazilian tarot.

A man who looked like Bobby Dunston's father was not only a Certified Master Hypnotherapist, Reiki Master, Theta-Healer, and Alternative Medicine Practitioner but also claimed to be an exceptional palm reader.

Still another woman who went only by her first name believed that her integrated palmistry/tarot readings were the clearest way to give me both broad and specific peeks into my destiny.

And then there were the dozen or so straight-up psychic mediums who all promised to connect me with loved ones who had passed over and, in most cases, to bring healing messages from the spirit world. They were scattered throughout the ballroom, each manning a booth that included a slightly out-of-the-way sitting area where they could meet with those clients that reserved time on their sign-up sheets. No two were side by side, and in most cases they were separated by several booths.

They all seemed to market themselves differently.

I walked up one aisle and found a psychic medium blessed with insight of intuition, clairvoyant, clairsentient, and clairaudient abilities who said that she had studied for a lifetime. Another claimed that she had forty years of experience traveling the world and doing energy work, readings, and ghostbusting. Another claimed to be "naturally gifted." Yet another boasted that she was one of the most admired psychic mediums by those in the know.

Walking down the next aisle, I found a woman—the majority of psychic mediums were women, I noticed—who dipped into her "spiritual toolbox" that included psychic, empathic, and mediumship abilities to best serve her clients; a woman with a direct and honest style that allowed clients to navigate through the fluff; and a woman who provided five-star integrity and an objective approach.

Across from them was a booth where two men worked as a team to provide clients with satisfying answers. Twenty yards to their left were three women who combined their individual gifts to give powerful and meaningful messages that would enlighten my journey.

I came close to laughing out loud a half-dozen times. Why wouldn't I? This was a universe of which I had no practical knowledge or experience, and because of that it was easy for me to dismiss it out of hand. Yet the place was packed with people both young and old. They couldn't all be crazy, could they?

I wandered around until I found a stand that served French beignets. I bought a couple and wandered some more.

Hannah Braaten had a booth just where Esti said it would be, except it was empty. My watch told me that she was still giving her lecture. The program I picked up at the door said that the festival offered three different fifty-minute-long lectures and workshops every hour on the hour. Hannah's was called "Spiritual Protection and Psychic Self-Defense: How to Protect Yourself in Daily Life." The title made me wonder if there might be something to all those movies I've seen over the years where the ghost hunters were attacked by the ghosts, a thought that would never have invaded my consciousness if Shelby Dunston hadn't insisted on telling me that a dead man had put a price on my head.

I finished the beignets and dropped the empty bag in a trash bin. Eventually the hall began filling with people who had just come from the lecture halls. The volume had already been high, the noise of a couple hundred people talking and moving about amplified by the walls and high ceiling of the ballroom. Now it shimmered with newfound excitement.

I found a spot where I could watch for Hannah.

"McKenzie?" a woman's voice asked.

I turned to find Kayla Janas approaching.

"It *is* you," she said. "What are you doing here?"

"I have an appointment to speak with someone. What are *you* doing here? Are you working one of the booths?"

"No, no, no, I don't have the experience for that yet. I came for the free workshops. The next one is about how the seven main chakras and the aura play a vital role in intuition, psychic abilities, and spirit communication."

"What are chakras?"

"The internal energy centers of the body. After that there's a workshop on reincarnation."

"Is your boyfriend here?"

"Kyle? He isn't really my boyfriend, although we do spend a

lot of time together." Kayla started chuckling. "No, he's not here. Ever since we met, he's been very supportive of me, yet I know, I just know, that he wishes I were a normal girl. My other friends, girlfriends, they're not here either. They say they love me and I believe them, but then they roll their eyes . . . I don't blame them. Growing up, all I ever wanted was to be like everyone else, too."

"Where's the fun in that?" I asked.

"I keep telling myself that we are all how God made us. If only I could convince my family."

"If nothing else, you'll fit in fine with this crowd," I said.

"Why's that?" Kayla asked.

"Look around. From what I've seen, the female psychics fall into two categories. They either look like your sweet old grandmother or they're babes. That sounds sexist, I know—"

"Which group am I in?"

"Stop it."

"I don't know about that," Kayla said. "They all look pretty normal to me. Well, there's Hannah. I was just at her lecture. She is so smart and so beautiful. Hey, that's who you're here to see, isn't it. Because she was the first psychic Ryan Hayes went to see."

"Yeah."

Kayla sighed dramatically. "I wish I knew how all this was going to work out," she said.

"Being a psychic, you're supposed to see the future, I thought."

Kayla reached out and seized my hand. She glanced around as if she were afraid someone was listening and lowered her voice.

"Sometimes I can," she said. "I don't know how or why, but sometimes . . . At the very beginning of the semester, we're all about to start classes after summer vacation; everyone's excited except for my roommate. She's distraught, so terribly upset. I asked her why. It turned out that her boyfriend back home dumped her the very night before she left Cedar Rapids, Iowa, to come back up here for school. She told me that she's had like a half-dozen boyfriends in high school and college and they all treated her like crap and she was blaming herself, saying she'd never find someone who loved her as much as she loved them. For some reason, I don't know why, I told her—there's a Caribou Coffeehouse just off campus—"

"I'm familiar," I said.

"I told her to go there. I told her to go there right now. I don't even know why; I just felt that's where she needed to be. She went. Probably she did it to humor me. She walked in the door, and standing in line to get a coffee was a guy she went to high school with in Iowa who she barely knew, didn't know he was going to the University of St. Thomas, didn't even know that he was in the Cities. They've been together ever since and couldn't be happier. Is that crazy or what?"

"A little bit," I said. "But in a good way."

"When I can make people happy it makes me happy, only I'm so terrified of unintended consequences. Readings that go badly. I mean, how happy have you been since I told you about Leland Hayes?"

"Kayla, this might make you question my sanity, but I'm actually enjoying myself. I live for this crap. God help me."

Kayla did something I didn't expect. She smiled and hugged me.

"I need to go to the next workshop," she said.

"Take care," I told her.

I watched Kayla walk out of the ballroom.

And watched Hannah walk in. She was wearing a rose-colored dress made of some magic material that clung to her curves yet managed to look loose-fitting at the same time. Her hair was up and her makeup was impeccable, and I thought, She's making an effort for the crowd.

That's when I noticed the cameras. Not cell phones held by fans looking for a selfie, hoping for something they could post on their Facebook pages, but professional video cameras. Hannah was being filmed. She was good at it, too, knowing how to play to the cameras, how to stand, to turn, to move without actually acknowledging their existence. I attributed her composure to her training as a model. The people who surrounded her were not nearly as skillful. They seemed genuinely intimidated by the cameras as well as the boom mics and the male director who attempted to choreograph everything without being noticed himself. Yet that didn't stop them from maneuvering around Hannah with the hope of being immortalized forever on high-definition video.

She stopped to speak to one woman in particular. The camera operators positioned themselves so that one was shooting Hannah, a second was shooting the woman, and a third was shooting them both with festival-goers in the background—all while keeping out of each other's shots. The conversation lasted for a good ten minutes and ended with the woman breaking down in tears and Hannah giving her a hug and a few encouraging words before moving on. Afterward, one of the cameras remained while a second woman, who I presumed was a producer, took a few minutes to interview the first woman, probably about her encounter with Hannah. The producer was holding a clipboard with a form that the woman eventually filled out and signed.

Hannah stopped to chat with a few more people, taking selfies and signing autographs as she made her way to her booth. Once there, she chatted, posed, and signed some more. Hannah's mother stood near her, yet always out of camera range. She saw me and gave a wave as if I were a waiter and she was ready to order dessert. I took two steps forward, then stopped when she raised her hand as if she had suddenly decided to go on a diet. A moment later, she left the booth and maneuvered through the crowd toward me.

"Mr. McKenzie." She held out her hand and I shook it. "It was kind of you to come."

"Ms. Braaten."

"You're probably wondering what's going on."

"No," I said. "Not really."

Esti seemed intent on telling me anyway. Apparently a production company with close ties to a cable TV network had arranged to follow Hannah during the festival. They were filming her interacting with her fans, giving lectures, giving readings, and generally emoting for the cameras—"emoting" was the word Esti used—against the possibility of turning her work into a reality TV series.

"You're telling me that all of this amounts to an elaborate screen test," I said.

"In a way," Esti said. "The producers hope to put together a pilot, and if it scores well with preview audiences, we could be on the air by next fall. The producers are hoping to call the show *Model Medium*, but neither Hannah nor I approve of the title."

Call it "Psychic Babe," my inner voice said. *No, no. "MILF." Medium I'd Like to—*

"That's exciting," I said aloud. "When did all this come about?"

"We've been talking about it on and off for a few months now, but the decision to go ahead didn't come down until Monday morning." Esti waved her hand at the film crew. "TV people seem to take forever to make up their minds, yet once they do, they move in a hurry. Mr. McKenzie, you've involved us with the police. As you might imagine, involvement with the police cannot be to our advantage at the present time."

"It rarely is at any time. What did they tell you?"

"Very little. Mostly they asked contentious questions and became accusatory when we couldn't answer them to their satisfaction."

Contentious and accusatory—that sounds like Shipman.

"I am sorry about Mr. Fogelman," Esti said.

"Fogelberg."

"However, we had nothing to do with his demise, Hannah had nothing to do with it, and we deeply resent that you've involved us."

"Look at it from my point of view, starting with the very real possibility that Fogelberg might have been killed because he was mistaken for me."

I explained why in detail.

"My daughter did not tell Ryan Hayes what his father told her during the reading," Esti said. "That was someone else's mistake. We are not responsible."

"Why was Karl Anderson following me?"

"How should I know?"

"I thought he might have told you when you chatted with him outside of your house twenty minutes after you and Hannah returned from the reading in Excelsior Thursday afternoon."

Esti gave it a few beats before she gritted her teeth and hissed between them. "You followed us," she said.

"No. I followed Anderson because I thought he was following you and your daughter, and I genuinely feared for your safety. I didn't know you were pals."

"Anderson is no friend of ours. I told him to stay away from us or I would call the police. McKenzie . . ." Esti closed her eyes and took a deep breath. She seemed to visibly relax as she slowly exhaled and gradually reopened her eyes. "McKenzie."

Instead of a hiss, her voice now had a nurturing quality, like a teacher trying to reach a troublesome yet promising student.

You should learn how to do that, my inner voice told me.

"McKenzie," Esti said, "when I first encountered Anderson at the community center, I assumed he was just another stalker."

"Stalker?"

"Perhaps that is too harsh a word. Unfortunately, they're attracted to my daughter like insects to a bright light, men who claim to fall in love with her at first sight and somehow expect her to reciprocate. This was especially true when she worked as a model. I've learned to spot them at a distance. Mr. Anderson attempted to charm her. Hannah was polite. I wish she would be more firm, but . . . In any case, Anderson quickly steered the conversation to the reading. He wanted to know what Leland Hayes told Hannah. He wanted her to contact Leland. Hannah refused to cooperate, which made him angry. That's when I stepped in. I told Anderson to leave or I would have him escorted from the premises, which was a bluff, of course. How many community centers have a security detail? He did leave, however. Then I saw him parked outside my house. I told him again to leave. I said next time I wouldn't bother to speak to him; I would simply pick up a phone and call the authorities. I didn't know he was a private investigator until you told me."

Why didn't you tell us this story when we asked about him the other day?

"Is Anderson working for Ryan Hayes?" I asked.

"He didn't say. I didn't ask."

"Perhaps I should."

"At the risk of seeming rude, McKenzie, I don't care what you do. Just don't involve my daughter."

"Fair enough."

"Often, the people who come to Hannah do so for very specific reasons and will feel cheated when their expectations go unmet. But this is—" Esti began to laugh and I didn't know why until she finished her thought and I realized that she was using words she must hear herself a hundred times a week. "This is nuts."

I laughed with her. Esti rested a hand on my wrist and bid me farewell. I watched her walk back to the booth and the fans and cameras that surrounded Hannah, and I thought I liked her more than I liked her gorgeous daughter.

Oh well.

By then another round of lectures and workshops was letting out, and the population and volume in the ballroom had increased precipitously. I thought of buying a second bag of French beignets for Nina. They weren't bad, and the woman did love her pastries. I gave another glance toward Hannah's booth as I moved down the aisle. I stopped when I saw that she was doubled over in a metal folding chair and holding her stomach. Esti moved quickly to her side and began rubbing Hannah's back in an attempt to comfort her. Cameras filmed her from three different angles. Festival-goers formed a semicircle around the booth and watched.

I moved toward her because, well, that's what I do. As I approached, Kayla came quickly to my side and grabbed my wrist.

"I'm so glad you haven't left yet," she said. "I'm a little frightened by all of this."

"Frightened by what?"

"He's here. I saw him wandering down the aisles and sneaking into the lecture halls like he's looking for someone."

"Who?"

"Leland Hayes."

My hand went immediately to my hip where I normally carried my SIG Sauer. Unfortunately, I'd left it in the trunk of my Mustang because the hotel banned guns on its premises. Or fortunately, depending on your point of view. I mean, who was I going to shoot at? I spun around looking for Leland Hayes and saw nothing.

"Where is he?" I asked.

"I don't know. I lost him a few minutes ago. What do you think he wants?"

I glanced back at Hannah, who was still doubled over in the chair and clearly suffering a great deal of discomfort.

"Payback," I said.

TWELVE

I moved toward Hannah. Kayla followed closely behind. We managed to filter through the crowd. Hannah looked up and saw me. She wrapped her arms around her stomach and rocked back and forth as if she were trying to hold herself together.

"I don't know what's happening," she said. "I opened myself up to do some readings and I became so nauseous. This has never happened to me before." Hannah continued to rock. "I had to shut down. It was too much."

"He's standing behind you," Kayla said. "He's smiling."

Hannah's eyes found Kayla's face. "Who?" she asked.

"Leland Hayes."

Hannah studied the younger woman for a few beats.

"You can see him?" she asked.

"Yes. Can't you?"

"I don't want to see him. It hurts too much."

Hannah took a deep breath as she uncurled herself until she was sitting straight. She continued to study Kayla's face as if searching for an answer to an unspoken question.

"What does he look like?" she asked.

"He has half a head."

"How do you communicate?"

"Words and pictures."

"Not feelings?"

"No."

"You're lucky." Hannah began rubbing her temples. "That hurts. What's he saying?"

"Nothing. He's just smiling. Now he's leaving. He's . . . He's gone."

"I don't think he came from the other side. I think he's earthbound."

"So do I."

"Who are you?"

"My name is Kayla Janas. I attended your lecture. I wish I could turn it on and off, like you do. I've never been able to."

"I try to stay in normal mode most of the time, because mediumship is extremely draining and sometimes I get physically sick if I stay open all the time," Hannah said. "I've learned how to set clear boundaries with the other side. You can, too."

All the while the cameras rolled. The director whispered into the ear of the man holding his camera on Kayla, and he nodded and moved slightly to his right. Next he whispered to the man holding the boom mics over Hannah's and Kayla's heads, and he nodded, too. He pushed past me and found a folding chair that he set in front of Hannah, again without speaking a word. Kayla must have received the message, though, because she sat down. A cameraman moved to his knees so he could shoot up at the two women.

"I screwed up," Kayla said.

"It was you who told Ryan Hayes about Leland's message, wasn't it?"

"It didn't occur to me to withhold it at the time."

"That's something else you can learn."

A look of concern crossed Esti Braaten's face as she realized that the entire exchange between her daughter and Kayla was being filmed.

"You need to rest," she said.

Hannah glanced at her. Apparently mother and daughter had a private language, because she nodded in recognition and slowly stood up. So did Kayla. The cameras followed them.

"I don't understand this," I said. "Leland shouldn't be here, should he? You told me that there almost always needs to be a personal connection to draw a spirit out."

"That's usually true," Hannah said. "On the other hand, I've had spirits contact me hours before I'm supposed to do a reading, especially gallery readings. That's why I always have a driver. Some of the spirits, they'll ride in the car with me."

"Yes, but the spirits are connected to the people you're going to read. Or am I mistaken?"

"No, you're not mistaken."

"So why is Leland here?" I asked.

Part of the answer came from a few booths down. The two male psychic mediums who were working together began to speak in loud voices.

"McKenzie," they said. "Is there a McKenzie here?"

The female psychic medium who was blessed with insight of intuition, clairvoyant, clairsentient, and clairaudient abilities asked the same thing. "McKenzie?"

The psychic medium with five-star integrity gripped her head in the same way that Hannah had and called my name as if it caused her pain.

The woman whose reputation everyone was supposed to know said the same thing, except instead of sounding like someone in pain, she seemed to be attempting to locate the owner of a freshly brewed café mocha. "McKenzie, please."

Not all of the mediums were chanting my name, however. Most of them seemed as puzzled as I was.

Festival-goers began talking to themselves, confused looks on their faces. Some of them repeated my name as if saying it out loud would bring clarity.

The director of the film crew spun in a circle, looking above the heads of the festival-goers as if the answer could be found in the distance.

"What's going on?" he asked.

My name echoed through the ballroom.

"Who the hell is McKenzie?"

I found Esti's terror-stricken face. I don't know why I laughed, yet I did.

"This is nuts," I said.

"Who's McKenzie?" the director asked again.

I had no intention of answering. Unfortunately, Hannah, Kayla, and Esti were all focused on me, and the director took a chance.

"Are you McKenzie?" he asked.

"I'm going to take off," I said.

The director grabbed my arm. "No, you're not," he said.

I looked down at his hands and then up at him. "Don't do that," I said.

He must have heard something in my voice that resonated, because he released me and took a step backward. The cameramen weren't as easily intimidated, however. They continued to point their cameras at me.

"It's possible that Leland has attached himself to you," Hannah said. "I've seen it before." Hannah glanced at Kayla.

Kayla shook her head. "I don't see him," she said.

The other psychic mediums continued to ask for me. The director sent a camera out onto the ballroom floor to record them asking for me. Another filmed a wide shot of all of us; the third camera stayed close on Hannah.

"It's possible Leland's in hiding," Hannah said.

"Why would he be hiding?" I asked.

"This place is crawling with ghostbusters. Someone might decide to take him on."

"Are you listening to yourself?"

Once again I was challenging Hannah, and she wasn't happy about it. Neither was her mother. I expected some sort of retaliation, yet none came.

Esti continued to rub Hannah's back.

"Why is this ghost contacting all of the other mediums?" the director asked. "What does he want?"

"Why don't you go and ask them?" I said.

I was hoping the director would leave. Instead, he sent his producer, the young woman with the clipboard.

"I don't think McKenzie is a negative person," Kayla said. "He's skeptical, that's all."

"I've noticed," Hannah said.

"He wants to believe. He just can't let himself do it."

Hannah waved more or less at the entire festival and the psychic mediums chanting my name.

"Despite all the evidence right in front of him," she said.

"You'll notice I'm standing right here," I said.

"I can't help you if you don't trust me."

"What are you, Tinker Bell? I have to clap my hands to prove that I believe?"

Hannah glanced at the younger woman.

"I don't know how to help him either," Kayla said.

The producer returned and whispered into the director's

ear. The director repeated her words loudly enough for the festival-goers close to the booth to hear.

"A ghost is offering a reward to anyone who shoots McKenzie?" he said.

The crowd gasped.

"This is great," the director said.

"I'm going home," I said.

"No, no, no, no, no . . ." the director chanted.

"You know how to reach me if you need me," Hannah said.

"Wait." The director was clearly annoyed. "Let's just wait a minute."

Hannah turned toward Kayla. "Would you like to have lunch with my mother and me?"

"I don't want to intrude," Kayla said.

"We welcome your company. Don't we, Mom?"

Esti didn't seem to care one way or the other.

It was clear from Hannah's tone that the invitation did not include the director and his crew.

"Ms. Braaten," the director said, "we need to talk."

I don't know if he meant mother or daughter. It was mother who answered.

"Hannah needs to take a break," Esti said. "We will return by one."

"Wait a moment. We had an understanding."

"One P.M."

Hannah, Esti, and Kayla left the booth and moved toward the exit at the corner of the ballroom. I guessed that they would have lunch in the hotel's restaurant.

I went toward the exit in the opposite direction while trying to ignore the gawking expressions of the festival-goers as I moved past them. I had no doubt they thought the entire scene was well worth the twelve dollars they paid at the door, ten in advance.

The director stood in the booth behind me, surrounded by his crew and their equipment.

"This is so unprofessional," he said.

I moved through the ballroom, across the crowded lobby, and into the parking lot that wasn't crowded at all. I headed for my car. Two young men and a woman followed me. I was nearly halfway to my car when I turned to challenge them. Probably that was a foolish thing to do; if it had been just the two men, I wouldn't have done it. The girl, though, made me think they were more curious than confrontational.

"Can I help you?" I asked.

They halted about ten yards short of me. The hands of the two men were empty. One was wearing gloves; the other was not. The woman was carrying a large bag over her shoulder. She was holding the strap with one hand, but her other hand was inside the bag.

My inner voice said, *When are you going to learn that women are just as dangerous as men?*

"Are you McKenzie?" the taller of the two men asked.

"Yes."

The woman removed her hand from her bag. She was holding a cell phone.

Lucky you.

"May I take your photograph?" she asked.

"No."

"Please. I'm taking a sixteen-week class, Psychic Spiritual Development. Next week we're doing a section on reading photographs."

"What does that mean?"

"Energy is captured in a photograph, and this energy can reveal secrets about you to those people who know how to read it, and I thought, given what just happened in there, I would really like to try to read yours."

"No," I said.

The woman seemed disappointed by my response. Her two friends seemed like they were willing to make an issue of it.

"Are you sure that's all you wanted?" I asked.

The two young men glanced at each other.

"I have a question for you," I said. "Assuming you're foolish enough to believe what those mediums were saying about me, how are you going to collect the money? Are you going to find a psychic to dial up the spirit of the dead man? And then what? Confess to committing murder and demand the dead man pay up? What if he doesn't? What are you going to do? Threaten his life? Oh, wait."

"We didn't mean nothing," the taller man said.

"The lady just wanted to take your pic," the shorter man said.

I was paying so much attention to the two men that I didn't notice the woman bring her cell up and snap my photo until I heard the metallic sound that her phone made.

"Thank you," she said.

I shook my head at her audacity. Normally I would have admired it. Instead, I spun around and stomped off toward the Mustang. A quick glance over my shoulder told me that the trio was no longer following me.

When I reached the car, I popped the trunk, retrieved the SIG, and hung it on my belt behind my right hip even as my inner voice spoke to me.

Who are you planning to shoot? The girl with the cell phone? Her two friends? Leland Fucking Hayes? What you need is a crucifix. Some garlic. A mallet and a wooden stake.

I don't know why I thought that was so funny, yet it made

me laugh just the same—the idea that I would fight off Leland Hayes the way vampire hunters fought off Dracula, the way Peter Cushing went after Christopher Lee in all those great old Hammer movies.

"McKenzie," I said aloud, "you need a plan."

THIRTEEN

I didn't have a plan. Certainly none came to mind as I drove back to the condominium.

I stopped at the security desk, where I found out Smith and Jones were off for the next few days. I asked the woman working the desk if they had left a message for me. She said they hadn't, so I didn't know if they'd found the red Toyota Avalon or not. I might have called Bobby Dunston, except I didn't want to talk to him, or anyone else, for that matter. I couldn't think of a conversation that wouldn't make me sound like a lunatic.

I returned to the condo and started walking in a large circle again. By the third lap, it occurred to me that I had no basis on which to judge the reliability of any of the things that I'd seen or heard in the past few days.

"What you need to do is some honest research," I said aloud.

Unfortunately, of the thousand or so books Nina and I had collected for our library, not one was devoted to the paranormal, except for some Stephen King, Dean Koontz, and Neil

Gaiman, and I didn't think that they counted. There was the internet, of course, but after a half hour of surfing all I found was links to movies, books, psychic mediums, and TV shows. So what the hell, I decided, let's watch some TV. Except, where to begin? I found the titles of 167 TV series devoted to ghosts, psychics, and the paranormal broadcast in the United States since the midseventies, and the only one I recognized was *In Search of . . .* with Leonard Nimoy.

I browsed episodes of a handful of the more recent reality shows that I could watch on demand. There seemed to be a lot of contradictions. In one, an exorcist was brought in to cleanse a haunted house of a particularly pesky demon in an elaborate ceremony that included hand-holding, prayer, and burning sage. In another show, the owners were told that they should simply tell the ghosts they were not wanted and the ghosts would leave. In yet another, a psychic medium and an ex–New York homicide cop working together told the homeowners that nothing could be done and they should move. In the fourth show I watched, a group of ghost hunters confirmed that a bed-and-breakfast was indeed haunted, as the owners had surmised, but the spirits weren't particularly malicious, and they, the B&B owners, and their guests could happily coexist if they simply treated one another with courtesy and respect.

I suppose you could learn to live with a ghost, my inner voice told me.

Stop it, I told myself. There are no such things as ghosts.

Who told you that?

My parents.

So Hannah and Kayla and all those other psychic mediums chanting your name at the Twin Cities Psychic and Healing Festival were just making up all this crap?

This time I spoke aloud. "There are no such things as ghosts."

It was at that precise moment that my baseball was swept off the shelf of a bookcase onto the hardwood floor.

It occurred so quickly and so unexpectedly that it took a few beats before I was able to register what had happened.

This wasn't just any baseball, mind you. This particular baseball had been autographed by the seven Minnesota Twins that played on the teams that won both the 1987 and 1991 World Series. It was enclosed in a clear acrylic square box near my desk.

I crossed the room, picked up the box, and held it up to the light. There was no damage.

My first question: What the hell?

My second: Really?

I told myself that there had to be a logical explanation for what happened that had never happened before. I returned the ball to its place on the shelf even as I entertained a theory involving street vibration and the weight of my building.

Didn't Minnesota Public Radio get something like $3.5 million from the Metropolitan Council to deal with the vibration caused by Green Line trains rolling past its studios in downtown St. Paul?

I took a few steps backward, all the time watching the box.

After a few seconds, I announced again, "There are no such things as ghosts."

The box began to tremble.

Then it stopped.

Then it flew off of the shelf and landed at my feet. We're talking at least a five-foot flight.

Three-point-five million bucks, my inner voice repeated.

Mind you, I had just spent a long Saturday afternoon fast-forwarding through over a dozen TV shows arguing that there really were ghosts and that most of them were assholes. Some of the shows even employed electronic devices to prove it, like EMF meters, EVP recorders, REM pods, IR lights,

FLIR thermal imaging cameras, and a lot of other stuff with acronyms that I didn't know. So while this might have freaked me out last Saturday, at the time it seemed perfectly reasonable.

Although, I had to wonder, why was I being haunted now when I'd never been haunted before?

What was it that Hannah Braaten said? It's possible that Leland attached himself to you.

Are you saying that Leland Hayes followed me home? I asked myself.

Hannah said she's seen it before.

I flashed on the episode where the psychic medium said that you needed to be firm with the spirits that invaded your space, that you had to let them know who was in charge.

"Hey, asshole." I spoke loudly. "Yeah, I'm talking to you, Leland Hayes, you godless prick. You ruined your life, you ruined your son's life, and now you want to fuck with me? Screw that. I want you out of here. This is my home, not yours. In the name of God, get out. In the name of the Father, the Son, and the Holy Spirit, take your worthless ass out of here and don't ever come back. Go to the other side and take responsibility for your crimes, you chickenshit."

I stood quietly and waited.

Nothing happened.

I waited some more, thankful that there was no one around to see or hear me—at least no one that I could see or hear.

Some people liked the sound of silence, whatever that was. It made me nervous, which probably said something disturbing about my personality. After a few more minutes of it, I said, "Got nothing to say for yourself? Fine."

I looked down at the acrylic box at my feet.

There are plenty of things that can't be explained, my inner voice reminded me. *That's why ancient cultures invented gods.*

I picked up the box and walked it back to the bookcase. I told the computer to play random songs from my playlist, and she settled on the Frank Sinatra–Aretha Franklin duet of "What Now My Love" to start. I arranged the box on the shelf so that Kirby Puckett's autograph was facing outward.

I was interrupted when the door to the condominium opened behind me.

For some reason, the light metallic sound of lock and door handle sounded as loud as gunfire.

I spun toward it and stared.

Nina looked back at me.

"You okay?" she asked.

"Hmm? Sure. Fine."

"What are you doing?"

"Looking for something to read. What brings you home so early?"

"I don't know." Nina dropped her bag and coat on the chair where she usually dropped her bag and coat. "I just felt like I should be here."

I flashed on the story Kayla Janas told me about her roommate, about how Kayla sent her to the coffeehouse because Kayla felt that's where she needed to be.

C'mon, McKenzie. It doesn't always need to be a thing.

"How was your day?" I asked.

"Not bad," Nina said. "How 'bout yours? How was the Twin Cities Psychic and Healing Festival?"

"It had its moments."

I walked toward Nina. She walked toward me. We kissed. Instead of I'm-happy-to-see-you, it felt more like I'm-happy-that-you're-in-my-life-and-please-don't-ever-leave-it.

"And what can I do for you?" I asked.

Nina smiled broadly, and I immediately thought of our master bedroom and the recent acceleration of our sex life.

"Take me dancing," she said.

"Is that a metaphor?"

She rapped my chest. "You always say you're going to take me dancing and you never do," Nina said. "We used to dance all the time when we first started dating."

I gripped my knee. "Did I ever tell you about my hockey injury?" I said.

"The one that kept you from playing hockey last night? C'mon, McKenzie. Step up. You owe me."

"All right, all right, I'll take you dancing."

"I expect you to do it with a smile."

I smiled.

The phone rang. Nina read the caller ID before answering.

"Hey, Shel," she said. "Before you say anything, McKenzie has promised to take me dancing, so . . . You and Bobby are welcome to come with, but . . . No . . . No, Shelby. If you want to join us . . . Threaten his life. That always works for me . . . Okay, okay. I'll see you then."

Nina hung up the phone.

"Here's the plan," she said. "They're hosting a Swing Night at the Wabasha Street Caves on the south shore of the Mississippi across from downtown St. Paul, the old speakeasy built into the sandstone bluff."

"I've been there."

"First, we're stopping at Shelby's, though. She and Bobby may or may not join us, she doesn't know yet, but she wants to see us."

"Why?"

"Who knows? Maybe she's had a vision. I need to change. Are you going dressed like that?"

FOURTEEN

I've seen Nina take an hour or more to get dressed and I've seen her do it in less than three minutes, yet she always looked great. At least, that's what I told her as we drove I-94 going east. We used the Cretin-Vandalia exit, which was starting to make me nervous, and a series of side streets to get to Bobby's house across from Merriam Park in St. Paul, which made Nina nervous.

"What?" she asked.

"Nothing. Just being careful."

"Why? You know what? I don't want to know."

"Okay."

I took a left and then a right. There was no one behind me.

"All right, why?" Nina said.

I told her.

She closed her eyes and leaned back against the seat.

"You don't believe me," I said.

"I didn't say that."

"In the TV shows I watched, it's always the other way

'round. The woman says she's being haunted, and it's the husband or boyfriend who blows her off."

"I'm not blowing you off, McKenzie. But you're asking me to believe a lot of stuff that I've been taught isn't true, isn't real."

"Believe me, I know exactly how you feel. I'm having a hard time dealing with it myself."

Nina smiled.

"This is certainly a lot different than the usual miscreants you attract," she said.

"You mean like the guy you pushed down the stairs at the Minnesota Club that one time?"

Nina chuckled at the memory.

"Yeah, well, he had it coming."

Hugs and greetings were exchanged at the front door. Nina and Shelby stayed upstairs while I made my way to Bobby's man cave, which I had helped him build in his basement. He had the Minnesota Timberwolves on the big-screen TV; they were getting toasted by the Boston Celtics.

"What's going on?" he asked.

"Same old, same old. Not watching the Wild?"

"Between periods. Why are you dressed so nice?"

"Why aren't you?"

"Why would I be?" Bobby asked.

"Nina's making me take her dancing. I thought you were coming with."

"Ha. By the way, your pals Smith and Jones contacted me the other day. Did they tell you?"

"I haven't seen them."

"Turns out they had video that you told them to send me

of a red Toyota Avalon circling your building thirty minutes before Mr. Fogelberg left Friday."

"So it wasn't about me, then," I said.

"They sent us a copy of the footage, but there's not enough of it to confirm that it was the same car that followed Fogelberg."

"How many Toyota Avalons can there be?"

"One million three hundred and seventy thousand in the United States alone, including hybrids."

"In Minnesota? In the color red?"

"I don't believe in coincidences," Bobby said. "Neither do you."

"Yet they happen all the time."

"McKenzie, what are you doing here?"

"You invited me."

"Why would I do that?"

Bobby stared at me for a few beats. I stared back. He moved to the foot of the stairs and called up.

"Shelby?" he said. "Shelby."

She appeared at the top of the stairs. She was grinning the way she had just before she shouted "surprise" at Bobby's fortieth birthday party.

"You guys should come up to the living room," she said.

We walked up the stairs, through the kitchen, and into the living room. Hannah Braaten was sitting in Bobby's favorite chair. Shelby was standing behind her. Esti Braaten was sitting across from her daughter, and Kayla Janas was standing near the front door. She was the only one who appeared uncomfortable.

"Robert," Shelby said, "this is Hannah Braaten and her mother, Esti. I told you about Hannah."

Bobby glared at his wife much the same way as when he learned that he wasn't going to have the quiet fortieth birthday he had hoped for. Bobby hated surprises.

Hannah rose from her seat and extended her hand. "Commander Dunston," she said.

Bobby shook her hand, but I could tell his heart wasn't in it.

"McKenzie, it's good to see you again," Hannah said. "I hope you weren't too upset by what happened at the festival this afternoon."

"Meh," I said.

Bobby glared some more. "What are you doing here?" he asked.

"I told Hannah that she could come over and speak with you," Shelby said.

"Why would you do that without asking me first?"

"They told me they wanted to help you, and I thought—"

"You know better than that."

They were the starkest words spoken in the harshest tone I've heard Bobby use to his wife in all the days I've known them and they jolted me. At the same time, Shelby shrugged as if she knew she had done wrong yet expected to be forgiven.

I glanced at Nina, who was leaning against the railing of the staircase that led upstairs. She made a big production out of looking at her watch.

"Well, you kids have fun," I said. "Nina and I—"

"This concerns you as well, McKenzie," Hannah said.

"In what way?"

"The reason Leland Hayes was at the festival this afternoon spreading your name around—Ryan was there," Hannah said. "He arrived just as you were leaving."

"Did he?"

"This time, though, he wasn't looking for a reading. He didn't want to speak to his father. He hates his father."

I glanced at Nina again. This time she was actually tapping the face of her watch with one finger.

"What did he want?" I asked.

"He apologized, Mr. McKenzie," Kayla said. We all turned to look at her standing next to the front door. She was the only one who hadn't bothered to remove her winter coat.

"Apologized?" I repeated.

"He said he didn't know why he behaved the way he did, grabbing my shoulders and shaking me, threatening me," Hannah said. "He said it was like an outside force was controlling him. His father, perhaps."

"He said that he was sorry and that he wanted to help if he could," Kayla said.

"Help who?" I asked.

"Help you."

"Me?"

"Leland Hayes isn't just telling his son to kill you anymore," Hannah said. "He's telling anyone who will listen."

"Leland Hayes who was shot dead over two decades ago," Bobby said. "That Leland Hayes?"

"I know you're skeptical," Hannah said.

"Skeptical isn't the word for it. I've been a police officer for nearly twenty-five years. I've seen psychics come and go, all of them with information that they promised would help me solve a crime, usually a high-profile murder extensively covered by the media, and not one of them told me the truth. The Wetterling kid, Jacob Wetterling, who was killed back in '89, the crime solved twenty-seven years later—psychics started coming out of the woodwork forty-eight hours after he was abducted. And they kept coming. For years. Clairvoyants, tarot card readers, Indian medicine men, people with witching rods, Satanists, voodoo priests, witches, psychic mediums—and they were right about precisely nothing."

"There are frauds, that's true," Hannah said. "And some well-meaning people without the skills—"

"Well-meaning, my ass. This is a two-point-two-billion-dollar industry. You pretend to open a direct line to the after-life and deliver messages from dead loved ones to vulnerable people who are in mourning and in grief solely for the cash."

"Commander Dunston—"

Hannah's voice had a hard edge to it, as if she were about to deliver a vigorous defense, only Bobby was having none of it.

"Should I explain how you perform your magic tricks?" he asked. "With cold readings before a large crowd, you throw out simple generalities, a father who embarrassed you in public, a mother who died unexpectedly, because the broader the generalities, the greater the chance they'll resonate with someone, and when they do you can use their responses and nonverbal cues to make narrower and narrower guesses. We do it all the time in law enforcement. The Reid technique. The PEACE method. The kinesic interview. Pick your favorite interrogation process.

"With hot readings, you research the specific individual you're going to read, doing deep dives into the individual's social media history, often going back years and years. Not just theirs, but all of their family's Facebook and Twitter pages, too, searching for those tiny tidbits of information that they can't remember ever telling anyone. You find a pic of all the male members of the family wearing bow ties at Dad's funeral, you tell the subject, 'Your father liked to wear bow ties,' and the subject says, 'Oh my God, how did you know that?' I know how it's done because I do it every day to catch criminals."

"Are you calling my daughter a criminal?" Esti asked.

"Mother, please," Hannah said.

"We came here because we feared for Hannah's safety. Ryan Hayes threatened my daughter. That didn't get him what he wanted, so now he's pretending to be cordial, but he could easily turn on her again. He's the criminal, not Hannah."

"If you wish to file an incident report, there's a police sub-station less than two miles from here," Bobby said. "Or you could always call 911."

"Bobby," Shelby said, "I believe her."

"Four out of ten Americans believe her, and nothing I say is going to change their minds. Evidence—"

"Like the kind you take to court?"

Bobby lowered his voice. "Yes, evidence like the kind we take to court isn't the reason that you believe her, and it won't be the reason that you stop." Bobby moved next to his wife and gently stroked her shoulders. "Anyway, where's the harm in telling you that your grandfather loved you, that he didn't mean to die on your birthday, that it was just bad luck? Except it doesn't end there."

Bobby turned to Hannah. "Does it?" he asked.

"It was a mistake to come here," Hannah said.

"Why *did* you come here?" Nina asked. She was no longer looking at her watch. Instead, her arms were folded across her chest and she was leaning backward against the staircase as if she were surrendering to the inevitable. "Why didn't you call 911 if you felt threatened?"

"We believe if we can help the police find the stolen money, the money that Leland Hayes hid—without it, he has nothing to offer his son or anyone else. Without it, he has nothing with which to threaten McKenzie's life. Or mine." Hannah spun to face Bobby again. "I would think you'd want to find the money."

"Not me," he said. "I'm just a lowly local cop. Armored truck robbery is a federal beef. You should be talking to the FBI. Want me to give you some names?"

"Hannah," I said. She turned to face me. "This search for

the hidden loot—would it be conducted in front of the cameras I saw at the festival?"

"What cameras?" Shelby asked.

"They're thinking of making a TV series based on Hannah's life," I said. "*Model Medium.* They've been following her around with a camera crew, director, producers—"

"That has nothing to do with this," Hannah said.

"The woman, the young woman, with the clipboard . . ." Shelby was looking up to her right as if trying to remember. "At the reading. The one who stayed behind when all the others left. She was taking notes."

"I saw a woman at the festival with a clipboard, too," I said. "If we're thinking of the same person, she's a producer."

"What a coincidence," Bobby said.

"One thing has nothing to do with the other," Hannah said.

"You know what? I'm going to take your word for it."

"I'm sure you will. Good-bye, Commander Dunston. Mother?"

Esti rose from the chair, and together mother and daughter moved toward the front door.

"I'm sorry," Shelby said.

"Think nothing of it," Hannah said.

She opened the front door and Esti passed through it. Kayla Janas did not move, however. She stood as if fixed to the spot, her eyes staring off into the distance. Her lips moved slightly as if she were talking to herself.

"Kayla?" Hannah said. "Are you coming?"

Kayla's response was to take several steps forward until she was standing in the center of the living room, her arms held loosely at her sides. Her eyes were wide and moist and unblinking. She looked like someone about to do something that frightened her.

"Commander Dunston," she said, "Ruth Nowak says she's waiting for you to find her."

"What did you say?" Bobby asked.

"Ruth Nowak—"

"Don't do this."

"She's cold. She's alone."

"I don't know who you think you are—"

"She's wrapped in the quilt that her mother gave her for Christmas three years ago, purple and gold with a football helmet and the name Vikings stitched in the center."

Bobby moved toward the young woman until he was close enough to strike her. His fists were clenched, yet he did not raise them.

"Get out of my home," he said.

"Ruth needs you to find her."

"Let me guess—she's in a wooded area not far from running water, and there's an elementary school and train tracks and—"

"She's hidden in the trees between a small pond and the back fence of a farm near New Richmond, Wisconsin. A woman owns the farm. Animals live on it. Ruth doesn't know her name or what kind of animals."

Bobby stared for a good ten beats. I was a little speechless myself. Kayla had been so specific.

"Who are you again?" Bobby asked.

"Kayla Janas. I'm a student over at Macalester. Commander Dunston, please don't be angry. I'm new to all of this, and it scares the heck out of me."

Bobby stared some more.

"Good night, Ms. Janas," he said.

"Good night, Commander."

Kayla turned and walked out of the door that Hannah was still holding open despite the winter cold. After she passed, Hannah looked up at me.

"I've never seen skills like hers," she said.

Then she too left, closing the door behind her.

Bobby stared at the door for a long time. The look in his eye, the expression on his face—they told me that his cop's brain had left the room and he was now doing exactly what he'd told Deputy Chief Hodapp he was doing—working the case.

"That was fun," Nina said.

"I'm sorry, Bobby," Shelby said. "I didn't mean—"

Bobby spun around, moved to his wife, and wrapped his arms around her.

"Bobby . . . ?"

"I gotta go," he said.

"Go where?"

"McKenzie, you're coming with me."

"I am?"

"You're driving."

"I am?"

Bobby left the living room. He returned moments later wearing boots and putting on a heavy winter coat.

"Let's go."

"Go where?" I asked.

"Wait a minute," Nina said. "I thought we were going dancing?"

"Nina," Bobby said, "forgive me, please. I don't know how to explain this. It goes against my better judgment, yet I just . . . I have to go do this. Shelby, I just . . . There's someplace I need to be. McKenzie . . ."

I followed Bobby to the front door.

"Where are we going?" I asked again.

"New Richmond."

FIFTEEN

The road to New Richmond, Wisconsin, began for us back at the Cretin-Vandalia entrance ramp, where I regained I-94 and went east until we encountered I-35E and went north. At Highway 36 we drove east toward Wisconsin. Bobby didn't have much to say except "Nina's mad at you now. That's on me. Tell her I'll make it up to her."

"Oh?" I said. "Are you going to take her dancing?"

He didn't say if he would or wouldn't. I had the hockey game on the radio. The Wild rallied to beat the Maple Leafs in a shootout. Bobby didn't have anything to say about that either.

"Why are we doing this?" I asked.

We were fast approaching the St. Croix Crossing, the bridge over the St. Croix River that connected Minnesota to Wisconsin.

"That young woman, Kayla . . ."

"Kayla Janas," I said.

"She was so sure. So specific, telling me where Ruth Nowak was. There was no hemming and hawing, no probing to see if anything she said resonated."

"Did anything resonate?"

"Robert Nowak, Ruth's husband, has a receptionist working in his office. Molly Finnegan. She lives in New Richmond on a forty-acre alpaca farm."

"Alpaca?"

"You know, like llamas."

"I know what they are."

"Finnegan has a side hustle selling alpaca fleece. She has pictures of her animals on her desk."

"Let me guess—she's also young and pretty."

"No, she isn't. She's over fifty and looks it. Also, there wasn't any history of calls from Nowak to her cell, work phone, or landline. That's why it didn't click that she and Robert might have had a relationship beyond employee-employer."

"'Course, this doesn't answer my original question," I said. "Why are we doing this? You don't believe any of this psychic-medium crap."

"It's just a feeling I have. McKenzie, c'mon. Half the decisions you make are based on feelings that you have. Give me this one."

"Okay, but why do we have to explore your feelings in the dead of night? Why can't you do it with your team tomorrow morning?"

"I don't mind looking ridiculous in front of you."

"I think there's a compliment in there somewhere."

Once we crossed the bridge, Minnesota State Highway 36 became Wisconsin State Highway 64. We followed it through the town of Somerset, passing softball fields where we once competed in a tournament when we were kids. I mentioned them to Bobby, but he was busy working the case.

About forty-five minutes after we started, we reached the outskirts of New Richmond. Bobby used the GPS app on his phone to direct me north after we passed the municipal golf course, then west, north, east, and north again. We slowly passed a farmhouse sitting on a high hill. After a half mile, Bobby had me stop on the narrow shoulder of a country road. There were no lights to be seen, only the flickering stars in a brilliant night sky.

"Look at this." Bobby showed me a satellite image of the area on his smartphone. "This is Molly's farm. Her house, some kind of a barn, pond, wooded area, fence."

"Okay," I said.

"Follow this fence here. That's the neighbor's property. Follow it to the far corner here. Cross under the fence over to the wooded area. See what's there. Do you have a flashlight?"

"I do."

"Don't use it unless you have to. Try to keep the beam low."

"Bobby, why me?"

"Do I need to explain the rules of evidence to you? I can't search this woman's property without a warrant."

"So get a warrant."

"Based on what? A psychic medium's vision? Get up the hill, McKenzie."

"Bobby, look at me. I'm dressed to go dancing."

"Whose fault is that? Get going. Oh, and leave your keys so I can start the car if it gets cold."

There was snow and ice in New Richmond. Not a lot, but enough to make my dress shoes inadequate for the task of following the fence line for a half mile. They made a disconcerting crunching sound as I walked on the frozen grass.

It was all of fifteen degrees above zero, and it didn't take long before my feet became cold, followed by my legs beneath the thin dress pants. I was wearing a sports jacket beneath a gray trench coat, so there was that. And gloves. Yet I wasn't wearing a hat, and by the time I reached the corner of the property my ears were numb. I was also breathing harder than you'd expect from the short distance I traveled. I was sure the puffs of breath escaping into the night sky must look like smoke signals to anyone watching.

The fence consisted of three horizontal strands of heavy barbless wire, and I wondered if it was electrified. I reached out and gently tapped the top wire. I wasn't immediately electrocuted, so I tried again, holding it longer this time, prepared to feel a painful electric shock that didn't come. Satisfied, I slipped between two of the strands and made my way to the wooded area.

It was darker there; the light from the stars overhead had a difficult time penetrating. Plus, it was quiet. The only sounds I heard were made by me.

I moved slowly from tree to tree, seeing very little. I flicked on my flash, pointed the beam at the ground, saw nothing but shallow snow, grass, and trees, turned it off, and kept moving until I reached the far edge of the tree line. The pond was located at the bottom of a gentle slope; the frozen water reflected the stars like a mirror. Beyond the pond was Molly Finnegan's farmhouse. I didn't see any lights burning in the windows, yet decided not to take any chances and slowly backed into the woods.

Again I used the flash, holding it close, my body positioned between the light and the farmhouse, as I chose a path among the trees. I flicked the light off and continued exploring.

I walked carefully, the way a blind man might in unfamiliar country. It was because I was being so careful that I didn't trip when the toe of my right foot caught on something. At first, I thought it was a tree root. When I turned on my flash, I saw that it was a shovel with a pointed tip made for digging. Next to the shovel was a purple-and-gold quilt rolled up around what I knew was Ruth Nowak's body. Both the shovel and the body were pushed up against two trees. Even in broad daylight they would have been difficult to find.

I wrapped my hand over the business end of the flash so that only a tiny bit of light could escape and squatted down next to the quilt. After a moment, I turned it off entirely, hoping the beam hadn't alerted anyone like, I don't know, the bitch who lived in the farmhouse on the hill overlooking the wooded area. Of course she was a bitch. She helped murder Ruth. At least, she helped the boyfriend dispose of the body.

It was obvious what had happened, too. Robert Nowak and Molly Finnegan had carried Ruth up to the wooded area where they planned on burying her. Only the damn ground was frozen, so they had just dumped her there, probably thinking they could finish the job come spring.

"I'm sorry, Ruth."

'Course, I didn't know her, any more than I knew her husband or Molly. She might have been a terrible human being. Only, she had deserved better than this.

God rest her soul, I thought.

Except her soul isn't resting, is it? my inner voice suggested. *Not if it's following homicide cops around and making itself known to psychic mediums that would be better off worrying about their college classes and not talking to the dead.*

"Jesus," I said aloud.

I stood slowly and edged away from the body. I hadn't touched the quilt or the shovel, and I hoped my wanderings wouldn't confuse the crime scene guys when they came to investigate. My intention was to make my way through the woods back to the fence.

The noise stopped me—a crunching sound of someone walking on the frozen grass and snow.

I remained still.

The crunching sound was on my right.

I listened hard, tilting my head in that direction.

It stopped.

Next I heard it on my left.

My head turned toward it even as my hand moved to my hip. Only, I was unarmed. I had hoped to go dancing with my girlfriend, after all, not search a dark grove for the body of a murdered woman.

The crunching sound on my left slowly circled me until it was on my right side again.

It grew louder before stopping altogether.

I flicked on my flashlight and pointed it at the noise.

I was startled enough by what I saw that I nearly cried out.

Two alpacas were staring back at me with huge brown eyes.

They were just over three feet tall with long necks that made them look bigger.

One was rust colored. The other looked like a pile of dirty snow.

"Fucking scared the hell outta me," I said.

They hummed at me like polite cows. It was such a soothing sound, I nearly apologized to them.

Then I thought, Do they bite?

I started backing away from them just in case.

"Nice alpacas," I said.

I flicked off the light, quickly returned to the fence, and slipped back through the two heavy wire strands. The alpacas followed me, until they were stopped by the fence. For a moment they reminded me of bored dogs looking for a pat.

"'Night, fellas," I said and started following the fence line back toward my Mustang parked on the country road.

I climbed inside the car and slid behind the steering wheel. The car was running. I hadn't realized how cold I was until I felt the warmth of the heater.

Bobby had been working his smartphone. He slid it into his pocket. "Well?" he said.

"I was nearly assaulted by two giant alpacas."

"Alpacas are among the gentlest creatures on earth. They have them in petting zoos, for God's sake."

"If you say so."

"What did you find?"

"Mrs. Nowak is there, wrapped in her purple-and-gold quilt just like Kayla said. They left her against the side of a couple of trees because the ground was too frozen to bury her."

Bobby stared at me for a few beats. Either he thought I was kidding him or he was having a difficult time digesting the news.

Finally he said, "She was telling the truth, then. Kayla Janas. She actually knew. How is that possible?"

"Kayla said that Ruth told her where we should look."

"How is that possible?" Bobby shook his head as if he needed to dislodge a thought. "When she told me about Mrs. Nowak, my first impulse was to slap her in the mouth. I had this feeling, though—something told me I needed to be here. Do you have any idea what I'm talking about?"

"I'm starting to."

"We can't tell anyone about this," Bobby said. "Can you imagine what the assistant county attorney would say? I'll have to find a way to connect Finnegan with Nowak and use that to get a warrant to search her property. Dammit. How is this possible?"

"I don't know. If one thing is true, though, does that mean all the other things they've been saying are true as well?"

"You're asking me, after the speech I gave Hannah Braaten in my living room?"

I put the Mustang in gear and started working my way back toward St. Paul. We didn't have much more to say to each other until we reached the St. Croix Crossing.

"Hey, Bobby," I said, "I did you a favor. Now you need to do one for me."

"What?"

"Tell me where I can find Ryan Hayes."

SIXTEEN

Ryan Hayes worked for one of those big-box chain stores that sold everything you could possibly need to take care of your house and yard, which kind of threw me. He had spent the last twenty-two years of his life in federal custody. I wouldn't think he'd have much experience with landscaping, carpentry, or plumbing. If someone asked him for a thingamajig to attach the whatchamacallit to the doohickey beneath the kitchen sink, how would he know what to tell them?

I found him in the millwork aisle. I didn't know what millwork was, although the doors, molding, trim, wall panels, and flooring suggested that it had something to do with wood.

He turned to face me. Hayes was about five years younger than I was, but he could have easily passed for ten, maybe even fifteen. He was wearing a cheerful smile, an orange apron, and a Santa hat. His name tag was on one side of the apron, and a button proclaiming that he was Employee of the Month was pinned to the other.

"How can I help you?" he asked.

"I'm McKenzie."

I didn't know what I was expecting. Fear? Anger? Indifference? What Hayes gave me instead was an even brighter smile.

"I thought you'd be taller," he said.

"I thought you'd look older."

"Nah. In prison you have regular meals, regular exercise, a good night's sleep, free medical care, a general lack of stress—it does a body good."

"I'll have to take your word for that."

" 'Course, I'm talking about federal prison. I have no idea what goes on in those state shitholes."

"I hear you're looking for me," I said.

"Why would I do that?"

"I can think of 654,321 reasons."

"Do you believe in ghosts, McKenzie? Do you really believe the old man would come from the grave to pay that kind of coin to zero you out?"

"I don't know what to believe."

"You're here, so you must believe somethin'."

"Mostly I'm here to find out what you believe."

"I owe you one, McKenzie, so tell you what. There's a snack bar towards the front of the store. Why don't you meet me . . ." Hayes looked at the silver watch around his wrist. "Thirty-five minutes? Is that too long a wait?"

"No. I'm fine."

"You might want to take a look over in electrical. We're having a sale on all of our light bulbs, including the ones that your computer can turn on or off. Brighten up your life, McKenzie."

I gave him a nod and walked away.

Now you know how he got to be Employee of the Month, my inner voice told me.

I killed some time wandering through the store. It had so many "perfect" Christmas gifts for sale that I began to reevaluate the meaning of the word. Plus the music; one Christmas song after another played over invisible speakers. It made me want to run out into the cold. On the other hand, it also reminded me that I still had plenty of shopping to do. What could I get Nina that was better than a brick of nickels? Two bricks?

Eventually I wandered over to the snack bar. It sold what you'd expect: hot dogs, Polish sausages, popcorn, chips, candy, coffee, soft drinks, ice cream bars and cones. I bought a small bag of popcorn and sat on a metal chair next to a round metal bistro table like the kind you could buy in the store's outdoor furniture department. Five minutes passed before Hayes appeared. He gave me a wave and went to the snack bar. A couple minutes later, he sat across from me. He had a paper boat filled with a Polish sausage in a bun with mustard, ketchup, and relish, a bag of barbecue potato chips, and a black coffee.

"In prison, all of the meals are nutritionally balanced," Hayes told me. "The first time I ate fast food, I thought I had died and gone to heaven. But after eating it for a solid week or so I thought I really would die. It made me feel sick and lazy. Just wasn't used to it, I guess. All that sugar and salt. I had to go back to the diet I've known for the past twenty years. Every once in a while, though . . ."

Hayes took a bite of the Polish sausage and hummed almost exactly the way the alpacas had hummed at me the night before.

"Other stuff," Hayes said. "I have no taste for pop, Coke, Pepsi, whatever. Those energy drinks, too—they just zap me, man. It's all just too damn sweet. And alcohol—I drank two beers the day I got outta the joint and threw 'em both up. I suppose I could develop a taste for it, but what's the point? Really, the only thing I can drink is coffee. Black coffee, too. I can't doctor it up like they do in all those coffeehouses, Starbucks and Caribou and Dunn Brothers and—I can't believe there are so many coffee shops. How the hell do they all stay in business? In them Hallmark movies, the coffeehouses are always about to go out of business till the women who own 'em find the men of their dreams and they work together to save 'em, you know? Coffeehouses and bookstores."

"You watch the Hallmark Channel?" I asked.

"Not when I was at Big Sandy. That was all community TVs, and I watched whatever the other inmates watched; didn't say a word about switchin' no channels, either. You learn to pick your battles inside, and I sure as hell wasn't gonna fight over *Law & Order: SVU*, you know?

"In Sandstone, I was able to watch TV in the cell; forty channels, man. I bought myself a thirteen-inch flat-screen from the commissary for $200; paid for it outta my wages working maintenance, forty cents an hour. That's how I got the experience for this job. Whaddaya think, McKenzie? On the Hallmark Channel, even the villains are nice people. Think it's like that in the real world?"

"No."

"I learned that in a hurry. Gotta tell ya, though, gotta tell ya—if you're nice to most people, mostly they'll be nice to you. Am I talking too much, McKenzie? I've been told that I have a tendency to talk way too much."

"I don't mind."

"Lot of people do. They don't wanna hear the sound of someone else's voice when they can hear their own, you know? So what do you want to talk about? My old man, who came to me when I went to see the psychic? Hannah Braaten? Man, I've never seen anyone as beautiful as her. Growin' up in prison, I thought women like that only existed on TV, you know? Somethin' created by the special effects guys. I had sex only once before I went inside, and she was pretty but not that pretty. I didn't get laid again until—I hired a prostitute after I got out. She wasn't as pretty, either."

"Why did you go to see Hannah?" I asked.

"There was this woman I met, nice woman; met her after my thing with the prostitute. She heard about this Hannah Braaten and said we should go, kinda like a date, and I said sure because, well, a date. Then I fucked it up, grabbing Hannah like that and yelling. Shoving that guy. I don't know what I was thinking, what came over me. Never done anything like that, not even when I was inside. It was like I was possessed. Do you believe in possession? Anyway, the woman . . . I don't blame her for telling me to get lost.

"Then I did it again when I went to see the other psychic, the young one. She was pretty, too, but real, you know? Not like Hannah. And I lost it. Well, I didn't lose it; I didn't start screamin' like I did the first time. But I was rude to her, tellin' her to fuck the money, like who gives a shit, really? It's the fucking old man being an asshole. I don't give a shit about him. I didn't go to the psychics to see him, anyway. I wanted—you want to know the truth, McKenzie? When the woman suggested going to see a psychic, my first thought was that this was a chance to talk to my mom.

"All I really know of the world is what I've seen on television, 'kay? I watched all them shows about psychics talkin' to the dead—the woman on Long Island and the kid in Hollywood and the guy drivin' the taxi and the other woman, the big woman, I don't know where she lives. Saw the paranormal shows on TLC and Destination America and the Travel Channel. The Travel Channel, no kidding, like they're expecting people to visit all those haunted houses when they go on vacation or something. I believe it, too, you know? I mean, they can't be making up *all* of this stuff, can they? So when the woman mentioned seeing a psychic, I thought maybe I could talk to Mom."

"I get that," I said.

"Do you?"

"I'd like to talk to my mother, too. She left me when I was twelve, just like yours."

"Did she leave you with a sadistic sonuvabitch who spent the rest of his life fucking up yours?"

"No."

"Well, then we don't have as much in common as you think. My mom, all I had of her was a single photograph that I kept hidden beneath the floorboards of this shed we had out back where I'd go to hide from the old man, which was stupid because that was like the first place he'd look when he wanted to give me a beating. He'd find me, but I made sure he never found the photograph. I knew he'd tear it up or something if he did.

"I'll tell you, McKenzie. The reason I'm even here talking to you is because I figure I owe you one for putting a round in that bastard's head. The best thing that ever happened to me. That piece of shit—the only person I've ever hated. Except for maybe that prick judge who put a seventeen-year-old kid in prison for twenty-five years and one month for somethin' his fucking old man made him do. Ahh, you can't dwell on it. Can't dwell on it. Gotta move forward."

"Speaking of which . . ."

"Speaking of which, what exactly do you want, McKenzie?"

"First, I'd like to know that you're not going to shoot me for the reward your old man offered."

"What the cops wanted t' know, too. Did I shoot some guy named Fogelberg thinking it was you cuz I wanted to collect a reward from a dead man? Whaddaya say to a question like that?"

"What *did* you say?"

"I asked 'em when the murder took place, and then I showed 'em my time card to prove that I was here when it happened. Got the boss to vouch for me, too, which was hard cuz then I had t' explain what was going on, all the time wondering if I was going to lose my job because, you know, cops comin' here thinkin' I'm a person of interest every time somethin' goes down, the boss ain't gonna like that. He was cool, though.

"McKenzie, I'm not a criminal. I know that asshole judge slapped the word across my forehead and stuck me inside, but tellin' the truth, man, I never hurt anyone in my life, except for maybe that guy I shoved at the reading, and I'm really sorry 'bout that. That's why I went to that thing yesterday, that fair, and told Hannah I was sorry. I ain't my old man, 'kay?"

"You went to see Hannah?"

"I didn't want her t' think I was this raving lunatic, you know? She was cool about it, though. Friendly. Way friendlier than I thought she'd be. What else do you wanna know?"

"I'm thinking about going after the money," I said. "If I find it, it'll take the incentive out of shooting me. Want to help?"

Ryan chuckled. "That's what Hannah wanted, too; probably why she was so friendly," he said. "She wanted me to help her find the money. I nearly said yes because—have you seen Hannah? I mean seen her up close?"

"Yes."

"Wow."

Wow, indeed, my inner voice said.

"But you know what?" Ryan said. "I haven't thought about the money once in all these years. Why would I?"

"It would give you a nice start on the rest of your life."

"No, man. What I told Hannah, it would just chain me to the past, you know? Besides, even if I did know where it was and went out and dug it up, I couldn't keep it. If I tried, they'd toss my ass back inside. You're not allowed to profit from your crimes, McKenzie. Don't you know that?"

"What if I found a way around the statute?"

"A legal way?" Ryan asked.

"Yes."

"I don't know, man. I gotta think this would only dig up a load of bad shit for me, you know?"

"Worse than your old man calling your number from the grave—one one eight eight zero zero four one?"

"That's another thing. All this is based on the idea that the ghost of my old man is speakin' from the other side and that he's tellin' the truth, which he'd never done once when he was alive. I still have a hard time believin' it even after goin' to the second psychic to get, you know, confirmation. I just wanna forget the whole thing. Gotta move on, man, like I said."

Another employee wearing an orange apron walked up next to our table. He was about thirty with Hispanic features and looked as if he spent a lot of time outdoors even in the winter. His name tag read ROGER.

"There you are," he said.

Ryan looked quickly at his watch. "Am I takin' too long a break?" he asked.

"No, no." Roger set a hand on Ryan's shoulder. "No, God, take as long as you want. If everyone was as conscientious as you my job would be a breeze."

"If there's somethin' that you need . . ."

"I need you to move a display, no problem. It can keep." He offered his hand. "Roger Flores."

I shook his hand.

"McKenzie," I said.

"Yeah, yeah, boss, this is the McKenzie I told you about," Ryan said.

Roger's face lit up as if he'd just discovered that the Tooth Fairy was real after all. "No kidding," he said.

"Listen, I gotta get back to work," Ryan said.

"No hurry, kid," Roger said.

"I've already wasted too much time." Ryan stood and gathered up the remains of his snack. "Good t' see you, McKenzie. You take care."

"If I find a way for you to keep the money . . . ?"

He waved at me. "I don't want it," he said.

I stood abruptly and reached into my pocket. Ryan waited while I withdrew a card with my name and cell phone number. I offered the card and he took it.

"If you change your mind or if there's anything I can do for you," I said.

"Why would you do anything for me?"

"If you're nice to most people, mostly they'll be nice to you—words to live by."

Ryan waved the card at me in a kind of salute. A moment later, he deposited his debris in a waste can and disappeared deep into the store. I sat back down. Roger sat across from me.

"'Kid,'" he said. "Ryan's eight years older than I am and I call him kid. I suppose it's because everything seems so new to him that he's like a kid. The world today is way different from the one he knew when he was sent to prison a couple of decades ago. He's still trying to figure out how computers work, smartphones. Heck, he just got a driver's license last month. If you're McKenzie, you know all about that."

"A little," I said.

"He told me about you and what happened to his father and all that nonsense with the psychics. Ryan's not very good at keeping secrets. You'd think he would be after spending all that time behind bars. In prison, he said, you don't talk to anyone about anything. Out here, all he wants to do is jabber. He won't talk about prison, what happened to him in there. He'll talk about everything else, though. What he had for dinner last night. I can see that."

"Still . . ."

"Yeah, probably not the best thing. He'll grow out of it. Listen to me—he'll grow out of it. Like he really is a kid. So, you're McKenzie."

"I am."

"None of my business, but you mentioned money. Are you talking about the money Ryan's father stole?"

"If Ryan told you what's been happening, then you should know, it is not about the money. Rather it's about what some people might try to do to get the money."

"Ryan's a good kid. He's trying to get past all that. I wish you'd let him."

"Unfortunately, it's not just me. There seems to be a growing movement toward finding all that cash. Others might want to see if Ryan is interested in joining it. Just so you know."

"All right."

"He looks like he's doing okay."

"My wife keeps trying to line up women for him, but I don't know. Can you imagine being thirty-eight years old and having been on a grand total of three dates?"

"It's nice of you to look out for him."

Roger shrugged the way some people do when you congratulate them on being decent human beings, like it was no big deal. But it was.

"Good-bye, Roger," I said. "Thanks for your time."

A few moments later, I was in the parking lot and walking to my Mustang. Out of my peripheral vision I noticed a man moving quickly on an intercept course. It was twenty-two degrees and cloudy, yet his jacket was unzipped and he wasn't wearing a hat or gloves. That suggested he just threw on his coat when he saw me.

Had he been waiting in a car or the store? my inner voice wanted to know.

He couldn't have followed me, I decided. I had checked my car for a GPS transmitter before I left the condominium and was extra careful ensuring that I wasn't being tailed. Which meant he had been sitting on Ryan or . . .

The man reached me just as I reached the Mustang. I quickly raised my hand, a cop stopping traffic. He stopped and stared.

Amateur.

"If you're a friend of Ryan's you have no problem with me," I said. "Just ask him. If you're not a friend you should walk away right now, because I'm feeling a little cranky."

He smirked and moved forward. His hand dipped into his coat pocket.

"You think you're so fucking smart," he said.

I pulled the fingers of my right hand back and tucked in the thumb, preparing for what the karate guys call *Shotei Uchi.* As soon as he was within striking distance I drove the heel of my palm hard under his nose, knocking his head back. The blow wasn't necessarily meant to break his nose, but a cracking of cartilage suggested that I might have. He staggered and brought both hands up. He took two steps backward and sat on the dry pavement. Blood began spilling between his fingers.

"What are you doing?" he wanted to know.

"What are *you* doing?"

I stepped next to him and reached into his jacket pocket. Instead of a gun, I found a thin wallet. I opened the wallet. It contained a gold coplike badge with the word DETECTIVE embossed on it and a laminated card with a name, address, photograph, physical description, and the words PRIVATE printed across the top and INVESTIGATOR across the bottom in block letters reversed out of black bars.

"Karl J. Anderson, Private Investigator," I said. "Why are you following me?"

Anderson pinched the soft part of his nose just above his nostrils and tilted his head forward so the blood would drain through his nose and not down the back of his throat. Breathing through his mouth made him sound like he had just finished a race.

"I'm not," he said.

"Maybe not this time, but before."

"I don't know what you're talking about."

"That wasn't you following the Braatens all the way from the Minnetonka Community Education Center in Excelsior last Thursday? That wasn't you waiting for me outside Gracie's Power Academy Friday? C'mon."

Anderson didn't have an answer for that.

"Esti Braaten told me that you were stalking her daughter," I said.

Anderson tilted his head toward me and lowered it back down again.

"If she said so, it must be true," he said.

I nudged his leg with the toe of my shoe.

"C'mon, Karl," I said. "May I call you Karl?"

"May I call you asshole?"

"You should have identified yourself *before* you put your hand in your pocket."

"You've got a point. Look, Esti wanted me to keep an eye on Hannah from a distance. She was worried because of what happened with Ryan Hayes, but she didn't want her daughter to worry. Afterward, she asked me to check you out. She wanted to know if you were going to be a sail or an anchor."

"Sail or anchor?"

"Words she used."

"For what?" I asked.

"To find the money."

"What money?"

"I can't believe I let someone so dumb get the jump on me."

"Yeah, okay, the money that Leland Hayes stole. Why do they want to find it?"

"Guess."

"So they can give it back in front of every TV camera they can find."

"Was that so hard?"

"You're starting to annoy me, Karl."

"You have no idea how upset that makes me."

"When did the Braatens hire you?"

"None of your business."

"C'mon." I nudged him with my toe again. "Let's be friends."

"With friends like you . . ."

"Partners, then, to go after the money."

Anderson tilted his head again to look up at me. "Did Ryan tell you something?" he asked.

"He told me a lot of things; said he owed me for shooting his old man."

Anderson lowered his head again.

"When did the Braatens hire you?" I asked again.

"I met them for the first time last Monday."

The day before the reading that Shelby attended, my inner voice reminded me. *Before Leland Hayes made his appearance.*

"Did you tag my Mustang with a GPS transmitter?" I asked.

"The St. Paul cops asked me the same question. I didn't give them a straight answer either. McKenzie, I had nothing to do with what happened to Frank Fogelberg. As soon as I realized that I was tailing a silver Lexus, I knew you pulled a fast one and I let it go."

"Can you prove it?"

"I already have, to that female homicide dick—what was her name?"

"Jean Shipman."

"Yeah, yeah," Anderson said. "A real ballbuster, but I like her."

"I can't imagine why."

"She's smart. She's pretty. She's a good cop."

"If you say so. Why are you here?"

"After Esti decided that you were an anchor, they asked me to sit on the kid, Ryan Hayes. They were hoping that he might have a brainstorm and go searching for the money or that someone might come looking for help in finding it. Imagine my surprise when you showed up."

Anderson released his nose and snorted a couple of times. The blood stopped flowing. He slowly stood up. I could have helped him up but decided against it.

It's not like we're friends all of a sudden.

"This is where I warn you to stay out of it," Anderson said.

See?

"Hannah and Esti came to me last night and asked for help," I said.

"And you turned them down, so now you're out of it. Stay out of it, McKenzie."

"Since you asked so nicely . . ."

"Next time I won't give you the benefit of a doubt."

"Next time you had better not let me see you coming."

Anderson stared at me.

I stared back.

"We're having some fun now, aren't we?" I asked.

"Shut up."

Anderson turned around and walked off. I watched him go. Once I became bored, I slid inside my Mustang and started it up.

Now what? my inner voice wanted to know.

I made a hands-free phone call even though I hadn't left the parking lot yet.

A man's voice said, "Special Agent Brian Wilson."

"Harry," I said. "About those Minnesota Wild tickets I mentioned . . ."

SEVENTEEN

Harry agreed to help me—sorta. He refused to expend so much as an iota of FBI resources on what he termed "another one of your leisure-time pursuits," but he gave me the name of someone who might. In exchange, though, I had to give him both of my hockey tickets, which meant that, instead of our attending the game together, I had to spend Monday evening watching it on TV while Harry took his wife. I didn't mind too much. Harry's wife once called me a wastrel. I wasn't sure what the word meant, so I looked it up—a wasteful or good-for-nothing person, spendthrift, squanderer. The following day I sent three dozen long-stem American Beauty roses wrapped in baby's breath to her office. The next time we met she asked what she'd get if she called me a penny-pinching skinflint. We've been friendly ever since.

I didn't bother to call, but instead drove to the headquarters of Midwest Farmers Insurance Group bright and early Monday morning. I managed to finagle my way upstairs, where I was stopped by an officious woman who demanded to know my business. I told her. She told me not to move. I didn't, not even to sit in one of the chairs in a lobby that was tastefully decorated for Christmas, while she disappeared into a suite of offices. A few minutes later, she returned and escorted me to an office with a splendid view of the Mississippi River as it flowed between downtown St. Paul and Harriet Island. There was a desk in the office. On the desk was a nameplate that read MARYANNE ALTAVILLA. Behind it sat a young woman dressed·in a severe black jacket and skirt and white dress shirt. Her hair was nearly the same color as the jacket and skirt. It was pulled back in a ponytail.

"Mr. McKenzie," she said.

I waited for my escort to depart before I replied.

"Really?" I asked. "Mr. McKenzie? How 'bout a little love?"

Maryanne left her chair, circled her desk, and gave me a hug.

"How are you?" she asked. "It's been a long time."

"I'm well. You?"

"Couldn't be better." Maryanne returned to her chair. "How's Nina?"

"Spectacular." I glanced around her office. It looked like she had moved in three days ago; there were very few personal touches to be seen and not a single Christmas decoration in sight. "I love what you've done with the place."

"You don't like my office?"

"You've only been here, what? Fifteen months? I thought you millennials were all about your creature comforts."

"No, that's you boomers."

"Hey, hey, hey. Gen X."

"No kidding? I thought you were older than that."

"Really, Maryanne?"

"Anyway, millennials are minimalists. We like to keep it simple."

I stared at her for a few beats. Maryanne was pretty enough to be a psychic medium. She was also the smartest woman in the room no matter what room she was in, which was a big reason why she was named chief investigator in Midwest Farmers' Special Investigations Unit before her thirtieth birthday.

"So?" she asked. "To what do I owe the pleasure?"

"Two words—the Countess Borromeo."

"That's three words. What about it?"

"How much money did I save your insurance company when I recovered it?"

"Four million, give or take a few dollars. Why? Have you heard about another missing Stradivarius?"

"No, but I'm in a position to save you some more money."

"I'm listening."

"Leland Hayes."

"I don't know who that is."

"He robbed an armored truck for $654,321. A friend with the FBI told me that Midwest Farmers took the hit."

Maryanne retrieved the electronic tablet that was lying on top of her desk and transcribed what I told her.

"When did this happen?" she asked.

"About twenty-two years ago."

That made her pause.

"I was in the second grade twenty-two years ago," Maryanne said.

"I bet you were at the top of your class, too."

"I could go all the way up to five on the multiplications table. McKenzie, I don't know anything about this."

"If I could see the case file . . ."

"No."

"I might be able to recover the loot."

"How much would that cost us, I wonder."

"Less than $654,321."

Maryanne stared at me while she drummed a tuneless solo on her desk with the fingers of her right hand. I waited.

"You have a track record with us going all the way back to that embezzler, Teachwell," Maryanne said. "The Countess, the Jade Lily—that cuts you some slack."

"How much?"

She drummed some more, stopped abruptly, and looked at her smartwatch.

"Buy me lunch," Maryanne said. "Twelve thirty. Kincaid's."

"Owwww, pricy."

"You said it yourself, McKenzie—we millenials like our creature comforts."

Kincaid's was one of the more upscale restaurants in St. Paul, as its prices suggested. You wouldn't think that a guy with my money would care, but I've discovered that the older I get, the more I reflect the blue-collar values I learned growing up in Merriam Park. I managed to get a window table with a view of the Landmark Center and Rice Park beyond, both decorated for the holidays, plus an outdoor ice rink where couples skated hand in hand in large circles. Maryanne Altavilla joined me five minutes later. She ordered a cup of lobster bisque and an open-faced crab sandwich. I had a Wagyu sirloin with crispy green-onion potato cakes and roasted green beans. It was very good. Not as good as the steak you can get at Rickie's, but still . . .

"The question at the time—did the money belong to or was it in the care, custody, control, management, or possession of a federally protected financial institution?" Maryanne said. "It was ruled, against the strenuous objections of our legal team, I hasten to add, that the money had not yet reached its destination even though the crime had taken place in the parking lot, that it was not in possession of Midway National Bank at the time of the robbery. Therefore, according to the contractual relationship between the bank and the messenger service, it fell upon the armored truck company to make good the loss, which meant it fell on us. By the way, the vocabulary has changed since then. The armored truck business is now known as the cash-in-transit industry or simply referred to as the cash management business."

"All this means . . . ?"

"Midwest Farmers had to write a check—$654,321."

"And?"

"We'd like to get it back. I ran it by my supervisor before I came over, and he said exactly what I thought he'd say—if you find it, he's sure that we can come to a mutually beneficial arrangement."

"That's what I figured, too," I said. "How much help are you willing to give me, though?"

Maryanne reached into her pocket and pulled out a flash drive. She set it on the table next to her plate. I reached for it, but she set her hand on top and drew it back.

"McKenzie," she said. "We both know how this works. The money belongs to whoever digs it up."

"Finders keepers, losers weepers."

"Especially if it's not still conveniently stashed in the canvas bags used by the armored truck company so the rightful owner can easily be identified. There's no law that says you'd have to turn it in. If you take this, though, I will consider it a personal contract between you and me that you will return the money to Farmers."

"For a substantial reward, you might add."

"Half, maybe more. Anything we can recover at this point would be a bonus."

"My lawyer would tell you that a verbal contract isn't worth the paper it's written on," I said.

"So would ours, and we have hundreds. Do we need a paper contract, you and I?"

"This is where it gets complicated."

"In what way?"

"To find the money, I might need to enlist Ryan Hayes."

"The son?" Maryanne said. "The son who helped Leland Hayes rob the armored truck in the first place?"

"He did it against his will."

"Is he out of prison?"

"The BOP kicked him loose about six months ago. He's now an upstanding member of society."

"I'm sure."

"Convincing him to help will be a problem," I said. "I might need to offer him an incentive."

"This is an issue because . . . ?"

"It's against the law for a criminal to profit from his crime."

"*Riggs v. Palmer, Plumley v. Bledsoe*, the slayer rules—I see where you're going."

"So . . ."

Maryanne started drumming her fingers again. Because of the white linen tablecloth it didn't sound nearly as loud as it had in her office.

"Our business arrangement is with you," she said. "Recover the money and you'll be handsomely rewarded. Whatever you do with the reward is none of our business. I don't even want to know."

I plugged the flash drive into my computer back at the condominium and pulled up the contents. In Minnesota, an insurance company has thirty business days in which to conduct an investigation and either accept or deny a claim, and Midwest Farmers Insurance Group used every damn one of them to find the money Leland Hayes stole before agreeing to pay off Midway National Bank. It had half a dozen investigators working the case. At least that's how many handwritten field reports were scanned into the case file Maryanne Altavilla had given me.

There was no evidence of fraud, so the Special Investigations Unit spent all of its resources attempting to track Leland's movements before and after the robbery took place, more often than not retracing the efforts of the FBI. There were documents, of course, and plenty of them. Plus transcripts of witness interviews, photographs, and even video.

A lot of time was also spent trying to follow the money. The $654,321 came in denominations of $1 to $100 bills that had been gathered from cash-intensive businesses like supermarkets, check-cashing stores, and other banks. And it was unmarked. No one had bothered to paint a tiny blue dot in the upper right corner of each bill or taken the time to make Xerox copies of them—remember Xerox? Also, this was long before 9/11. There was no Patriot Act, no Homeland Security, and the Financial Crimes Enforcement Network, aka FinCEN, was just getting started. However, the Bank Security Act was in place, as well as the Annunzio-Wylie Anti-Money Laundering Act and the Money Laundering Suppression Act, which demanded that banks report cash transactions of $10,000 or more, as well as any suspicious monetary activity. The FBI couldn't find a single Suspicious Activity Report in the greater five-state area that could help lead them to the cash, however.

Nor could it answer the basic question—why did Leland Hayes come back to St. Paul?

He could easily have left Minnesota in the hours between the time he robbed the armored truck and when I encountered him. He could have driven north and crossed into Canada, for that matter. In those days, a passport wasn't required; you could do it with a driver's license. Even if he loved his son, which he clearly didn't, there was nothing he could have done for him. Plus, he must have known that Ryan would give him up the first time he was asked, which he did. So what was he doing on Arcade Street—without the cash—three hours after the heist?

I took notes.

It was my intention to reconstruct Leland's movements myself, interview all of his known associates, as the cops would label them, along with his neighbors, and visit his old haunts. It was the coldest of cold cases. Most of the people who knew Leland were probably long gone by now, and those who weren't—let's just say memory is a tricky thing and let it go at that. On the other hand, the statute of limitations had long ago rendered everyone involved in the heist not guilty on all counts. Witnesses who had nothing to say twenty-two years ago might have plenty to talk about now. At least, that's what I was hoping for, although, honestly, I didn't like my chances.

I was reading a transcript of an interview with a woman named LaToya Cane, described by the investigator as an "unco-operative, unmarried African American woman"—"unmarried" was underlined twice as if that meant something—when my cell started playing "West End Blues." The caller ID read NINA TRUHLER.

"Hey, you," I said.

"McKenzie, you should drop by the club," Nina said. "Butch Thompson is playing solo piano during Happy Hour. You love Butch Thompson."

"I do."

"I'll even buy you a beer."

"Why?"

"What do you mean why?"

"You know I hate surprises almost as much as Bobby Dunston does."

"Can't a girl just want to spend time with her beau?"

"Beau? Does that make you my belle?"

"I like that—*ma belle amie*."

"Nina . . ."

"There's a man here. A young man, old enough to drink but just barely. He asked members of my waitstaff if they knew who you were. They said they did, but you weren't around and they didn't know if you were going to be around. He said he'd wait. They shouldn't have done that. Sorry."

"That's okay. What about the man?"

"My people said he was very nice, very polite. Right now he's sipping a beer and listening to Butch. He's African American, not that that matters."

"What does matter?"

"McKenzie, he's carrying a gun."

"Call the police."

"What? Why?"

"You have a sign on your door, don't you—management bans guns on these premises?"

"Yes."

"Call the cops. I'll be there in ten minutes."

EIGHTEEN

I saw them in the parking lot beneath an LED light mounted on a tall metal pole, a young, light-skinned African American dressed for success and two older white men wearing the colors of the St. Paul Police Department. No shots or angry words were being exchanged when I arrived. In fact, it looked as if everyone was getting along just fine.

I found a slot for the Mustang, parked, and strolled up to them. The kid saw me coming and smiled. The cops were somewhat anxious, so I made sure they could see my empty hands as I approached the circle of light. It was only about 5:30 P.M., yet in Minnesota in December it might as well have been midnight.

"Are you McKenzie?" the kid asked. He told the officers, "This is the man I came to see. Listen, I'm very sorry about all of this. I certainly didn't mean to frighten anyone. But I do have a license to carry a concealed firearm."

"Not in private establishments that have posted a sign banning guns on their premises," the taller officer said. "The owner here doesn't think guns and alcohol should mix."

"I appreciate that," the young man said. "That's why I'm content to lock my gun in the trunk of my car. At the same time— there are no legal penalties for entering a private property or business that has posted these signs."

"Funny how you know only those parts of the law that benefit you."

"Again, I apologize. I'm sure you officers have more important things to do than hassle me."

"Is that what we're doing, hassling you?"

The kid grimaced. An African American male trying to make nice with white cops and not doing a very good job; I didn't blame him for being concerned.

"A poor choice of words," he said. "I apologize again." The young man turned from the officers toward me. "Mr. Mc-Kenzie?"

"Yes."

"I've been looking for you."

"With a gun?" I asked.

The young man sighed as if it were a topic he had long grown tired of.

"I meant nothing by it, as I just explained to the officers," he said. "I have since secured my firearm in the trunk of my car—"

"So I heard."

The young man sighed some more.

"Can we talk?" he asked. "Officers, again I apologize for taking you from more important duties."

The two cops stared as if they wanted to slap the cuffs on him for something, anything, yet couldn't think of a good reason or even a bad one. "Have a nice day," one of them said, even though it was evening. The other didn't speak at all, at least not to us. He did speak quietly to his colleague, though, as they walked off. Probably discussing how they'd like to put an arm on the kid for violating the jackass ordinance, if nothing else. After a moment, they separated, went to their respective patrol cars, and drove off.

"Let's talk," the young man said.

"Start with your name."

"That's right. We haven't been introduced. I'm Jackson Cane."

He offered his hand, but I didn't take it. Instead, I flashed on one of the names I had just read in Maryanne Altavilla's SIU case file.

"Are you related to LaToya Cane?" I asked.

My question jolted the kid, although he tried to hide it.

"That's my mother," he said.

"Okay."

"How do you know my mother?"

"She lived next door to Leland Hayes."

"That was before I was born."

"Okay," I said again, trying to not give anything away.

"Can we go inside?"

"No."

"It's twenty degrees out."

"Winter in Minnesota, get used to it."

Jackson was wearing a thigh-length quilted nylon parka with a fur-lined hood large enough to fit over a suit coat, black slacks, and black dress shoes, but no hat or gloves. He reminded me of a bank teller as he rocked back and forth against the cold. I, on the other hand, was perfectly comfortable in my leather coat, leather gloves, boots, and a maroon knit hat emblazoned with the gold *M* of the University of Minnesota pulled over my ears.

"This is ridiculous," Jackson said.

"Tell me what you want. Tell me why you came to this place looking for me with a gun."

"The gun—I have a right to carry a concealed weapon."

"So do I. Why did you come here?"

"I knew this was a place where you hung out."

"How did you know that?"

He paused before he answered, "Research."

"If your research told you that, it would also tell you where I live. Why didn't you go there?"

Jackson didn't answer.

"Was it because of the guys sitting at the security desk?" I asked. "Was it because of all the cameras? Guess what. You're standing beneath a camera right now."

I pointed upward. Jackson's gaze followed my finger to the camera mounted to the light pole.

"Tell me what you want," I told him.

"I have a business proposition for you."

"Go on."

"About the money."

"What money?"

"McKenzie, you know what money. The $654,321. It belongs to me."

"How does money stolen from an armored truck before you were born belong to you?"

"Anyone who finds it can keep it," Jackson said. "I know how the law works."

"That doesn't answer my question."

"I'm willing to give you a portion if you help me."

"How much is a portion?"

Jackson hesitated before he answered, "Twenty-five percent."

"You big spender, you. What, pray tell, do I need to do to earn it?"

"There's someone we need to talk to, someone that knows exactly where the money is hidden but refuses to say."

"What do you expect me to do about it? Make him an offer he can't refuse?"

Jackson's response was to stare at me.

"For God's sake," I said. "Who told you I was that guy?"

He didn't reply.

"How the hell do you know who I am in the first place?"

He refused to answer.

I moved a few steps toward him.

Jackson moved a few steps backward.

I was thinking how much fun it would be to drive the palm of my hand against his nose the way I had done to Karl Anderson. Jackson must have been reading my mind, because he abruptly pointed up at the camera above our heads. He wasn't grinning as if he had won something, though. Instead, he looked like he was afraid I was going to punch him anyway. Which is why I didn't.

"You had a business proposition for me," I said. "Okay, here's one for you—I'm going after the money myself, for no other reason than to keep someone else from getting it. You can help. Start by telling me who told you about me, who told you my name. I'll give you a portion."

"The money belongs to me."

"Not if I get it first."

"The money belongs to me," Jackson repeated.

"Have it your own way," I said. "Oh, just so you know—I have a gun, too."

I turned and walked toward the entrance to the club. I was tempted to look behind me to see if the kid was impressed with my parting line, yet resisted just in case he wasn't.

Rickie's was crowded. It was Monday night, and the elegant upstairs dining room and performance hall were closed; a red sash was fixed across the entrance of the carpeted spiral staircase that led to it. All of Nina's customers, instead, were gathered in the comfortable downstairs bar. Most of the small tables, wooden booths, and comfy chairs and sofas gathered around the fireplace were taken.

Butch Thompson was playing Scott Joplin from the small stage set in the corner, working "Sunday Rag" before sliding effortlessly into Jelly Roll Morton's "Winin' Boy Blues No. 1." I stood just inside the door and listened to him. Butch was one of the last great ragtime and stride jazz pianists. I wondered briefly who would replace him when he moved on and couldn't think of a single name. It made me sad.

I pulled off my hat and turned toward the bar. There was an empty spot at the corner, and I asked myself if it had been reserved for me. I answered yes when the bartender set a fresh Summit Ale in front of me without asking if I wanted it. But then, Nina's people had always been good to me. We had an arrangement. They would take my order, yet never give me a bill. In return, I would always leave a tip large enough to cover the order and then some.

"The place is hopping," I said.

"Partly it's Butch," the bartender said. "He always draws a crowd. I think it's mostly the weather, though. People are enjoying it before the real winter sets in. Do you want to see a menu or just order or what?"

"I want to talk to the boss first."

"I'll tell her you're here."

Only, he didn't need to. Nina stepped around the corner where the restrooms and her office were located. She took a deep breath and exhaled as if she were relieved to see me.

What did she expect? my inner voice asked. *To find you lying facedown in her parking lot?*

The woman worries too much, I told myself, but not her. I knew it would only start an argument.

Nina moved to where I was sitting. She rested a hand on

my shoulder and smiled. She was not one for public displays of affection, but then neither was I.

"Hey," I said.

"What happened?"

"The kid wanted me to help him find Leland's loot."

Leland's loot—I kinda like that.

"Why you?" Nina asked.

"I don't know. He wouldn't say, and I resisted the urge to beat the truth out of him."

"That was nice of you."

"I thought so."

The bartender appeared in front of us.

"Anything, boss?" he asked.

"No," Nina said. "I'll be in the office."

She asked me to join her by yanking my arm. I grabbed the ale, slipped off the stool, pulled a ten from my pocket, dropped it on the bar, and followed after her. Once inside her office, Nina closed and locked the door. The locking surprised me. She had never done that before.

"Nina," I said.

She took the glass from my hand, made to set it on her desk, thought better of it, and put it on a shelf instead.

"Nina," I repeated.

She wrapped her arms around me and brought my head down close enough to kiss my mouth.

"This is not like you," I said.

"I know."

NINETEEN

The next morning, I was sitting at my computer, rereading Maryanne Altavilla's case file, and taking more notes, especially addresses. Nina was dressed for work. She sat in the chair across from me.

"I think I need to talk to someone," she said.

"About what?"

"You know about what."

"Nina . . ."

"I had sex in my office. Who does that?"

"According to the adult film industry . . ."

Nina took her face in both hands. "Oh, God," she said.

"You make it sound like a terrible crime was committed."

"Not a crime, but, but . . ."

"Should I tell you what I think?"

"I know what you think," Nina said. "You think what we did was great fun."

"I think there are only two kinds of sex, regardless of what the evangelicals might tell you. There's sex with love and there's sex without love. I love you—"

"I love you, too."

"That's all that matters, not the where or the when or the how or anything else."

"I agree with you."

"Well, then?" I asked.

"It's just that lately, I've been thinking about sex all the time. It's like suddenly I'm a guy."

"Um . . . ?"

"An article I read in *Psychology Today* said that men think about sex an average of thirty-four times a day."

"That sounds about right. Still, is that any reason for you to see a therapist?"

"I didn't say I wanted to see a therapist. McKenzie, do you think I could be possessed?"

"Excuse me?"

"When I was looking up psychic mediums the other day, I read this piece about a woman who was doing all kinds of things that were out of character, including having sex any time of the day or night, and it was decided that she was being possessed by a woman who had died in the house that she and her husband bought. They eventually took care of her. She was fine. But ever since, I've been wondering if I might not be possessed by my dead mother."

"I have no idea what to say to that."

"Shelby's into all this paranormal stuff. I'll ask her."

"No, no, geez, Nina, don't do that."

"Why not?"

"You can't tell Shelby what we do in private."

"Oh, for God's sake. You don't think she knows we have sex? Now that her girls are older, she and Bobby practically—"

"Noooo," I said. "Too much information."

"Men. You guys think about sex all the time, yet you never want to talk about it. I have to go."

For one of the very few times in my life, I was actually glad to see her walk out the door.

A few minutes later, I left the condominium myself. I checked the Mustang for GPS transmitters again just because, left the parking garage, and drove toward South Minneapolis. Along the way, I listened to Minnesota Public Radio and heard this:

The body of a fifty-four-year-old woman, who had been missing from her St. Paul home for nearly two weeks, was discovered by investigators late Monday in a farm field near New Richmond, Wisconsin. Mrs. Ruth Nowak was found wrapped in a blanket by officers of the New Richmond Police Department who were acting on a search warrant requested by the St. Paul police. A spokesperson said the circumstances surrounding the woman's death were not yet known and the Ramsey County Medical Examiner will determine her cause of death. He refused to speculate on who put the body in the field or if a relationship existed between Nowak and the farm's owner. The search for Nowak began twelve days earlier when Robert Nowak reported his wife missing from their Crocus Hill home. Nowak is the owner of RN Management Group, a business-consulting firm based in Shoreview. The couple had been married for thirty-two years.

"I wonder how Bobby managed to get a search warrant," I said aloud.

Two of the addresses I had written down were in Ventura Village, a neighborhood more or less in the center of Minneapolis that took its name from the Spanish word for happiness or luck and had never experienced much of either. Case in point—I found statistics suggesting that nearly one out of every twelve residents experienced a violent or property crime in the past year. The neighborhood association actually paid off-duty cops to patrol the high-crime areas neglected by on-duty cops.

The first address belonged to Leland Hayes, and the second was next door, where LaToya Cane had lived. I didn't actually expect to find her there, or anyone else who knew Leland, for that matter. Eighty percent of Ventura Village's residents were renters squeezed into five ten-story towers, about fifty additional apartment buildings, and a hundred or more duplexes, triplexes, and quadruplexes, which gave the place a transient vibe—30 percent of the residents were replaced every year. I was pleasantly surprised when I discovered that both Leland's and LaToya's places were single-family dwellings.

Leland had lived in an ugly rust-colored clapboard house with rotting trim boards surrounded by a spotty lawn and a cyclone fence. At least, it was rust colored now. It might have been a bright yellow twenty years ago. It had a garage that seemed too small for a standard SUV and a short driveway leading to it that was located outside the fence, go figure. There was a small wooden shed leaning against the garage; Ryan's hiding place, I told myself.

A sign hanging on the fence said the house was for sale. I parked my Mustang and went up to it. There was a sleeve attached to the sign filled with red and black trifolded sheets of paper that provided specific details—two bed, one bath, 672 square feet, partially furnished, one-car garage, built in 1913, foreclosure, est. $89,000, $5,000 assistance grant available to homeowners who purchase a house in Ventura Village and live in it for five years, tour by appointment only. I didn't know it was possible to buy a house for less than $100,000, but what do they say? Location, location, location.

There was a gate in the fence. I opened it and walked to the front door. I knocked. There was no answer. I didn't expect there would be. I pressed my face against the glass. Despite the sofa, stuffed chair, and coffee table that I saw, the place appeared empty.

I walked back. There was a black man standing at the fence watching me. He was big enough to play the defensive line for the Vikings. On the other hand, the dog he was walking was about the size of his right foot.

"You ain't thinkin' of buyin' this place, are ya?" he asked.

I stepped outside the fence, closed the gate, and bent to pet the dog. He wagged his tail and growled at the same time.

Mixed messages, my inner voice told me.

I decided to let the dog be.

"I haven't decided," I said aloud. "The price is right."

"You gotta know—the place is haunted."

"Haunted?"

"I know what you're thinkin', but I ain't makin' this shit up, man. Place has had at least a dozen owners in the past twenty years. That's gotta tell ya somethin'."

"People come and go, don't they?" I said. "Especially in Ventura Village."

"Not like that, man. I've been here ten years now. Live right over there." He pointed at a small well-kept house across the street and down a couple of lots. "This one time, musta been what? Three years ago. It's night. Summer. I'm havin' a cold one on the porch. All of a sudden these people come runnin' out the front door screamin' their heads off. They see me and come runnin' my way like I was supposed to protect 'em or somethin', and I'm like, I told you not to buy the place."

"What frightened them?"

"Oh, they was yellin' that there was this guy inside the house with half a head tellin' 'em to get out, get out."

"Half a head?"

"What they said."

"Did you go and take a look?"

"Fuck no."

Do you blame him?

"So what happened?" I asked aloud.

"They moved out, whaddaya think? Place is fuckin' haunted, I'm tellin' ya. Next people that moved in, nice couple. Hispanic. They lasted two months. Just packed up and drove away; didn't even take all their furniture. Let the bank worry about it, man. You know, in some states, they gotta tell ya if a house you want t' buy is haunted. It's the law. They call it— are you ready? Ghoul disclosure."

I don't know exactly why I laughed, but I did.

"Ain't funny," the man said. "Maybe it is a little, but I'm tellin' ya—you don't want t' move here."

"The guy with half a head, did you ever find out what that was about?"

"Oh, yeah. Woman who lived next door told me. Guy what used to live there, I can't remember his name, he got hisself shot robbin' a bank in St. Paul. Guard took his head off wit' a shotgun. Boom. Now he's like, you know, a permanent resident. Hanging around a shitty place like that, you gotta wonder what he's thinkin'."

"Maybe he has nowhere else to go."

"Yeah, but if you're gonna haunt someplace, go to the Mall of America, someplace like that, you know? If it was me, I'd be hangin' over t' Target Center watchin' them Timberwolves play."

"The woman next door, does she still live here?" I asked.

"Naw, naw, naw, Ms. Cane"—he spoke the name with respect—"she moved over t' Standish-Ericsson, only three miles away but might as well be on the far side of the moon. Why? You wanna ask 'er 'bout the ghost? I'm tellin' ya, man."

"The askin' price is pretty reasonable."

"That's just the starter. You could git this place for seventy-five. Less even, if you negotiate."

"What I'm saying."

"I don't know Ms. Cane's home address, but she's got a business over on Thirty-fifth Street near Twenty-third. I was over there once just to say hi. Sells all kinds of ghost shit."

"Ghost shit?"

He held his hands up like he couldn't believe it either.

"I know, I know," he said. "Right? Somethin' else. You know the area where her store is, what they're startin' to call it now? The Witch District."

TWENTY

The Witch District was populated by a wide variety of shops that catered to customers with more than a casual interest in witchcraft, not to mention communication between the living and the dead. One displayed a number of T-shirts in its window that read GHOSTS ARE AWESOME, I WILL HAUNT YOU, WITCHY WOMAN, and THE WITCH DISTRICT KEEPS IT WEIRD. Another featured a library filled with books on magic and tarot cards and magazines like *Sabat,* which claimed to fuse witchcraft with feminism. I'm not sure why, but the fact that the area was also well decorated for Christmas made me go "Hmmm."

LaToya Cane's store was called Good Spirits, and my first thought was that it was schizophrenic. On one side, it sold most of the stuff that I had seen at the Twin Cities Psychic and Healing Festival; I wondered if it had a display there and I hadn't noticed. There were lavender and frankincense incense cones, astro dice sets, crystals, healing stones and jewelry, chrome altar bells, lunar calendars, tarot cards and books that teach you how to read them, Wiccan guidebooks, charcoal, small cast-iron cauldrons, single-spell kits with instructions, and all kinds of potions, including love spells—anything and everything needed to contact spirits and enlist their aid.

On the other side, though, a wide assortment of electronic gear including spirit boxes and EMF meters was displayed next to all the things one might buy to combat ghosts, including palo santo wood splinters, sage smudge sticks, smoky quartz and black tourmaline chips, white candles, salt, brick dust, white roses, prayer cards, religious talismans like rosaries and crucifixes, holy water, and banishing-spell kits.

I met an African American woman in the aisle between the two sides. She was about as old as me and wasn't dressed witchlike at all. She looked like a floor rep for Macy's.

She smiled and asked, "How may I help you?"

"I'm McKenzie."

She kept smiling.

"Are you LaToya Cane?" I asked.

"Have we met before?"

"No, but I met your son last night."

I noticed that her skin was darker than his.

"Jackson?" LaToya said. "Did he send you to me?"

"Not exactly."

LaToya kept smiling.

"This is going to sound ridiculous," I said.

Her eyes flitted right and left at the merchandise surrounding us and settled back on my face.

"People come to me with all kinds of troubles," she said. "I don't think they're ridiculous."

"I'm the former police officer who shot Leland Hayes in the head. Now he's using psychic mediums to tell people that he will show them where he hid the money he stole if they kill me."

LaToya's smile didn't diminish one bit. If anything, it grew even brighter.

She shook a finger at me. "I have to admit, of all the stories

I've heard since I opened this place . . ." She shook her finger some more. "I knew Hayes."

"I know. That's why I'm here."

"Step this way."

LaToya led me toward the back of her store, where there was a counter with a cash register. Behind the counter was a single stuffed swivel chair in front of a long desk stacked with several CCTV monitors so she could watch her customers without being intrusive about it. There was also a laptop, plus wire baskets filled with invoices that made me wonder if LaToya trusted it. Next to the desk was an old-fashioned percolator set on a small table.

"Coffee?" she asked.

"Bless you."

She filled two cups and gave me one.

"Mr. McKenzie?"

"Please, just McKenzie is fine."

"Call me Toy."

"Thank you, Toy."

"Do you actually believe that Leland Hayes is threatening you from the grave?"

"I'm just telling you what I heard."

"From whom?"

"A psychic medium named Hannah Braaten."

"She's a lightweight," Toy said. "I'm not sure how seriously I would take anything she says."

"Kayla Janas?"

"I don't know her."

"Okay."

"Why did you come to me?"

"You said you knew Leland Hayes."

"Yes. I lived next door to him for I don't know how long, a few years anyway."

"You told the FBI that you never heard of him," I reminded her.

"Did I?"

"According to the report."

"The FBI report?"

"No," I said. "Actually, I'm working off a file generated by Midwest Farmers Insurance Group. A field agent wrote that you were uncooperative when they went to see you after Leland was killed."

"I don't remember the FBI, but I remember them. They all but accused me of stealing Leland's money, the bank's money, actually. Stealing it and hiding it in the house I was renting. They demanded that I let them search it. When I refused, they said they would come back with a warrant."

"They didn't, though, did they?"

"No," Toy said. "They were just trying to intimidate me. It nearly worked. I was twenty-two years old and living alone and they were threatening prison and whatever. But you grow up poor and black in neighborhoods like Ventura Village, you learn when people are bullshitting you and when they're not."

"What can you tell me about Hayes?"

"He was a vile, despicable sonuvabitch. Loudmouth—some of the things he said to me, screaming at me over his fence just to hear the sound of his own voice. He was the only person who ever called me nigger to my face."

"Did he have any friends?" I asked.

"Sure. Men just as loathsome as him hangin' around, doin' their shit. The cops knocked on his door at least a half-dozen times that I know of. He always blamed me for calling them, although I never did. Another thing you learn when you're young and black."

"Do you remember any of their names, Leland's friends?"

"Just one. Bastard named Stuart Moore. He caught me once

out by the curb and told me that he wasn't a bigot like the rest of them, and to prove it, he offered to pay twenty dollars if I would take him around the world. I slapped his face. He slapped me back. He hit me harder than I hit him, but it was satisfying just the same."

"Yet you told the Feds and the insurance investigators that you barely knew Hayes and his friends."

"What part of young, poor, black, and living alone in the projects did you not get?" Toy asked.

Good point, my inner voice said.

"Hayes had a son," I said aloud.

"Ryan." Toy made the name sound filled with sadness. "Poor kid. Leland beat him down, not just physically; he was always carrying bruises, but mentally, too, emotionally. He walked around like a zombie. He didn't even have the strength to run away. When Leland was gone, and he was gone a lot, I'd make Ryan come over to my house. I'd feed him, talk to him. I found out his mother had died a couple of years before I moved there. It just shattered him. And then his father . . . I was only five years older than him, but I became—I was going to say his substitute mother, but no, that's not right. Friend is better.

"McKenzie, I didn't have the best childhood myself; one of the reasons I was living alone. Nothing like what he had to go through, though. He went through it alone, too. He contacted me after he was convicted of the truck robbery and asked if I would find a photograph of his mother that he had hidden from Leland. He said I could give it to his public defender, but I brought it to him personally. 'Course, they wouldn't let him keep the frame, only the picture. I met him in the jail where they were holding him before they sent him to Kentucky. Seeing him like that—it made me cry. I still get sad when I think about him."

"He's out, you know."

Toy's head came up and she looked hard into my eyes. "I didn't know," she said. "When?"

"About six months ago."

"Have you seen him?"

"Yes, just the other day."

"How'd he look?"

"Good. Strong." I told her that he was working, that his employers named him Employee of the Month. "He seems to be doing all right."

Toy nodded her head as if it was what she had expected to hear. "Do you have a phone number, an address?" she asked. "I'd like to see him again."

Normally I'd keep private information like that to myself, but the expression on her face told me that I would be a real jerk if I kept Ryan and Toy apart. My notebook was in the inside pocket of my leather coat. I pulled it out and recited Ryan's current address and where he worked. I didn't have a phone number. Toy scribbled it down on a notepad.

"Thank you," she said.

"My pleasure."

"So are you going to tell me why we're talking about Leland Hayes, or what?" Toy asked.

"I'm trying to find the money he stole before he can pay it to someone else."

"Is that why you went to see Ryan?"

"Yes."

"What did he say?"

"He said he wanted nothing to do with it."

"Good for Ryan."

"Anything you can tell me . . ."

"I probably already told you everything I know," Toy said. "Leland and I were not friends."

"The day of the attempted robbery . . ."

"What did the report say?"

"It said you caught the bus on Franklin Avenue at seven thirty in the morning and got home at six that night just in time to meet the Feds when they knocked on your door."

Toy spread her hands wide.

"Yeah, that's what I was afraid of," I said.

"Tell me about Hannah," Toy said. "Tell me about the reading."

I did.

"Do you believe her?" Toy asked.

"Don't you?"

She wagged her hand as if to say it was fifty-fifty.

"Toy," I said, "I am in desperate need of enlightenment."

"I believe in the paranormal," she said. "I believe that ghosts walk the earth. My experiences living next door to Leland's house after he was killed, that's what got me interested. Well, not my experiences. My neighbors. There were a lot of them, too, moving in and out of that place over the years. One by one they told me about being haunted by him.

"So, yes, I believe in the paranormal, McKenzie. I believe there are psychic mediums that can communicate with the dead. I do not believe, however, that it's anywhere near as common as it appears to be on TV and in the movies. Hannah and her colleagues—there is no doubt, at least I have no doubt, that a blessed few of them can and do communicate with the spirits of the dead every single day of their lives. But the rest? I don't believe their gifts are as substantial. Some can do it most of the time; others can do it some of the time; still others can't do it all.

"Except they have a product to sell, don't they?" Toy added. "People pay them for readings, pay them to contact their loved ones. Often a great deal of money. What are they going to say if the spirit doesn't come through? Sorry, better luck next time?

Some of these psychic mediums do group readings in huge halls, casinos even. What if they can't actually contact a spirit or if they can only contact a few? What do they tell a thousand people who paid, what, a hundred dollars or more to see a show?"

"Toy," I said, "are you telling me that the less gifted psychic mediums will investigate the lives of some of their customers so they have something to fall back on if they can't give them the real deal?"

"If a customer comes in and asks for a Come to Me Love Spell Kit and I'm all out, I might steer her to a bottle of Self-Love Potion #9 or even my Vibrant Pulse Pussy Tonic if I thought that's the way she was leaning."

I flashed on Karl Anderson.

He said the Braatens hired him the day before they did the reading that brought Leland into your life, my inner voice reminded. *But he could have been feeding information to Hannah about the people she was reading long before then, couldn't he?*

"Tell me about Hannah Braaten," I said.

"I don't know her. We've never met."

"You said she was a lightweight."

"Yes, but I didn't say she was a fake, did I?"

No, she didn't.

"Toy, I'm not a cop anymore. I'm not a lawyer or a journalist. Nothing you say to me will be held against you. I won't even repeat it."

She stared at me over the brim of her coffee cup for a few beats, took a sip, and set it down on her desk.

"McKenzie, no psychic medium has ever told me that they cheat," Toy said. "No friend or acquaintance of a psychic medium has ever told me that they cheat. I have no tangible evidence to prove that they cheat. We're just talking."

"Okay."

"People come in all the time and they tell me things. They tell me when a psychic was spot-on and when the psychic got a few things right and some things wrong and when a psychic was just plain faking it. A woman came in Sunday and told me about a reading where her grandfather was supposed to have come through. The psychic gave the woman specific details about the grandfather that rang true, but then she said that he was sitting next to his wife. The woman asked, 'Which one?' The psychic answered, 'The second one.' The woman said, 'Funny, I had tea with her last week.' See what I mean?"

It was my turn to stare over the brim of my coffee cup. I also took a sip and set the cup down.

"Hannah Braaten," I said again.

"Hannah is exciting and beautiful; people are talking about her. She's the next big thing, and I'm sure she's enjoying the moment. For what it's worth, no one has ever told me that she was a phony. What they have said was that she usually delivers the readings people expect, but sometimes she doesn't, and when that happens she'll apologize."

"She's convinced certain people that Leland Hayes will pay a lot of money to see me dead without apology."

"What people?"

"Your son, for one."

That jolted her.

"What are you talking about?" Toy wanted to know.

"Jackson came looking for me last night. He wanted me to help him find Leland's stash. He believes the money rightfully belongs to him."

"Jacks said that?" Toy said.

"Yes."

Toy moved her head quickly to her left, looked down, and became very still. "I can't imagine why," she said.

She's lying, my inner voice told me.

"He tracked me down," I said aloud. "I found it very disconcerting. It makes me think others might try to do the same thing."

"McKenzie, I don't know why Jackson wants to find Leland's money after all of these years, why he thinks it belongs to him—except maybe he heard about it so many times while growing up, while living next to Leland's house, that it seems like his. What I do know is he would never hurt you. Or anyone else. Not because of this."

"Okay."

"Jacks spent his first twelve years in Ventura Village; this was before we moved over near Roosevelt High School. I gave him everything I could, a good education and the discipline to benefit from it. I made sure he stayed out of the gangs, that he didn't get involved with drugs. I taught him not to feel sorry for himself or think that he was entitled, like the world owed him something. You know how hard that was to do, a single mother? Now he's studying economics at Macalester College while interning at an investment bank in downtown St. Paul. Every time I see him I feel like I might cry, he makes me so proud."

Toy waved at her store. "At the same time, Jackson thinks all of this is silly. Well, not the profits, only the idea behind them. I worked retail all my life, McKenzie, behind God knows how many counters and eventually behind the desk. When Jackson and I finally got a little bit ahead, I took that experience and what I learned studying all that paranormal stuff and opened this place. I was in the right place at the right time because of the explosion in TV shows about paranormal activities, the movies, the books, the websites—did you know there's a Facebook page devoted strictly to haunted houses?"

"Of course there is," I said.

"It all generated an enormous amount of customer interest. Even people who don't believe a word of it, who think the paranormal is a joke, will come in to buy love potions for Valentine's Day and spirit boxes for Halloween. They think it's fun. And it is."

"I used to think so, too," I said.

"But Jacks believing that Leland Hayes is talking from the other side—I doubt that, I really do. Maybe he heard the story and that got him thinking about the missing money."

Maybe he heard it at Macalester, my inner voice suggested.

"Did you know he carried a gun?" I asked aloud.

"I tell him not to. A young black man carrying a concealed weapon the way the police are today . . ." Toy shook her head as if she could see the future and it terrified her. "I know he doesn't carry it all the time. He doesn't carry it at school or work. Even so . . . It comes from growing up where he did. I can't make him understand that the whole world isn't Ventura Village or even South Minneapolis."

"Toy, I'm not here because of your son. If he finds the money, God bless him. I hope he buys his mother something nice. I just want all of this to go away."

"You shouldn't be talking to me, then," Toy said. "Or Jackson. You should be talking to Hannah."

TWENTY-ONE

I went back to my car, sat behind the steering wheel, and thought about Hannah Braaten. Could she have made all this up just to entertain the audience at her reading?

If she did, how do you explain Kayla Janas and all those other psychics at the Twin Cities Psychic and Healing Festival? my inner voice asked. *And Leland's haunted house?*

A lightweight, Toy had called her.

Still...

"I don't believe in ghosts," I said aloud just to hear the words.

What do you believe?

I believe that Leland Hayes stole $654,321.

And hid it where?

I pulled my notebook from my pocket again and reviewed what I had written there.

What are you looking for?

Stuart Moore. LaToya said that he was a friend of Leland's, yet I don't recall seeing his name listed in the insurance company's case file.

Maybe he's a ghost, too.

I started the Mustang and drove back to my condominium to find out.

Smith and Jones were working the security desk. I thanked them for finding the footage of the red Toyota Avalon and sending it off to Bobby Dunston. They asked if anything had come of it.

"Not that I heard," I said. "But then the cops don't necessarily confide in me."

"You're saying you and Detective Shipman aren't bosom buddies?" Jones asked. "What's that about, anyway?"

"She's jealous of my storied exploits," I said.

"Aren't we all?" asked Jones. "What about the psychic medium thing? How's that working out?"

"I'm no further along than when I started."

"So we didn't miss anything," Smith said.

"I'll keep you posted," I told them.

I bid good-bye to the boys and took the elevator to the seventh floor. I went directly to my computer after entering the condo and fired it up. I skimmed all the Midwest Farmers field reports while carefully searching for names. I found two that I had already entered into my notebook—Fred Herrman and Ted Poyer, plus their addresses from twenty years ago. I couldn't find Stuart Moore no matter how hard I tried, so I Googled his name. There were sixteen matches in Minnesota. I narrowed that down to six within the greater Twin Cities area. Using Facebook, LinkedIn, and a couple of other social media sites, I was able to reduce that number to two, one in Minneapolis, one in St. Paul.

What are the odds that a friend of Leland Hayes is intimate with the legal system? my inner voice asked.

Pretty good, I decided, which was why I accessed the website of the Minnesota Judicial Branch. A couple of clicks brought me to a page designated as Minnesota Public Access, which allowed me—or anyone, for that matter—to search through most of the court records in the State of Minnesota Court Information System. I clicked on the tab labeled MINNESOTA DISTRICT (TRIAL) COURT CASE SEARCH, accepted the terms and conditions, and was sent immediately to a page that allowed me to choose the types of case records I wanted to search. I selected criminal/traffic/petty and was sent to still another page with blank information fields that the website wanted me to fill in. All I had was a name, so I entered the one belonging to Moore in Minneapolis and hit SEARCH.

A second or two later, I was told that Moore had been charged and convicted of four, count 'em, four traffic violations in the past nine years—failure to obey a traffic control signal, parking within five feet of an alley or driveway, passing a parked emergency vehicle on a two-lane street without moving to the far lane, and violating a winter parking ban.

Clearly a menace to society.

I also discovered that he was thirty-two years old, which meant he wasn't the hardened criminal I was looking for. So I repeated my search, this time using the name of Moore from St. Paul.

My, my, my . . .

Stuart Moore had been a jerk in three different counties. The search engine told me that he had been convicted of multiple counts of domestic assault, disorderly conduct, driving under the influence, pawning another's property, and obstructing the legal process with force, earning him a bunch of fines and a few jolts in various county jails. Then came a big fall: criminal sexual contact in the second degree. He had copped a plea, which suggested that the evidence must have been pretty compelling—ninety months in Stillwater and registered as a sex offender when he got out, which occurred about a year ago.

The fact that he was registered meant that I could look him up online, and I did, first by accessing the website of the Minnesota Department of Corrections. Next, I clicked on the SEARCH FOR OFFENDERS AND FUGITIVES tab, followed by the PUBLIC REGISTRANT SEARCH bar. I typed in Moore's name and was immediately told where he lived in Ramsey County as well as his age, color of his eyes and hair, height, weight, build, and ethnicity, none of which was necessary because, in addition, the site featured colored mug shots. The page also gave me Moore's MNDOC offender ID and offense information :

Offender engaged in sexual contact with victim (female, age 16). Contact included penetration. Offender gained access to victim by following her home after she exited a city bus and asking to use her phone. Offender gained compliance through threat of physical force. Offender was not known to victim.

I headed for the door. And stopped.

What did they teach you in the Boy Scouts before kicking you out for having a problem with authority? Oh yeah—be prepared.

I crossed the condo to my bookcase, pressed hard, listened for the click, and swung open the massive door. I stepped inside the secret chamber, moving to the gun cabinet. I retrieved the nine-millimeter SIG Sauer and holstered it on my hip. I didn't know if that fit the other parts of the Scout motto, the ones about keeping myself physically strong, mentally awake, and morally straight, but it seemed like a good idea at the time.

Sixty years ago, the East Side of St. Paul was a virtual boom town unto itself. Ten thousand multiethnic employees earned a comfortable middle-class living from their jobs at three thriving neighborhood businesses—Theo. Hamm Brewing Company, Seeger Refrigeration Company, which later merged with Whirlpool, and 3M, formally known as Minnesota Mining and Manufacturing Company and called "the Mining" by the East Siders. Dozens of shops, banks, drugstores, barbers, restaurants, and bars thrived along Arcade Street, Payne Avenue, and East Seventh Street. You could get anything you needed within a six-block radius. Only, the national recession that closed out the sixties pounded the local economy into dust. Plant closings and layoffs became regular news. 3M moved. Whirlpool shuttered its Arcade Street plant. Hamm sold out. One by one the little shops and restaurants closed their doors. Crime soared, property values plummeted, infrastructure crumbled. Still, it was better than Ventura Village. Here, at least, you only had a one-in-thirty-two chance of being a victim of a crime per year.

Stuart Moore lived in the heart of the East Side in one of those small, affordable bungalows built during the Great Depression that had walls loaded with asbestos and lead. Several of the homes surrounding him were decorated for the holidays; his was not.

Stuart's front door was only a couple of steps from the boulevard, which was only a couple of steps from the street. He was sitting outside in a white plastic lawn chair despite the cold and sucking on a cigarette. I knew from the court documents that Stuart was sixty-six, yet he looked as old as his house. He also looked as if he wanted to pick a fight with someone, anyone.

I pulled to a stop in front of the bungalow and stepped out of the Mustang.

"What the fuck do you want?" he asked.

"Mr. Moore?"

"You deaf, boy? I asked you a question."

"I'd like to talk to you, if you'd allow it."

"I don't talk to no fucking cops."

"Hey, man," I said. "Do I call you names?"

That caused Stuart to laugh, which caused him to cough, which prompted him to take a long drag of his cigarette. By then I had crossed the narrow boulevard and stood a few feet in front of him.

"I don't like fucking cops," Stuart said.

"There are days when I don't care much for 'em myself."

"Who you?"

"My name's McKenzie."

I watched closely to see if he recognized my name, only his wrinkled face gave me nothing. I didn't offer my hand; I didn't think he'd shake it anyway.

"Do I know you?" Stuart asked.

"We've never met."

"Whaddaya want?"

"Leland Hayes."

"Fucker's dead."

"That's what I heard."

"Got his head shot off twenty year ago up over t' Lake Phalen, can't be more than a mile from here."

"Yeah, I heard that, too."

"Whaddaya wanna talk 'bout him for?"

"Actually, what I want to talk about is the money he stole before the cops put him down."

Stuart laughed some more, which brought on another coughing fit followed by still another drag from his cigarette.

"Fuckin' one of them treasure hunter types, ain't ya?" he said.

"You could say that."

"You askin' me where the money is? If I knew I sure as hell wouldn't tell you. I'd go dig it up myself."

"Did you dig it up yourself?"

Stuart gestured at his modest surroundings; his winter coat looked as if he had bought it from the Salvation Army.

"Fuckin' look like it?" he asked. "You know, I don't think I've ever gone more than a week or so without thinkin' of all that cash, fuck. Wanna know what I think?"

"I do."

"I think them Feds took it."

"The Feds?"

"F-B-fuckin'-I, yeah. Sayin' they can't find it after all these years—you believe that shit?"

I squatted down next to Stuart, setting a gloved hand on the arm of his plastic chair to steady myself.

"Maybe they did," I said. "If they didn't, though—you say you've been thinking about this for a long time. You knew the man. What do you think he did with it?"

"Who says I knew the man?"

"A woman named LaToya Cane."

"Where have I heard—oh, yeah, the bitch what lived next door to Hayes back then. She remembered me?"

Careful, my inner voice said. *You're not going to get the intel you came for by calling out the sonuvabitch. Save it for later.*

"Apparently you made an impression on her," I said.

"Yeah, I remember her, too. Good-lookin' but racist. Wanted nothin' to do with no white man."

I wonder why?

"She was right, though," Stuart said. "I knew Hayes. We had some business dealin's and whatnot."

I took a guess on the whatnot based on what I knew of his criminal activities.

"Pawned some stolen property, I heard."

Stuart Moore spread his arms wide and grinned. "We didn't steal nothin'," he said. "We found it. Prove it ain't so."

Remember, you're on his side.

"Something falls off the back of a truck, what are you going to do?" I asked. "Let it just sit there in the street? It's a traffic hazard, man."

Stuart smiled at me and patted my knee. At the same time, a car rolled slowly down the street. Stuart watched it creep past. I couldn't see a face, but I could feel the driver's eyes on us.

"What the fuck you lookin' at!" Stuart shouted.

The car picked up speed and moved halfway down the block to park. A woman got out of the driver's side carrying a white plastic bag with the red Target logo on it. She hurried to the front door of her house and let herself in.

"You better run," Stuart said. "Bitch. Like any man wanna touch you."

Keep pretending.

"Do you get that a lot?" I asked.

"Fuckin' courts. Bad enough I gotta tell the cops where I live, they gotta put my name and photograph on a list you can get off the internet. Busybodies like that bitch down the street look it up and spread the word, so now everybody looks at me funny."

"What are you? Level Two?"

"Yeah, fuck. It's all bullshit. Little bitch wanted me to come into her house. Then, when mommy and daddy found out, it was all 'he raped me, he raped me' so she wouldn't get into no trouble."

Yeah, that's why you copped a plea instead of arguing that the sex was consensual like ninety-eight percent of the other assholes.

"You know," I said aloud, "it seems to me that a piece of all that money Leland stole would improve your life dramatically."

"How big a piece?"

"Half?"

"What I gotta do?"

"Just remember, man. You know, the statute of limitations has expired. Even if you were in on the heist, the cops can't say boo after all these years."

Stuart patted my knee again. "I remember better when I've had a drink," he said.

"I passed a place up on Payne Avenue coming over here. Everson's. What is it? A block away?"

"That'll do. But you know what? Why don't I meet you there in a little bit? I gotta step inside and take care of some shit."

"I can wait."

"No, no, no." Stuart patted my knee some more. "I'll see you there in a minute."

TWENTY-TWO

Everson's Cozy Corner was one of those joints built in the 1940s with windows placed high on the walls to let daylight in without allowing the teetotalers passing by to see who was inside. Stuart said he wanted to walk there, get some exercise, which made me happy because it meant I wouldn't have to let the asshole inside my car.

After I parked, I went to the front door, hung around on the sidewalk for a minute, then opened the door and stepped inside. I was immediately slapped in the face by the odor of industrial disinfectant. I tried not to react to it. My shoes ground peanut shells, stale pretzels, and popcorn kernels into the thick rubber tiles that covered the floor. The tiles told me that they didn't sweep up the debris at Everson's, they used a hose. I tried not to react to that either.

I found a spot at the bar, sat down, and shoved my gloves into my pockets. Before I had a chance to order, Stuart Moore arrived. He claimed the stool next to mine.

"Shot of rye and a PBR," he said.

The bartender set a couple of cardboard coasters in front

of us without speaking. He pointed his chin at me, his way of asking for my order. The bartender needed a shave, his eyes were unsteady, and his enormous belly strained the buttons on his shirt. I nearly asked if he was Everson before deciding that I didn't care.

"Jack," I said, a tough guy's drink. "No ice."

The bartender turned his back to us. I turned my back to him and perused the bar. Everson's was racist, and you didn't need a sign in the front window to figure it out. Sixty-four percent of the population of the East Side of St. Paul identified itself as being a member of one minority or another, yet the dozen or so men sitting at the bar and in the booths and at the small tables were all white. None of them seemed happy, either. They weren't there for a quick midafternoon beer or to watch ESPN on the flat screen mounted in the corner above the bar. They were there to nurse their grievances against humanity and plot their revenge. It made me recall all the times I was dispatched to quell disturbances in joints just like this when I was working the Eastern District. I gave the SIG Sauer holstered behind my hip a reassuring pat.

"You got a permit for that?" Stuart asked me.

"You care?"

"I'm supposed to stay outta trouble, the state says."

"Yeah? How's that workin' out?"

Stuart started laughing again, which led to another coughing fit. There was no cigarette to lean on, but by then the bartender had served our drinks. He picked up his shot of rye, and I hoisted my glass of Jack Daniel's.

"Fuck it," he said.

Stuart threw down his shot and chased it with a couple of swallows of Pabst Blue Ribbon out of the can. Apparently Everson's didn't offer bottled beer, a smart policy, I decided. Having been attacked with both over the years, I can testify that aluminum cans are definitely less lethal than broken glass. I took a sip of the whiskey.

"Your party," Stuart said. "Whaddaya wanna know?"

I glanced first at my watch and then at the front door while wondering if Stuart was really interested in the treasure hunt or if he was just killing time. I decided to go with my first thought.

"The place where you're living now, have you always lived there?" I asked.

Stuart gave me a look as if he knew where I was going and decided not to get in the way.

"Yeah," he said. "Well, not always. That's where I grew up. I moved away after I graduated from Johnson High School, but came back after I divorced my first wife." He smiled. "And my second. I inherited it when my parents passed while I was inside and moved in permanent after I got out. Nothin' the busybodies can do about it, neither."

"Were you living there twenty years ago when Hayes took the armored truck?"

"Why do you ask?"

"Hayes was spotted on Arcade Street three hours after the robbery. What was he doing on Arcade three hours after the robbery—without the money? Why wasn't he running to Canada? Or at least Wisconsin?"

"How should I know?"

"My thought—he had a friend living on the East Side that he trusted enough to leave the money with."

Stuart thought that was awfully funny. He laughed, coughed, took a sip of beer, and laughed some more. The bartender came over and pointed at the empty shot glass. I nodded for him to refill it because Stuart was laughing too hard to do it himself.

"Leland didn't trust nobody," he said. "Know why? Cuz he

was the biggest fuckin' asshole in the whole shitty world and he figured everyone was just like him."

"Okay."

Stuart leaned toward me.

"Besides, if I had all that money—$654,321—I would've spent it a long fucking time ago," he said. "Hos and blow."

Stuart laughed some more. The bartender refilled the shot glass, and Stuart swallowed half. At the same time, two men about Stuart's age entered Everson's. They stopped inside the door, looked around as if they were searching for someone they knew, saw us at the bar, and found a square table near the far wall where they could watch without looking like it. Stuart pretended not to see them. Instead, he drained his glass and took another sip of the PBR.

"You're buyin', right?" he asked.

"I am," I said.

I finished my own drink, motioned for the bartender, and made a circling gesture with my finger. When he stepped up to serve us another round, I pointed at the two men sitting at the table.

"I've got them, too," I said.

That seemed to jolt Stuart, although he tried hard not to show it.

"Are they the guys you called after you sent me away?" I asked. Stuart didn't say. "I'm just guessing, you understand, but—Fred Herrman and Ted Poyer?"

"You're one smart sonuvabitch, ain't you?" Stuart said.

"I practice a lot when I'm alone."

"I bet that's not all you do when you're alone."

By then the bartender had circled the stick and was standing in front of the square table. He threw a thumb in my direction to give Stuart Moore's friends the good news. The two men glanced at each other and made their drink selections. In

the back of my mind I could hear the old man chastising me—
"You never volunteer to pick up the tab until *after* your friends order."

Some people never learn, my inner voice told me.

"Should we join your pals?" I asked. "It'd be easier to talk at a table."

Stuart confirmed that he agreed with me by sweeping up his shot glass and the PBR, slipping off the stool, and moving toward where the two men sat. I followed with my Jack Daniel's.

"Hey," I said when we reached the table. "I'm McKenzie." I gestured at an occupied chair. "Mind if I sit there? I have phobias."

The occupant glanced at his comrades. When they shrugged at him, he moved from that chair to the one positioned next to it and I sat down. My back was now to the wall, with Stuart and his pals sitting in a semicircle in front of me. Granted, each man was at least twenty years older than I was, but there were three of them, and Dave Gracie had been right the other day—I was out of practice. The SIG Sauer gave me an equalizer, but I absolutely did not want to pull it.

"So is this one of those places where everyone knows your name?" I asked.

"The fuck?" asked the man who vacated his chair.

"Fred Herrman?"

He looked at his friends each in turn, a surprised expression on his face.

I spoke to the second man. "You're Ted Poyer."

"I know you?" he asked.

"This is fuckin' McKenzie, like I said on the phone," Stuart said. "He's the one who shot Leland in the head back in the day."

"You do remember me," I said.

"I remember you, too," Herrman said. "Leland was my friend."

(222)

I didn't actually believe that, but what was I going to do? Call him a liar?

"It's getting to be a long time to hold a grudge," I said. "Are you still holding a grudge?"

Before he could answer, the bartender arrived with drinks. Herrman stared at his for a moment as if he were looking for answers in the dark liquid. He picked it up, took a sip, and set it back on the table.

"I hate fuckin' cops," he said.

"People keep telling me that," I told him. "Truth is, I haven't been one for a very long time now."

"Why's that?" Poyer asked.

"Let's just say the St. Paul Police Department and I had a disagreement concerning working conditions and let it go at that."

The disagreement being that they wouldn't let you collect the reward on Teachwell while you wore a badge.

"What do you want?" Herrman asked.

"I want to find the $654,321 that Leland Hayes hid before I shot him. Like I told Stuart here, I'll share equally with anyone who helps me."

That caused the three men to communicate with each other using nods and shrugs and frowns.

"All I know is that he didn't leave it with me," Stuart said.

"Leland did come to you after the robbery, then," I said.

"He was lookin' for a place to hide, like he expected me to put 'im up in my mother's house while the world was lookin' for 'im."

"Without the money?"

"He said that he stashed it in a safe place and he'd give me some once the heat was off. I didn't believe him, the part where he said he'd share. I told him to fuck off. Fucker actually pulled a gun on me. Didn't shoot, though."

"Why not?" Poyer asked.

Stuart shrugged as though he couldn't think of a single good reason.

"Wait a minute," I said. "Didn't Leland know what he was going to do *after* the robbery? Didn't he have a plan?"

"The plan was that he wouldn't get caught," Herrman said. "He didn't know Ryan would be left behind to identify him."

"All right, all right," I said. "But why involve his son in the first place? I was told Ryan wasn't exactly an enthusiastic volunteer."

Stuart and Herrman both stared at Poyer.

"Because Leland was an asshole," he said.

"Tell 'im," Stuart said.

"Fuck."

"Tell 'im."

"It was supposed to be me," Poyer said. "Look. I thought Leland was fuckin' jokin'. We all did. Tellin' us how he had it all mapped out, hittin' an armored truck when it was the most vulnerable, he said. At the bank. And drivin' away like nothin' happened. And I'm like, sure, sure, why not? And then the day came and I'm like, are you fuckin' crazy? It's a goddamned armored truck. With armed guards. Even if we got away with it, the FBI would be chasin' us forever. So he says, 'Fuck you, I'll take care of you later,' and made his kid do it. I always felt bad about that. His kid. Ryan. He didn't deserve any of this shit. He sure as hell didn't deserve a father like Leland, treated him like shit every day of his life."

"Maybe Ryan knows where the money is," Herrman said.

"I asked him," I said. "He said he doesn't."

"He's out of prison?" Poyer said.

"Half a year now."

Poyer nodded his head as if he were glad to hear it.

"Nah, nah, nah, nah, nah, Ryan wouldn't know," Stuart said. "Leland wouldn't have told him. No way. Besides, Leland left him there, didn't he? Left him in the parking lot for the cops to catch. Didn't give a fuck about him till later when he realized that Ryan was sure to rat him out. Said he shoulda popped Ryan before drivin' off. Pop his own kid. Fucker. Anyway, that's what Leland told me later, the reason he needed a place to hide until they stopped lookin' for him."

"The FBI never stops lookin' for you," Poyer said.

"Did Hayes have any other friends?" I asked. "Someone else he could have reached out to?"

The old men thought that was a pretty funny question; Stuart had another coughing fit.

"Yeah, okay," I said.

"What I think?" Herrman said. "I think Leland figured he might get caught cuz of leavin' Ryan like he did. So what he did, he buried the money somewhere, down by the river, who knows, thinkin' if the Feds caught him and he went to prison, he'd have a nice payday waitin' for him when he got out."

"But why shoot it out with the cops, then? With me?"

"Cuz he was an asshole," Stuart said. "Ain't you been payin' attention?"

"The question remains," I said. "Buried it where?"

No one had any theories.

I thanked the old men for their time and dropped three twenties on the table, more than enough to pay for the drinks plus another couple of rounds if they drank frugally.

Before I could move off, Poyer said, "McKenzie? If you see Ryan again, tell him I'm sorry."

I said I would and headed for the door.

Poyer called out to me. "You know what you need?" he said. "You need to find one of them psychics like they have on TV."

I gave him a nod as if I had been thinking that all along.

TWENTY-THREE

My cell pinged as I walked to the Mustang. I took a look—a text message from Bobby.

U busy? it asked.

No, I replied.

Come talk to me.

U home?

Yes.

K.

Twenty minutes later, I parked in front of Bobby Dunston's house, a large pre–World War II colonial with a wraparound porch directly across the street from Merriam Park. There was a low-slung community center in the park with a decent gym, plus baseball fields where Bobby and I played when we were kids. And a hill dotted with large oak trees where I kissed Mary Beth Rogers, the most beautiful girl of my childhood, for the one and only time. I don't think I have ever looked at that hill without thinking of her and that very first kiss.

I was greeted at the door with a hug by Victoria, the elder of the Dunston girls.

"How are things at Central?" I asked her.

"I'm way too smart for high school."

"I believe you."

"Seriously. They gave me permission to start taking Advanced Placement courses. If I work it right, I could be a college sophomore by the time I graduate."

"What about Katie?"

"Didn't you hear?" Victoria said. "She made the varsity basketball team."

"As a freshman? Good for her."

"It is, because the only way she's getting into college is with an athletic scholarship."

I draped an arm around Victoria's shoulder as we made our way into the kitchen.

"You're a mean girl, you know that?" I said.

"I've been told that I take after Mom."

I don't know why I thought that was so funny, yet I was laughing when I found Shelby chopping vegetables at the island in her kitchen.

"Nobody told me you were coming for dinner," she said. "You know how I hate last-minute surprises."

"I'm not staying for dinner," I said. "I just dropped by to chat with Bobby for a sec."

"What do you mean you're not staying? You're always welcome, you know that."

"Shelby—"

"Or do you have plans to . . . hook up with Nina?"

Shelby winked at me, something I don't think I've ever seen her do before, and in that instant I knew that Nina had spilled her guts to her.

"God help me," I said.

I moved toward the staircase leading to Bobby's man cave in the basement.

"We're having marinated chicken breasts," Shelby said.

"Leave me alone," I told her.

I found Bobby sitting in a recliner, his feet up, his hands clasped behind his head, watching ESPN's *SportsCenter* through half-closed eyes.

"Our tax dollars at work," I said.

"Not even you can ruin the good mood I'm in."

"I just heard about Katie. Very cool. Too bad she doesn't play hockey."

"Are you kidding?" Bobby asked. "Do you know what it costs just for hockey equipment these days? Start at fifteen hundred a year. That doesn't count the tens of thousands you could end up paying for camps and clinics and associations and travel and dry-land training during the years it takes just to get a kid ready to try out for high school hockey. On the other hand, the most I've ever spent for Katie to play hoops for a year was about eight hundred dollars, and that included shoes. I'm fine with basketball. One of the happiest days of my life was when Kate discovered she could shoot the J from anywhere on the floor. But that's not why I'm happy now."

"Why are you happy now?"

"I got that sonuvabitch. Robert Nowak. You should've seen his face, too. One of my favorite things—he opens his door and sees me standing there and he knows, he just knows I got him. Up until that moment, see, the suspect always thinks he got away with something. But when they see me smiling at them—it's priceless."

"How did you do it?"

"I went back to his credit card statements," Bobby said. "Nowak had an expense account with his business, RN Management Group. He owned the business; of course he had an expense account. Well, I looked further back than I had before. A couple of years. I discovered that he had purchased two prepaid cell phones and had been adding additional minutes to them ever since. We went to the retailer, learned the IMEI numbers, tracked the locations. Nowak had one; Molly Finnegan had the other. They used them so their everyday cells and landlines wouldn't provide evidence of their adultery. If they had treated them as burners like real criminals, paying for them with cash, making a few calls, and then tossing them into the trash, we wouldn't have been able to prove anything, but apparently Nowak was too cheap to replace the phones.

"Add that to the fact that they were both on record claiming that they had no personal relationship whatsoever outside of the office, an obvious lie—a judge agreed that there was enough probable cause to search Molly's property. The rest, as they say, is history. God, I loved the look on his face. Molly gave us nothing, but Nowak, once I told him we found his wife, he folded like a piece of paper. I couldn't keep him from confessing. I'm waiting for the evening news so I can watch the perp walk."

"What was it Dad used to say—the man who loves his job never works a day in his life."

"Him and Confucius."

"So what can I do for you?" I asked.

"This was a clean bust. We obtained the IMEI numbers legally. Tracked the phones legally. Obtained a search warrant legally. I read Nowak his rights and got him to confess on camera legally. The idea of trying to connect Molly Finnegan with Robert Nowak in the first place—that just came to me, as hunches often do when detectives work an investigation."

"Of course. That's how they got El Chapo, you know. The Mexican marines had a hunch and followed a takeout order of tacos to his front door."

"My point being—you and I did not go to New Richmond, Wisconsin, Saturday night."

"I don't even know where Wisconsin is."

"Just as long as we're on the same page."

"Always," I said. "But you knew that before you called."

"Yeah."

"So why did you call?"

"It would be inconvenient if a psychic medium went on TV and announced to the world and the suspect's defense attorneys that she told me where to find Ruth Nowak's body."

"You could always argue that's what prompted you to take a closer look at Molly and Nowak, where the hunch came from."

"I'd rather not if I could avoid it," Bobby said.

"I don't blame you. All the other kids might laugh."

"Can you reach out to Kayla Janas for me?"

"I can," I said. "I will."

"Thank you."

"I still can't believe she knew where Ruth was."

"I've been turning it over in my head ever since," Bobby said. "I even looked into her background to see if she was in any way connected to Nowak or Molly or even Ruth. Please, don't tell her I did that."

"Okay."

"This just rattles my view of the world and how it works, you know?"

"Mine, too," I said. "I understood—remember that online prostitution ring I helped bust a few years ago? And the wannabee drug cartel working out of Lakeville?"

"The Iron Range Bandits," Bobby said. "Don't forget them."

"All that I understood. But this?"

"Simpler times," Bobby said. "Simpler times."

"By the way, any word on the Fogelberg investigation?"

"It always has to be about you, doesn't it, McKenzie?"

"I shouldn't be concerned that someone is trying to shoot me—"

"For a reward offered by a dead man?"

"Yeah."

"A couple of days ago I would have told you that you were nuts. Now . . . Detective Gafford tells me that Frank Fogelberg's first divorce cost him half of his net worth, so he planned his second divorce more carefully. He took out loans against their home, vacation home, cars, and boat; he drained their savings and investment accounts and transferred all the money into an account in the Cook Islands and then convinced a judge that he was broke, leaving his ex-wife with nada. Later he funneled the cash through a couple of shell companies into an LLC, which paid him a healthy salary as a consultant."

"Clever," I said.

"His ex thinks so, too. So do a few former business partners who apparently were also taken for a ride."

"Do any of them have experience boosting red Toyota Avalons from the parking lots of Holiday Stationstores?"

"How much experience do you need?"

The Dunn Brothers on the corner of Snelling and Grand Avenue in St. Paul was the first coffeehouse built by Ed and Dan and remains one of their most iconic stores even though the chain has grown into one of the ten biggest in the nation. There were plenty of chairs and small round tables for the nerds, artists, and liberal revolutionaries that it catered to, plus a tiny stage where performers with guitars channeled the folk singers of the sixties and seventies. The boys were smart enough to roast their coffee in the store on a daily basis, so the place always vibrated with a mood of fellowship that few other aromas could conjure. Like just about every other retail business in the world, it was well decked out with Christmas decorations.

I parked in the lot next to the coffeehouse and walked inside. Most of the tables were filled, and there was a short queue in front of the cash register. The folk singer, apparently in between sets, was standing near the door and chatting with a couple that looked more like family than fans.

Kayla was sitting toward the back of the coffeehouse as she had said she would be when I had called earlier and arranged to meet her. She was wearing an orange sweatshirt with the name and logo of Macalester College, tight jeans, and knee-high boots. Her feet were propped up on the seat of the chair across from her; I didn't know if she was hoarding the chair for me or just trying to get comfortable. A large textbook was in her lap and she was sucking on a yellow highlighter as if it were a cigar while she read. The image made me smile, brought me back to when I was in school with Bobby and Shelby and everything seemed possible.

I bought a café mocha and joined her. Kayla removed her feet from the chair when she saw me approach and sat up.

"Hi," she said.

I gestured at the textbook as I sat across from her. "Studying?" I asked.

"Some people, boys I've dated, they think I can read minds." Kayla closed the book, placed it on the table, and set the highlighter on top of it. "I wish I could; then I'd be able to find out what the prof was putting in the test."

"Isn't it hard to concentrate with all this noise?"

"No, it's easier. When it's really quiet, like in the library or alone in my dorm room, that's when I get the most spooked."

"Spooked? As in ghosts?"

"You have no idea. What can I do for you, McKenzie?"

"You had a very profound effect on Bobby Dunston the other night."

"The commander? I did?"

"Because of you, he took a much harder look at a woman who was employed by Robert Nowak, a woman who just happened to own an alpaca farm near New Richmond, Wisconsin."

"It's true, then," she said. "What I read online. They found Ruth?"

"Yes."

"On a farm?"

"Yes."

"Wrapped in a purple-and-gold quilt? Hidden in the trees between a small pond and the back fence of a farm?"

"I don't know the exact details," I said.

I could hear Kayla even though she had covered her mouth with both hands.

"Oh God, oh God, it's true, it's true. I can do this." She removed her hands. "Hannah said I could. She said she had never met anyone with my gifts, my skills, I don't know what to call it. Not a skill. You learn skills. It's a, it's a . . . Well, a gift then. I don't know if I should be happy or scared to death. Both. McKenzie, is Robert Nowak going to prison for killing Ruth?"

"That would be my guess. Him and Molly Finnegan, provided no one screws up."

"Molly is the woman's name?"

"Yes. She and Nowak were having an affair. Bobby used those facts to get a search warrant to search her property."

"I helped the police, then."

"Yes, you did."

Kayla stared at me for a few beats.

"Would they want me to testify?" she asked.

"Absolutely not."

"What do you mean?"

"Jury trials are iffy things."

Kayla stared some more.

"They'll think I'm lying about Ruth talking to me," she said. "They'll think I'm making it up. People do, you know. Think I'm making it up. The principal in my high school, even my family. McKenzie, do you think I'm making it up?"

"No."

"Thank you."

"Neither does Commander Dunston."

Kayla picked up a paper coffee cup with both hands and brought it to her mouth, yet did not drink.

"He doesn't want me to say anything about this, though, does he?" Kayla asked.

"Not at the present time."

"Because he doesn't want to complicate the case. He doesn't want a defense attorney to tell the jury that I must have done all those terrible things myself even though there's not evidence to prove it, because how else would I have known where Ruth was—we all know there is no such thing as ghosts."

"It's possible."

"Hannah said that might happen, the attorney trying to create reasonable doubt. She said we should hold a press conference anyway, so I'll get credit."

"What do you think?"

Kayla didn't answer straightaway. Instead, she slowly set the coffee cup back on the table. It was because she took her time wrestling with my question that I believed her when she answered, "It's not about me. It's about Ruth. She deserves justice. If I fucked that up . . ."

Kayla clamped a hand over her mouth as if it was the worst thing she had ever said. "I'm sorry," she said.

"You're a good person," I said. "I think only good people should be allowed to do what you do."

She smiled weakly at the compliment.

"Hannah will not be happy," Kayla said. "Did I tell you? She's invited me to be a guest on her TV show. She thinks something like this would be a huge boost to our chances of getting an on-air commitment from the network."

"Hannah wants you on her show?"

"As a recurring character while she helps me develop my gifts. She wants to mentor me. There's so much I need to learn."

Who exactly would be helping who? my inner voice wondered.

"The producers—I'm talking to television producers, do you believe that?" Kayla said. "The producers think it would be a good idea, too. They made me answer a lot of questions, though. Made me read them. One at a time. I guess they wanted me to *prove* I could read people before they agreed to let me on the show."

"Did they do the same thing with Hannah?"

"I don't know. I didn't ask."

I wanted to give Kayla some sage advice about who to trust and who not to trust and how to tell them apart, yet for the life of me, I couldn't think of what that would be. There are some things you only learn as you go. I decided to change the subject somewhat.

"Speaking of which—do you know an African American kid named Jackson Cane?" I said.

"Jacks? Yes, I know him. He's a friend of Kyle's. Well, me, too, I guess. Economics major."

"Did you tell him about Leland Hayes?"

"No, well yes, I mean, he was one of the people in the dorms when I—McKenzie, what happened?"

"He came to me last night. He wanted me to help him find the money Leland hid."

"I don't believe it."

"It's okay," I said. "He was reasonably polite about it."

"But why? Why would he do that?"

"You said that Macalester is an awfully expensive college. Maybe he has student loans to worry about."

"I shouldn't have said anything, though. I shouldn't have. Not to, well, not to anyone. I talk about readings being like visits to a doctor or a lawyer and then I blab it around—"

"Blab?"

"That's a word," Kayla said.

"That's okay."

"No, McKenzie, it isn't. I have to be professional. Oh my God." Kayla reached across the small table and set a hand on my wrist. "McKenzie, I told him I would be seeing you here tonight. Well, I told Kyle, but Jacks was standing there at the time."

"Where's your boyfriend now? I thought he was your designated protector."

"Kyle is not my boyfriend or my protector. He's more like"—Kayla tilted her head back and glanced at the ceiling—"I don't know what he is." After a moment, she brought her head forward and looked at me again. "Like I said, there's so much I need to learn."

"Don't worry about it."

"But I do."

"Listen." This time I reached across the table and rested a hand on Kayla's hand. "You do need to learn discretion. *Give every man thy ear, but few thy voice . . .*"

"Polonius to Laertes in *Hamlet*."

"But you're going to be fine, Kayla. You're on the side of the angels."

"Thank you, McKenzie. Wait. Does that mean the angels are also on my side?"

"Yes," I said. "Yes, it does."

"I hope they're with me during my test tomorrow morning."

I thought that would have been a good time for me to thank her again and depart, only Kayla wouldn't think of it. Instead, she took hold of my arm and told me to finish my coffee. The folk singer had returned to the stage and was channeling Bob Dylan—of course she was—and doing a very nice job of it, I had to admit, giving "The Times They Are a-Changin'" an anarchistic tone. Next she slid into a nice rendition of Paul Simon's "American Tune," and I decided that I was way too hard on folk singers.

While I listened, Kayla leaned in close to me and whispered.

"There's a woman with long white hair standing on the stage," she said. "She's singing along."

"What woman?" I asked. "I don't see a woman."

Kayla looked at me and grinned.

"Oh," I said.

Apparently Kayla wasn't the only one who had a lot to learn, because I was taken completely by surprise when the kid rose up in front of me with a gun in his hand.

What happened, I had left the Dunn Brothers and walked east on Grand Avenue until I came to the lot where I had parked my Mustang. It was way in the back, the only empty slot I could find when I arrived. I aimed my key fob at it as I approached. In quick succession the lights flashed, the locks clicked open, and I heard a voice say, "Don't move."

Only, I did move, turning toward the voice, and found Jackson Cane pointing a semiautomatic handgun at me.

"Don't move," he repeated.

Yet again I ignored him, this time by cautiously raising my hands to shoulder height.

Jackson eased closer to me.

I waited.

"You're going to help me." Jackson's words came out as puffs of white vapor that drifted away into the night. There was the noise of traffic, but I heard no other voices.

"Okay," I said.

He moved closer.

"I mean it," Jackson said.

"So do I."

And closer still.

He raised the gun so that the barrel was pointed at my forehead.

"Don't mess with me, McKenzie."

I knocked the gun up and away with my left hand, even as I shifted my head out of the line of fire. I closed my hand on his wrist, keeping the handgun pointed upward, slammed my knee into Jackson's groin, and hit him just as hard as I could with a palm heel under his jaw.

He fell.

As he fell, I twisted the gun out of his grasp.

I ended up standing above Jackson as he writhed across the dark asphalt, holding his groin with both hands.

Take that, Dave Gracie, my inner voice shouted.

I glanced around to see if anyone had filmed the encounter with their smartphones or, worse, called the cops. I saw no one, heard no sirens.

I bounced the gun in my hands, a nine-millimeter Smith and Wesson, a member of its M&P series, very popular because of its ergonomics, reliability, and soft recoil.

"Nice piece." I shoved the gun into the pocket of my heavy leather jacket after making sure the safety was on. "I gotta tell you, though, Jacks, that was pretty sloppy for a kid who grew up in Ventura Village."

"Fuck you."

"I met your mother this morning. She told me that she was so proud of you that sometimes it made her want to cry. I wonder what she'd think if she could see you now."

"Fuck my mother."

I nudged him probably a little harder than I should have with the toe of my shoe.

"Don't you dare talk about her like that. What's the matter with you?"

He didn't say.

I reached down, grabbed him by his shoulders, and helped him to his feet. I half pushed, half carried him between my car and the one parked next to it and leaned him against the hood.

"You want to explain yourself, or what?" I asked.

Jackson was still breathing hard; the white puffs reminded me of the engine of a train.

"My mother lied to me," he said.

"About what?"

"About my father."

"Do I really need to know this?"

"She said it was a boyfriend who ran out on us after she became pregnant. But it was really Leland Hayes."

I have to admit, that was a bigger surprise than the gun, and for a few moments I didn't move; I didn't even breathe.

"What makes you say that?" I asked.

He didn't answer, just stayed bent over, his hands resting on his thighs, staring at the ground.

"Jackson," I said. "What makes you say that?"

"I grew up hearing Leland's name. Not from Toy, never from Toy . . ."

He calls his mother by her nickname?

"The neighbors, though. I heard what an asshole he was, what a racist, how he was supposed to be haunting the house next door. I didn't pay any attention. Why would I? Fuck 'im. But then I heard from Kayla about how Leland was supposed to be threatening some asshole from the grave, no offense."

"Why would I be offended?"

"So I looked him up. I found photos of him online because of the robbery—and I knew. The second I saw his photo I knew. Don't you think I look like him?"

"No."

"Look past my skin tone, I'm lighter than my mom. Look past the hair. My eyes. My mouth. My chin. I look like Leland Hayes."

"No, you don't."

"I know, McKenzie. I fucking know."

"Did you ask your mother about this?"

"Why? So she can lie to me some more?"

"Do you honestly believe that your mother had sex with Leland Hayes? Because I've known her for all of five minutes and I don't believe it, not a word."

"I didn't say it was consensual."

"You think she was raped and she didn't tell anyone?"

"Who would she tell? McKenzie, I was born almost exactly eight months after Leland was killed."

"Jackson, you need to talk to your mother about this."

He shook his head.

"Is this why you think the money he stole belongs to you? Do you think it's your goddamn inheritance?"

He shook his head some more.

"You pointed a gun at me, you little prick."

He glared at me with an expression that suggested he didn't like the word. I shoved him hard enough that he nearly fell down again.

"You talk shit about your mother and now you feel insulted?" I shoved him again. "You pointed a gun at me. Why?"

"I can't find Ryan on the internet," Jackson said.

"He hasn't been out of prison long enough to leave a footprint."

"You know where he is."

"Do you expect me to lead you to him? Why? So you two can have a family reunion? He's your half brother if what you're telling me is true."

Jackson didn't have anything to say to that.

"God, kid," I said. "You need to talk to your mother."

"Will you help me?"

"Do you need a lift to her place? Is that what we're talking about?"

"Never mind."

"Go home, Jackson."

"Give me back my gun."

"No."

"It's mine."

"Tell you what—I'll give it to Toy. You can get it from her."

"What are you going to tell her?"

"I'm sure she'll ask how I got your gun. If she does, I'll tell her the truth."

"Don't do that. Don't you do that."

"If you want to talk to her first, I'll be happy to give you a head start. Now get out of here."

Jackson wandered into the center of the parking lot and made for the exit. Halfway there he paused as if he wanted to come back and plead his case some more, then thought better of it and kept walking. As he left the lot, my cell phone started playing "West End Blues."

I read the caller ID—Ryan Hayes.

Why not? my inner voice asked.

TWENTY-FOUR

The big-box store where Ryan Hayes worked was all but deserted when I arrived. He had lingered at the entrance while his fellow employees filed out, telling them that he was waiting for a ride. "What's her name?" some of them asked, and Ryan would look embarrassed like a teenager might; only he wasn't embarrassed. He was frightened.

"McKenzie, I need this job," he had told me over the phone.

He also said that a trio of older men had appeared at the customer service desk an hour earlier and asked for him. Thinking that they were just that—customers looking for service—the clerk directed them to the milling department. Only instead of going there, they asked when Ryan would be getting off. She told them what time the store closed, and the men left. She mentioned all this to Ryan when she saw him later. He contacted me, using the number on the card I had given him.

"I didn't know who else to call," he said. "The only friends I have are the people I work with, but if I keep bringing trouble into the store . . ."

I holstered the SIG Sauer to my hip—I had removed it when I went to see Bobby and Kayla—and drove to meet him.

The lights near the entrance were as bright as they had been when the store was open. Ryan stood beneath them while he waited for me, wearing a heavy coat, gloves, and a hat yet still rocking against the cold. He was clearly visible from a distance, which I thought was a good thing. I didn't want the boys to become confused.

I pulled to a stop in front of the door. Ryan hesitated. I powered down the passenger window of the Mustang and called to him.

"Get in," I said.

He hesitated some more but eventually opened the door, and slid inside.

"This is a really nice car," he said.

"Thank you." I gestured at the half-dozen other vehicles still in the parking lot. "Are any of these yours?"

"No, I take the bus."

I put the car in gear and drove slowly toward the exit. One of the parked cars was started and began following behind us; it didn't turn on its headlights until it reached the street.

"What are we going to do?" Ryan asked.

"I thought we'd let them follow us around for a bit and then ask them what they want."

"You know who they are, right?"

"Like I told you over the phone, if I had to guess, I'd say it was Stuart Moore, Fred Herrman, and Ted Poyer."

"My father's friends."

"In a manner of speaking."

"How do you know them?"

"We had a lengthy conversation this afternoon."

"About what?"

"The money."

"That's why they want to mess with me, too, isn't it? The money."

"If they had just wanted to say hello, they would have walked right up to you and said hello."

"Bastards are as rotten as my old man."

"I got that impression, although . . ." I told him what Poyer had told me at Everson's Cozy Corner.

Ryan thought about it and said, "I don't believe him."

"It's possible that they don't mean you any harm whatsoever," I said.

"What do you think?"

"Better to be safe than sorry. Are you hungry? I know where we can get some great tacos."

Ryan stared at me as if he were trying to see inside my head.

"I could eat," he said.

"My treat," I told him.

When Ryan went to prison, Minnesota had about half a dozen breweries and no brewpubs; I'm not even sure they had been invented yet. Now there were more than one hundred and seventy, and while they were all happy to pour you a glass or a growler of craft beer in their taprooms, only a handful actually had kitchens. The rest made do by teaming up with an astonishing array of food trucks that served everything from soup to lutefisk in their parking lots or from the curbs outside their front doors. Some of them were so popular that customers tracked their movements on their smartphones. One of my favorites was called Street Legal Tacos.

The way I explained it to Ryan, when most people think tacos they envision crunchy hard corn shells or fluffy flour tortillas loaded with beans, cheese, veggies, and ground beef. Street

Legal stuffed their smaller tortillas with breaded and fried tilapia or slow-cooked pork or grilled chicken or chopped sirloin and very little else. I ordered one of each plus a side of Mexican slaw. Ryan didn't have a preference, so he ordered what I ordered.

He took a bite and said, "This is incredible."

"Right?" I said.

Street Legal was parked in the lot next to a brewpub that had taken over an aging factory inside an industrial park located along the northern border of Minneapolis and St. Paul; I had no idea which city we were in. Because of the fourteen-degree temperature, most of the truck's customers carried their food into the pub. Ryan and I were the only people sitting at one of the picnic tables arranged outside. That way I could carefully watch the car that had followed us there while pretending not to. It wasn't difficult. The industrial park was virtually empty at that time of night; nearly all of the traffic was centered on the brewpub.

The car was parked near the entrance to the parking lot a long way from the front door of the pub. The occupants remained inside while Ryan and I ate, their car running, its exhaust snatched away by the wind. They waited and waited and waited some more, and I began to wonder what they were waiting for. Did they think that once we were finished eating, Ryan and I would grab a couple of shovels and start digging?

Customers came and went, cars entered and left the parking lot, and still they waited. I sent Ryan inside the brewpub. Five minutes later, he returned with a couple of glasses of beer, which was illegal. The alcohol was supposed to be kept inside. No one said anything, though, so we sat at the table sipping our beverages. Ryan said the beer tasted better than the ones he had when the BOP first kicked him loose, yet he still wasn't sure if he liked it. I told him my girlfriend wasn't a beer drinker either, that she preferred European ciders. Ryan said he thought he might give one a try sometime.

After a few minutes, the doors of the parked car opened and three men slipped out. I couldn't recognize them from that distance in the dark, but as they approached I realized that I had guessed right—Moore, Herrman, and Poyer. They approached in a semicircle as if they knew what they were doing.

A fourth man emerged from a car parked several spaces to the left of where the boys had parked. He came up from behind them. My first thought was that he was a brewpub patron. I changed my mind when I noticed that he kept pace with the boys, neither losing nor gaining ground on them.

"Anything happens, I want you to make a run for the brewpub," I said. "Call for help."

"Why?" Ryan asked. "Don't you think I can take care of myself?"

"You just got out of the joint. Do you really want to deal with the cops?"

Ryan watched me watching the three men approaching us. I kept thinking of him as being much younger than he was. Probably that was a mistake.

"What are you going to do?" he asked.

"Whatever is necessary," I said. "Don't worry about it. I got this."

Since when? my inner voice wanted to know.

Moore, Herrman, and Poyer halted well beyond striking distance yet close enough so that we could talk without shouting, the picnic table between us.

The fourth man halted twenty yards behind them, lingering in the shadows.

"Hey, guys," I said. "What's going on?"

"We want to talk to Ryan," Stuart said.

"Go 'head."

"In private."

"Ryan, do you want to talk to these guys in private?"

"No," Ryan said.

"Don't be like that," Stuart said. "It's been a long time since we've seen each other."

"You say that like we're friends," Ryan said. "When were we ever friends?"

"We watched you grow up."

"You watched my old man abuse me every day of my life and did nothing about it except sometimes you laughed."

"Listen, kid—"

Ryan stood slowly.

"Who the fuck are you calling kid, you shriveled up old bitch?" he asked.

Herrman raised his hands like a man saying no to a second helping of pie. He did it so abruptly that my right hand sought the butt of the SIG Sauer. I released the gun when I was convinced that he meant nothing by it. Poyer saw me do it, though, and took a step backward.

"I'm sorry," he said. "I'm sorry, Ryan, for what happened to you. We should have looked out for you a little bit, and we didn't. We should have come forward when you were arrested to tell the court what Leland was all about, and we didn't. We're sorry."

"Yeah, we're sorry," Stuart said, although I didn't believe him.

"I'm sorry," Poyer said. "We didn't come here to dredge up bad memories."

"Why did you come looking for me?" Ryan asked.

"Cuz of the money, why else?" Stuart said.

"If I knew where it was, do you think I'd share it with you?"

"We were thinking if you didn't know where it was that maybe we could, you know, compare notes," Poyer said. "Try to figure it out. It would be good for everybody. You could take half; we'll split the rest."

The way their heads snapped toward him, I knew that neither Stuart nor Herrman had agreed to Poyer's plan for dividing the wealth, yet they didn't debate the issue.

"In that case, why don't you grab something to eat and join us?" I said. "They have a steak taco with lime and cilantro—"

"If I wanted spic food I woulda stayed on the East Side," Stuart said.

"That's why you have so many friends, Moore. Why your neighbors are so happy whenever they see you. You bring joy wherever you go."

"Fuck you, McKenzie."

Ryan edged past me and circled the picnic table. It took him three long strides to reach Stuart. Stuart started to speak but was unable to get a word out before Ryan slapped him hard across the face.

He wasn't wearing gloves, and the sound of skin striking skin was so loud that the guys in the food truck forty yards away looked up.

Stuart glared at Ryan with such anger that I knew if he had a weapon he would have killed him.

"Just so you know, my best friend is Hispanic," Ryan said. "Mexican, actually. His family is from Juárez."

"I don't give a fuck who—"

Stuart was interrupted when Ryan slapped him again, this time with the back of his hand. He stumbled backward. The expression on his face changed from anger to something else. From where I was standing, it looked a lot like fear.

"You were about to say something," Ryan said. "Go 'head."

"If you think—"

Ryan slapped him a third time. Stuart crumbled to his knees and cradled his face. He went into another one of his coughing fits.

"I can do this all day," Ryan said. "How 'bout you?"

Stuart shook his head. There were tears in his eyes.

Ryan turned and retreated to his place at the picnic table. He winked as he passed me.

Okay, not a kid. Not even close.

"Guys," I said. "You know, it takes a lot longer to heal when we get older. I play hockey—"

"Do you really?" Ryan said.

"When I was a kid I'd take a hit and get up the next morning like nothing happened. I take the same hit today and I feel like I've been run over by a truck. So instead of slapping each other around, whaddaya say we talk it over?"

Apparently Stuart didn't like the idea. He stood slowly, turned, and stumbled back toward the car; he looked as if he might die before he got there. The way he kept coughing, I was willing to take bets.

Herrman turned his gaze to Stuart, to Ryan, and back to Stuart again before he followed after.

They both passed the fourth man, who simply stood in the parking lot, his arms folded over his chest like a theatergoer wondering if this was it, if this was what he bought a ticket for.

I know you, my inner voice said.

Poyer, on the other hand, walked right up to the picnic table where Ryan and I were standing, the table between us.

"Aren't you afraid your friends will leave without you?" I asked.

He patted his jacket pocket where his keys were.

"My car," he said. "Ryan, I am sorry. I'm as big an asshole as you think I am. I wish I could go back and change that, but you can never go back, can you? I am sorry, though. As for the money—we didn't have anything to offer you. No ideas at all. The only thing we could think of was that Leland stashed it at your house, but the FBI searched that, didn't they?"

Ryan nodded.

"We were hoping you knew about secret panels or some shit," Poyer added.

"I don't," Ryan said.

"Yeah. We figured you were more likely to help us than we were to help you. I'm sorry. I know I keep repeating myself, but I don't know what else to say. I hope you have a good life for the rest of your life." Poyer offered his hand. "I hope you're happy."

Ryan shook Poyer's hand. "You, too," he said.

Poyer turned and walked back toward his car. Ryan and I watched him go. The fourth man waited until Poyer passed him before walking toward us.

"C'mon, McKenzie," Ryan said. "I'll buy you a beer."

We went inside the brewpub. It was loud and filled mostly with people who were fifteen to twenty years younger than we were. We found an unoccupied table, and Ryan ordered a beer made with puréed blueberries, strawberries, blackberries, and raspberries, which he claimed was the best thing he ever drank. Hell, maybe it was. I had a pint of pale ale that was nothing special.

It was brighter inside, and it gave me a chance to study Ryan's face under the lights without him noticing, especially his eyes, mouth, and chin.

Jesus, my inner voice said. *He does look a little like Jackson Cane. Could they really be half brothers?*

Should I tell him? I asked myself. Tell him about Jackson?

Hell no. Of all the things that are none of your damn business, this has to be number one on the list.

"So what happens next?" Ryan asked.

"I'm sure the boys will keep their distance from now on. Especially Stuart. I doubt you'll ever see them again."

"That's not what I meant."

I gestured toward the door. Ryan turned, and together we watched Karl Anderson glancing right and left as if he were searching for his friends. Instead he found us, smiled, and moved toward our table.

There was a tinge of concern in Ryan's voice when he asked, "Who's that?"

By then Anderson had reached the table.

"Gentlemen," he said. "I got tired of waiting. It's cold outside, you know?"

"Ryan," I said. "This is Karl Anderson. He's a private investigator working for Hannah Braaten."

"The psychic babe?"

"You know what?" I said. "That's what they should call the TV show. Not *Model Medium*."

"I agree," Anderson said. He gestured at an empty chair. "May I?"

I gestured at the chair, too, and Anderson sat.

"What TV show?" Ryan asked. "Wait? You work for Hannah? What are you doing here?"

"I followed you from the store. Actually, I followed the three men who were following you. For a second there, I thought I might have to step in, but you guys seemed to have the situation under control."

"But why were you following us?"

"The money," I said.

"Goddammit, I don't know where the money is," Ryan said. "Besides, why should you care?"

"Hannah—" Anderson said.

"The woman doesn't take no for an answer, does she?" Ryan said.

"It's because of the TV show," I said.

"What TV show?" Ryan repeated.

"They're hoping to make a TV show about Hannah's life—"

"You mean like that woman in New York?"

"She thinks that finding the money would go a long way toward getting it on the air."

"God, it's like a curse," Ryan said. "The curse of Leland Hayes. Forget TV. It should be a goddamn horror movie."

Just then the waitress returned, and we ordered more beers, including an IPA for Anderson. Ryan wagged a finger at the detective.

"You've been spying on me," he said. "Stop it."

"For what it's worth, I'll tell Hannah and Esti tomorrow that this is a waste of man-hours," Anderson said.

Ryan sipped more of his fruity beer and glanced around the brewpub as if he were at the Minnesota State Fair and this was the best people-watching he had ever encountered. Finally he turned back to Anderson.

"What should I do?" he asked.

Anderson shrugged.

Ryan turned his eyes on me. "McKenzie, what should I do?"

"I don't know. I'm at the point now where I'm ready to ignore all this nonsense and hope it goes away."

"Except now I really want to find all that money," Ryan said. "I didn't at first, but after everything that's happened . . ." A girl walked past, and Ryan's eyes followed her as if he had never seen one before. "I'd just like to put a period to it, you know? Slam the door on the first half of my life and get on with the rest, try to make it better. Finding the money and turning it in would help me do that."

"I get that, I really do," I said. "Only, I am fresh out of ideas."

Ryan continued to watch the young men and women sitting and standing around us.

Eventually he said, "I have a thought."

"Feel free to share," Anderson told him.

"What would you do if the old man were still alive?"

"I'd probably conduct close surveillance," I said. "Make sure there was nowhere he could go that I couldn't follow. And then I'd do whatever I could to rattle his cage."

"Why?"

"Leland wasn't the trusting type. I don't mean just trusting other people, I mean trusting the world. He'd want to stay close to the money. He'd want to be able to check on it every once in a while to make sure that it was still there. If you could agitate him enough, make him wonder enough, eventually he'd lead you straight to it."

Anderson hoisted his beer. "I like it," he said.

"Rattle his cage, then," Ryan told me.

"The man's been dead for twenty-some years. I wouldn't know how to go about it."

"There's a show I watch on the Travel Channel," Ryan said. "About ghost hunters. What they do, they set up their equipment at all these haunted hotels and asylums, whatever, and then they try to provoke the ghosts by insulting them, calling them names, questioning their manhood. 'Course, whenever they get a reaction, they start screaming like little girls. No—that's not fair. Most little girls are way braver then those guys."

"Do you think that Leland would respond to that kind of treatment?" I asked.

"He was a bully. I know bullies. Trust me on this, McKenzie. Most of the men I knew inside were bullies. They had to prove that they were tough every day of their lives. None of them could take an insult."

"Do you think insulting him would rattle Leland's cage?"

Ryan shook his head as if he weren't sure of the answer.

The three of us sat drinking quietly for a few minutes. Ryan spent most of them watching the young people around him. He was so engrossed that he didn't notice the waitress approach and ask if he wanted another beer.

"Sir?" she said.

"Hmm?"

"Sir?" She pointed at his near-empty glass. "Another?"

"Umm, no, I'm good, thank you."

The waitress moved away.

"I'm a 'sir' now," Ryan said. "I'm nearly forty and I've never been twenty."

I didn't know what to say to that, so I didn't say anything.

Ryan finished his beer and set the empty glass down on the table.

"Do you know what rattles my cage, McKenzie?" he asked. "Pretty girls."

TWENTY-FIVE

Shelby Dunston tucked her legs beneath her the way she does and smiled brightly.

"Who is the prettiest girl you know?" she asked.

"You mean besides Nina?" I said. "Your daughter Victoria, unless Katie's also in the room, in which case it's a tie."

Victoria called to me from the kitchen, "Good answer."

"I remember when you would have said it was me," Shelby said.

"It's time to face facts, Shel—the years have not been kind to you."

That's when she threw a pillow at me.

"Stop flirting with my wife," Bobby said.

"I just called her an ugly old crone," I said. "How is that flirting with your wife?"

"Ugly old crone?" Shelby repeated.

Victoria stepped into the living room and knelt at the coffee table between me and her mother. She had half a dozen sections from a tangerine on a small plate and started eating them one at a time.

"Personally, Mom, I think you look fantastic," she said.

"Thank you, honey."

"For a woman your age."

"There's an old saying," Shelby said. "If Mama ain't happy, ain't nobody happy. Mama ain't happy."

"They're just teasing you, Shel," Bobby said. "The truth is, if everyone looked like you do, the word 'beauty' would lose all its meaning."

"Oh, that's good," Victoria said.

I tossed the pillow at Shelby's smiling face; she caught it and set it in her lap.

"I wish I had said that," I told her.

"I'm sure you will," Bobby said. "The first chance you get."

"Okay, Mama's feeling a little bit better," Shelby said. "But you still haven't explained what you're going to do."

"About what?" I asked.

"About Leland Hayes. How are you going to rattle his cage?"

"There's a line that's been repeating over and over again in my head for at least a week now—'there is no such things as ghosts.'"

"I would think that after everything that's happened, you might have changed your mind."

"That's the thing, Shel—everything that's happened. Kayla Janas almost convinces me, the way she led us to Ruth Nowak, her sincerity. But what I've learned about Hannah Braaten and her private investigators and how her business works makes me think it's a load of BS like Bobby believes."

"Leave me out of it," he said.

"What? You're wavering?"

"Robert Nowak and Molly Finnegan are in jail today. Yesterday, they weren't."

"Still . . . My involvement in all of this goofiness began

because a couple of psychic mediums said that Leland Hayes would pay his son, and I don't know who else, a hefty sum of money if they would shoot me. I can't help but notice that no one has actually tried to do that yet. Except for maybe the guy in the red Toyota Avalon."

"Yeah, about that," Bobby said. "Turns out it was Frank Fogelberg's ex-wife's teenage lover who pulled the trigger. We have video of him snatching the Avalon from the Holiday Stationstore and a fingerprint on the back of the car's rearview mirror. Detectives Gafford and Shipman gathered him up late this afternoon. I'm waiting to hear if he did it on his own or if she put him up to it."

"Teenage?" Shelby asked.

"Old men date young women all the time," Victoria said. "Why can't old women?"

"Good point."

"You." Bobby pointed at his daughter. "You need to pick your friends carefully."

"Why is it that every time someone else commits a criminal act, it's Katie and me who get a lecture? I mean, all of our lives you've been doing this."

"Wait," I said. "You couldn't have told me about Fogelberg when I walked through the door? You had to wait for, what, a convenient time to slip it into the conversation?"

"Suddenly I'm the town crier?" Bobby said. "I'm supposed to deliver the news?"

"If Fogelberg's shooting was a coincidence—how often does that happen, by the way? If Fogelberg's shooting was a coincidence, that just adds fuel to the fire. Or rather takes fuel from the fire. Is that a thing? The point is, it's just another reason to leave Leland's cage unrattled."

"Do it for the money," Shelby said.

"Hell with it."

"The fun, then."

"What fun? All I've gotten out of this adventure so far is bad dreams."

"Bad dreams?" Victoria asked.

"It's why your father keeps lecturing you. He doesn't want you to do dumb things like we did."

"What do you mean, 'we'?" Bobby asked. He knew what I was referring to; he just wanted to move the conversation into less painful territory.

Thank you, Bobby, my inner voice said.

"The thing is," I said, "I'm now inclined to agree with Nina that it's all a load of hooey."

"Where is Nina?" Victoria asked.

"At the club, where else?"

"What are you going to do?" Shelby asked.

"About Nina?"

"About Leland Hayes. You're not just going to give up."

"Give up what, Shel? A ghost hunt? C'mon." I gestured toward Bobby. "Tell her."

He shrugged in reply.

"*Only those who attempt the absurd can achieve the impossible*," Victoria said. "Albert Einstein."

"You know, there's such a thing as being too smart for your own good," I told her.

"No, there isn't."

"Besides," Shelby said, "what do you have to lose?"

"My self-respect."

"Phfffff."

"Okay, letting that slide, even if I did decide to do this, I'm left with the obvious question—pretty girls aside, how do you rattle a dead man's cage?"

"The same way you rattle the living," Bobby said. "You threaten what's important to them."

Hannah Braaten seemed pleased to hear from me. Esti not so much. They agreed to meet me in the living room of their home on Mount Curve Boulevard, which was much tidier than it had been the previous time I was there. Hannah sat in a stuffed chair opposite me. She was wearing a short skirt and a tight top, and she kept crossing and uncrossing her long, shapely legs while we chatted.

Do you think she's trying to rattle your cage? my inner voice asked.

Esti sat in a chair positioned at a ninety-degree angle from mine, giving me the unpleasant feeling that I was being out-flanked. She was wearing jeans and a sweater and hardly moved at all.

Karl Anderson was nowhere to be seen.

"It seems to me that we did not part on the best of terms the last time we spoke," Hannah said.

"I'm not entirely sure that's going to change," I said.

"Then why are you here?"

"I'm asking for your help."

"Help to do what?"

"Contact Leland Hayes."

"I told you before," Hannah said. "I can't just Google his name. I can't dial him up. I need a personal attachment to draw on. Besides, haven't you heard? I'm a phony."

"I never said that."

"Your friend Commander Dunston did, in no uncertain terms."

"It's possible he's had a change of heart."

"Is that because we found Ruth Nowak?"

"*We* didn't find her. Kayla Janas did."

"Are you calling me a fake again, McKenzie?"

"No, I'm calling you a journeyman ballplayer. It's like the kid they have playing shortstop for the Minnesota Twins these days. He's pretty good. Actually, he's very good. But he ain't Derek Jeter."

"I don't know who that is."

"Hall of Fame baseball player, won four World Series rings with the Yankees. Never mind."

You're killing me, Hannah.

"My point is, you're inconsistent," I said. "From everything I've learned, though, you are honest. An honest woman. Except for the Leland Hayes reading. Only I think that was all about impressing the TV producer who was sitting in your audience at the time and taking notes."

I expected an explosion of anger and denial. Instead, Hannah stared quietly at me before turning her head and staring quietly at her mother. Esti squirmed for a few moments before rising to her feet.

"It was necessary," she said. "I told you."

"It was not necessary," Hannah replied. "I told you."

"It all worked out."

"No, it didn't."

"Yes, actually," I said. "It did."

Both women looked at me.

"It was on the Monday before the reading that you heard from the production company that they would begin immediately filming a pilot episode against the possibility of turning your life into *Model Medium.* You wanted to give them something dramatic, but not all of your readings are dramatic, are they? Sometimes you can't deliver. Only this time you felt that you needed to deliver, so you hired Karl Anderson to hedge your bet.

"Anderson researched the people who were going to be in the audience and found Ryan. He quickly learned about Leland, about the robbery, about me, and about the missing money. It took him all of a half hour to get the grisly details. I know because that's how long it took me to do the exact same thing with my own computer. It was just too good a story not to tell, a dramatic way to end your reading. How could you not use it?"

"It was all my idea," Esti said.

"I have no doubt, but it was Hannah who did the emoting."

"I'm embarrassed by all of this," Hannah said.

"The thing is—you hired Anderson the *day* before the reading. Not the week before, not the month or the year before. Based on that and what others have told me about you and your readings, I'm willing to believe that this was a one-off."

"Mr. Anderson doesn't work for us anymore," Hannah said.

As far as we know.

"Still, you need to be careful about stepping over the line," I said. "I speak from experience, Hannah. You step over the line once, it becomes easier to step over it again."

She nodded, yet I had no idea if she understood what I was saying or not.

"It probably would have all ended there," I said. "Except you didn't count on Shelby Dunston being at the reading, a dear friend of mine. Like any good actress, though, you played out the scene for your audience—the woman with the clipboard. A couple of days later, I went to see you. 'Course, you were expecting that; Shelby had warned you. That's why you had me checked out, why you were ready with Agatha and Mr. Mosley."

"No," Hannah said. "They did come to talk to you. I didn't fake that." She took a deep breath and finished her thought with the exhale. "I don't expect you to believe me."

Hannah is just trying to salvage at least some of her reputation, my inner voice said. *Unless . . . If Anderson didn't tell*

Hannah about Agatha and Mr. Mosley . . . Did they really come from the other side to see you?

I shook my head to dislodge the thought.

"I saw Anderson at the Minnetonka Community Education Center," I said.

"That was my doing," Esti said. "After the way Ryan attacked my daughter at the reading, I wanted him to watch out for her. She wasn't supposed to know."

"I didn't know," Hannah told me. "Not until you came to the house that one time. I didn't tell you I knew Anderson because . . ."

"You were embarrassed," I said.

"Yes. And a little ashamed."

"When I told you that a second psychic medium had confirmed what you told Ryan at the reading, that surprised the hell out of you."

"To say the least."

"Kayla Janas *is* Derek Jeter. She has crazy skills, you've said so yourself. She was able to conjure Leland—I still don't know how that's done. Except Leland didn't actually tell Ryan that he'd trade the cash for my head until *after* Ryan asked if that's what Leland wanted. It was you who planted the idea in Ryan's head, and it was Ryan who gave it to Leland through Kayla. Fortunately, Ryan's a good guy despite everything that's been done to him. He blew Leland off. Only I didn't."

"No."

"That's when you saw another opportunity."

Again Hannah stared at her mother.

"A way to score more points with the production company," I said. "Find the money. Save me from Leland Hayes. On camera. That's why you kept Anderson on the job. That's why you invited me to the festival in time to hear your less scrupulous pals chant my name."

"I didn't do that," Hannah insisted. "I promise you I didn't." She turned to glare at Esti. "Mother?"

Esti shook her head vehemently. "No," she said. "No. McKenzie, whatever you think of me, you must know I'm not so foolish as to involve so many people in a, in a . . ."

"Lie?" I asked.

Could that be real, too—all those psychics chanting your name? Is Leland that powerful? Maybe you should rethink this.

"In any case, finding the money, that's what the meeting at the Dunston house was all about," I said. "At least that's my story, and I'm sticking with it. You might have your own narrative, and you're welcome to it. Reveal it on TV. I don't care."

Esti sat down. She folded her hands and set them on her knees and leaned forward.

"What do you care about?" she asked.

"I want to find the money, too. Partly for Ryan's sake. Partly for my own reasons."

"Will Ryan agree to a reading?" Hannah asked.

"No. We had a long discussion about that last night. He wants the money found because he thinks it'll help him move on with his life. Except he doesn't want to have any contact with his old man ever again. Plus, he's concerned about being seen on TV, about having his name mentioned on TV. He said his life was tough enough already without him becoming even more of a curiosity."

"Are you willing to go on TV?" Esti asked.

"I was afraid you'd ask that question. I really don't want to. I was hoping we could do this on the sly, and after we find the money, then you could bring in the TV people, give an interview, explain it all as dramatically as you like in front of the cameras while you hand over the cash to the insurance company."

"No," Esti said.

"No?"

"If you want us, if you want Hannah, to do this, then you'll do it on our terms."

"Mother," Hannah said.

"I insist."

"I could always go to Kayla Janas," I said.

"The inexperienced twenty-year-old girl who sees dead people?"

"She's very gifted," Hannah said.

"She's a child playing with matches."

I would have been annoyed by the argument against Kayla except I had already made it in my head before I called the Braatens.

"Okay," I said.

"Okay, what?" Esti wanted to know.

"I'll appear on TV, but only if it's absolutely necessary."

"It will be. You'll need to sign some releases before we begin."

Are you really going to let them make you a reality TV star?

"As long as it's understood that Ryan's name is not to be mentioned, not once," I said. "You need to guarantee that."

"This is all moot anyway," Hannah said. "I cannot bring Leland Hayes over from the other side if he doesn't want to come. Even if Ryan had agreed to cooperate, I still wouldn't be able to make that promise."

"Leland isn't on the other side," I said. "You told me yourself that you thought he was earthbound."

"It doesn't matter where he is. I still need someone or at least something with a personal attachment to him, and even then, what if he refuses to come through, what if he refuses to answer our questions? I'm the one who's going to look like an idiot—like a fraud. Not you."

"That's where the threat comes in."

"How do you threaten a spirit?"

"I tell him that if he doesn't do what we ask, I'll buy his house and burn it to the ground, let the Minneapolis Fire Department use it for practice."

"What are you talking about?"

"Didn't I tell you?" I asked. "I know where the sonuvabitch lives."

TWENTY-SIX

I drove to Ventura Village earlier than I needed to—and no, it wasn't because I was excited about the prospect of being on TV. It's true that I did spend more time than usual making sure I was dressed just right and my hair was just so, but that was because, well, appearances matter, don't they?

There were two vehicles anchored in front of Leland's battered old house, a small white delivery truck that looked like something the U.S. Postal Service might use and a sparkling black TV van. I parked a half block in front of them and walked back. A young woman with a clipboard, the same woman I had seen at the Twin Cities Psychic and Healing Festival, moved to intercept me.

"You're McKenzie," she said.

"Yes."

She offered her hand and I shook it.

"I'm Jodi Steffen," she said. "I'm one of the producers. There's something that I need you to do for us, but not now. In a minute."

We moved closer to Leland's place. The sun was starting to dip toward the horizon, and it bathed the house in a golden light. Instead of making it appear inviting, though, the sun highlighted the structure's many imperfections, giving the impression that it was even more dilapidated than it was. There was a man recording the imperfections with a handheld camera, shooting them from a wide variety of angles. Meanwhile, a second man was setting up a bank of shaded lights on thin telescoping posts behind the branches of a tree, the lights aimed at the front windows of the house.

"What's he doing?" I asked.

"That's our special effects guy," Jodi said. "He's setting up GV shots that'll make the house look dangerous—trees casting menacing shadows on the wall, that sort of thing. We're trying to create an ominous atmosphere."

"I find it disconcerting that you have a special effects guy on a reality TV show," I said.

"You've never heard of the observer effect?"

"The theory that the mere observation of a phenomenon inevitably changes the phenomenon?"

"Listen, general view shots are anything that looks interesting, that helps create a sense of time and place," Jodi said. "They tell the viewer what part of the year it is, if it's hot or cold, what kind of neighborhood we're in, if the structure is old or new or in between, if the place is scary. They provide the editors with the necessary tools to help build an edit, to help move the story along."

I found that disconcerting, too, but kept it to myself.

We passed the white truck. It was filled with lights, grip stands, small sandbags to keep the stands from falling over, tripods, rags and frames, reflectors, generators, electric cords, microphones, and a lot of other equipment I couldn't identify.

Eventually we halted a few yards away from Leland's house. A well-dressed woman, only a few years older than Jodi, was standing in front of it just outside the cyclone fence. The FOR SALE sign had been moved so that it was peeking over her shoulder. There was a camera with a microphone mounted on its side pointed at her face. A second camera was pointed at Hannah Braaten. Hannah was holding a notepad that she kept referring to while she spoke to the woman. The director I had met at the psychic festival was sitting in a canvas chair a few feet behind Hannah and the first cameraman. He was wearing a set of headphones and watching a small video screen mounted on a folding table that revealed what the cameras were filming.

Jodi pressed an index finger against her closed lips and gestured for me to follow her to the black TV van. The door was open, and we leaned inside. There was a man sitting on a stool in front of a bank of CCTV monitors. He was also wearing headphones.

"This is Mission Control," Jodi said.

I could hear Hannah and the other woman talking over a pair of speakers as they were being filmed. It turned out that the woman was the real estate agent who had given the production crew permission to film Leland's house. She was telling Hannah that she'd heard all of the stories—the rumors, she called them—about the house being haunted. It was her hope that Hannah and her people would finally disprove the rumors once and for all.

"Nothing we do is scripted," Jodi said. "The only moments that are planned are the scenes between the performers and the people they're interviewing. That's standard while shooting any story, even documentaries. We use the interviews to establish the history of the house, to set the scene, if you will. If you had arrived a few minutes earlier, you would have seen the interview we filmed with a neighbor who claims to know the history of the house, who knows some of the people who have been haunted."

"Big black guy with a dog the size of his foot?" I asked.

Jodi smiled in recognition. "He was great," she said. "Very colorful. We'll need to bleep half the things he said, but that's okay. It adds"—she paused as she searched for the correct word—"authenticity."

"I hope you don't expect me to give an interview," I said.

"No. We have something else in mind for you."

"Something else?"

"You're going to be the innocent. The naïve victim lacking experience with spirits and the bad things they can do who seeks the help of the heroic yet world-weary psychic medium."

I started to laugh. The tech working the control panel turned his head and glared at me. I put my hand over my mouth to tone it down.

"You think I'm joking," Jodi said. "Hannah said that you would be in the house with her, that we'd hear you and film you. She also said that you absolutely refuse to be questioned on tape. So how else are we going to introduce your character? How do we justify your involvement? The plan is for Hannah to record a voice-over that'll explain your part in the story. You won't say a word. Okay?"

"I thought you said that all of this was unscripted."

"We don't fake anything, McKenzie. Other crews do; we all get that. But we don't. At the same time, the execs put pressure on us to keep it interesting and action-packed. That's what all the GVs are about. That's a major reason why we film at night, forget the so-called witching hour.

"You might have also noticed if you watch these kinds of shows that only the highlights of a paranormal investigation are shown on-screen. The audience doesn't see us sitting in the dark all night waiting for something to happen. They don't see us poring over hours of video to discover if anything paranormal was captured by the cameras. To keep it exciting without altering the actual content, we employ narrative tricks. Which brings me to what we need you to do . . ."

A few minutes later, I was in my Mustang and slowly circling the block. Jodi wanted to film me driving down the street, parking, stepping out of the car, and walking toward Leland's house.

"We're establishing your character," Jodi said.

All I could think of was a story I once heard about the actor Steve McQueen and how he practiced getting out of his Mustang over and over again so that he'd look super cool while doing it in the film *Bullitt*.

I positioned my own Mustang at the end of Leland's street and slowly drove down it, refusing to look at the camera as I had been instructed. I eased into the designated parking spot, turned off the engine, and opened the door. I slipped out, twisting my body so that I was looking over the roof of the Mustang toward the camera beyond. I paused for a moment as if searching for something, eased along the side of the car until I had room to close the door, and moved slowly toward the house, all while trying to keep my face expressionless. I left my leather jacket unzipped despite the crisp winter air, and it flapped open as I walked.

Jodi slowly applauded when I reached her. "Very nice," she said.

"Are you sure? I could do it again."

What is wrong with you? my inner voice wanted to know.

"We're good," Jodi said.

Next, they filmed me walking up to Hannah, who was waiting next to the gate of the cyclone fence. I extended my hand and she shook it, and we chatted, and then she hugged my shoulders as if we were friendly, yet not quite friends.

"How was that?" I asked.

Have you no shame?

After being assured that there was no need for retakes, I zipped my jacket and leaned against the fence. The sun was close to setting. Hannah moved to the director's side and they began a spirited back-and-forth. The director kept glancing at his watch. Hannah kept gesturing with her hands as if there were nothing to worry about. After a few minutes, the director called my name and offered his hand. I walked up to him and shook it.

"Good to see you," he said.

"Thank you."

"Are you clear on what you need to do?"

"Not even a little bit."

"Good. I like spontaneity." He glanced at his watch some more. "Now if only the other one would show up."

The other one?

The director turned his back to me and spoke to no one in particular. "Are we almost ready?"

A member of the director's crew said that he had just finished placing the cameras and infrared motion sensors in the house.

"Show me," the director said.

The two men and Jodi retreated to the black van.

Hannah smiled at me. "Nervous?" she asked.

I surprised myself by answering, "Yes. I'm not used to all these cameras."

"You're supposed to pretend that they're not there."

"I'll try."

"Are you sure it's just the cameras, McKenzie?"

"What else?"

"You're the one who wants to talk to Leland Hayes."

"What I want . . ."

"Yes?"

"Remember when we first met? I told you I was confused and that I didn't like being confused. I'm hoping after tonight I will be unconfused."

"One way or another."

I had to chuckle at that.

"Yes," I said. "One way or another."

"Once we get inside, follow my lead. I'll explain things as we go. It'll be all right. I'll take care of you."

"Because I'm so innocent and naïve?"

I didn't laugh the way I had when Jodi first told me what my role in the TV show would be, yet I did smile.

"Big, brave, gun-toting ex-cop—were you ever innocent, McKenzie?" Hannah asked.

"Probably not. You?"

"Oh, yes. When I was younger. Sweet and innocent. Not now, though. McKenzie, the stories I could tell."

"Where's your mom?" I asked.

"She'll be along."

A few moments later, a car parked across the street and Esti Braaten stepped out of it. She was followed by Kayla Janas.

I glanced at Hannah.

"She wants to learn," Hannah said. "She wants to help. Besides, if I can't read Leland, maybe she can."

"Aren't you afraid that Kayla will discover you're not the superstar you claim to be?" I asked.

"I've never claimed to be a super anything."

The women joined us. Hannah and Esti hugged as if they hadn't seen each other for a while, which I found refreshing.

"I'm sorry we're late," Esti said without offering an explanation.

Hannah and Kayla also hugged.

"Are you okay?" Hannah asked.

"No," Kayla answered. "This is all new to me, like I said when you called, so no."

"You'll be fine. Just keep yourself open. Tell us everything that you see or hear."

"I'll try."

"There are no locks on the door, Kayla. No one is forcing you to stay. If you start to feel that it's too much for you, just walk out of the house. All right?"

"All right."

Kayla turned toward me. "McKenzie," she said.

She hugged me close, but it wasn't about affection. Kayla needed someone to hold on to. She told me why in a whisper.

"I'm scared to death," Kayla said.

"Don't be," I said. "Didn't your parents tell you? There's no such thing as ghosts."

Kayla thought that was funny, but Hannah and Esti didn't.

I released the young woman when Jodi motioned me toward her.

"Take this," she said.

I took the electronic device that she offered and bounced it in my hand.

"What is it?" I asked.

"An EVP recorder."

"EVP?"

"Electronic voice phenomena. We use these to digitally record what the spirits say to us. We might not hear the spirit, but these devices are specially designed to capture voices and sounds that can't be detected by the human ear, voices and sounds that are considered paranormal or supernatural. We hope. Mostly everything we record will turn out to be a whole lot of nothing, just mushy static. Sometimes a producer will be convinced that he heard a spirit speaking from the other side and will replay the mush over and over again, telling us what it says. Then he'll throw up a caption on the screen that translates the mush and replay it a half-dozen more times and the audience will say, 'Yeah, I hear it, too.' But mostly it's mush."

"Are you saying that sometimes producers will fake EVPs?"

"I'm saying that you sometimes hear what you want to hear, and what you want to hear more often than not helps support a dramatic plot line. Except, this one time—I'll never forget it. We recorded an EVP of a woman's voice, speaking clear as a bell. She said, 'He's sleeping now.' It was captured near a fresh, unmarked grave that turned out to be a newly buried child. It still raises goose bumps when I think of it.

"Sometimes you wonder if it's your imagination, if it's playing tricks on you," Jodi added. "Other times . . . I've been involved with paranormal crews that have been able to document the existence of the spirit world over and over again. 'Course, scientists rarely accept our evidence as valid, for the simple reason that crews are all over the place. Nobody's tools, methods, and practices are standardized. Our conclusions can't be reproduced in a laboratory; they don't lend themselves to peer review. That doesn't make them any less true, though. McKenzie, I have a very good feeling about tonight."

Well, that makes one of us, my inner voice said.

"Okay," the director said. "Is everybody here? Is everybody ready? Hannah? Kayla? McKenzie?"

Jodi and I joined the others at the gate. Hannah had picked up a large leather purse and draped it over her shoulder. I didn't think she was going on a shopping expedition to the Mall of America, so I asked her, "What's in the bag?"

"A few necessities."

"Necessities?"

"A girl never knows when she'll be invited on a long weekend in Vegas."

Esti shook her head and turned away. Everyone else laughed.

By then the sun had set and night had settled over the Cities. There were plenty of streetlights, of course, and porch lights, and the lights streaming from the windows of houses where normal people were going about their business. There were no lights on in Leland's house. The show would be filmed in complete darkness with night-vision cameras because—drama.

I stood staring at the house for a few beats before I realized that Hannah and Kayla were doing the same thing. I wondered if they were thinking what I was thinking—that they would look fabulous in the spooky pale green color that night-vision cameras film in, while I'd probably resemble the alien in *Predator.* I found the idea disconcerting.

When did you become such a Hollywood baby?

"Remember," the director said. "Don't speak unless you have something to say. Audio is everything. We want to hear the things that go bump in the night, and we can't if the performers are talking nonstop."

I turned on the EVP recorder and stuffed it into the pocket of my jacket.

"Cameras," he added. "Keep on the performers when they're talking. If the editors hear a vital conversation and want to cut it into the show, they're not going to be happy if you're busy filming an empty corridor. Hannah, it's all about you. Make it happen. All right. Let's have a good show."

TWENTY-SEVEN

One of the cameramen went first. There were three of them, and I never learned their names, so I referred to them by letter.

Camera A went to the front door, opened it, stepped inside the house, and closed the door. A few moments later, the director said, "Action"—swear to God—and Hannah, Kayla, and I walked to the front door. I opened it and held it open for Hannah and Kayla, allowing them to pass through the doorway in front of me because that's how I was raised, not because I didn't want to go first.

Camera A had positioned himself halfway up the staircase, filming us from an overhead angle as we entered the house. The door was closed and we eased into the living room. There were a couple of chairs, a tall side table, and a sofa left over from the previous tenants, yet we didn't use them. Hell, I could barely see them. There was a brief pause as Cameras B and C entered the house and took positions around us. I used the time to close my eyes and cover them with my hands, applying slight pressure with my palms. It was something that Shelby had taught me from her caving days—it's supposed to help your eyes adjust to the dark, allowing them to see better with limited light sources.

"Keep yourself open," Hannah said. I presumed she was talking to Kayla. I leaned against the back of a chair.

Minutes passed without anyone else speaking; I couldn't tell you how many. Finally I removed my hands and opened my eyes. It wasn't as if the place was suddenly lit up like Target Field during a Twins game, yet now I could see shapes, if not distinct features, and the shadows on the floor and walls that trembled along with the branches outside.

Hey, my inner voice said. *The special effects guy is really good.*

"Do you feel it?" Kayla asked. "The air? It's very heavy."

Hannah stood in the center of the room, her arms raised and her head bowed as if she were calling on an ancient deity.

"Yes," she said. "There's real darkness here."

"I've never felt this before," Kayla said. "It's like the air is pressing down on me."

"I have. Kayla, you can feel this?"

"Yes."

"You told me that you communicate with the spirit world through words and pictures, not feelings."

"That's what normally happens. This—I don't know how this is happening. I can't explain it. What is it?"

"Nothing I haven't felt before."

"Hannah . . ."

"Evil, Kayla. We're in the presence of evil."

That caused my head to snap toward her. Hannah had lowered her arms and was adjusting the bag hanging from her shoulder.

That was pretty dramatic, my inner voice said.

Is she telling the truth or playing to the cameras? I asked myself.

The cameras, my inner voice said. *We hope.*

We remained standing in the darkness for I don't know how long. I had lost all sense of time. It could have been a few minutes; it could have been much longer. I flashed on something that Einstein once said to help explain his theory of relativity—*When you are sitting with a pretty girl an hour seems like a second. When you sit on a red-hot stove a second seems like an hour. That's relativity.*

I wondered what Einstein would think of what I was doing now.

He'd think you were nuts, my inner voice said.

"Something," Kayla said.

"What is it?" Hannah asked.

"There's an older man. He's angry, a very, very angry person. He's all about taking what's his, about keeping what's his. I can't see him."

"He's hiding."

"He enjoys tormenting the people who live here," Kayla said. "The people who live here—he doesn't like them. He doesn't like their religion or their politics or philosophies or—he doesn't like the color of their skin. He communicates with them mostly by yelling. He yells at them all the time. He yells at them so loudly that the furniture shakes. He stomps around so that it makes things move."

I heard a loud thud from the kitchen and jumped about six feet into the air.

Better hope a camera wasn't recording you, you wuss.

"What was that?" I asked aloud. It was the first time I had spoken since we entered the house, and I was surprised by the sound of my own voice. It was like I hadn't heard it before.

"Probably the wind," Hannah said.

"There is no wind tonight. Not much, anyway."

"Not every little noise we hear in the dark is the spirit world trying to contact us. Take a deep breath. Try to relax. I learned a long time ago that it's nothing until we can prove it's something."

Yeah, you innocent, naïve victim, you.

"But let's take a look," Hannah said.

Camera C went first, positioning himself in the kitchen so that he'd have good video of Hannah, Kayla, and me as we entered the small room. I went last again, just to be polite.

The kitchen had a white refrigerator and a white stove, reflecting what little light seeped through the narrow windows. The cabinets were made of dark wood. At least they seemed dark. There was nothing lying on the floor or on the kitchen counters or in the sink, nothing that might have fallen from the walls.

So what made the noise?

I was tempted to pull out my cell phone, turn on its flashlight, and take a good look around, but I knew no one would like it.

We stood in the kitchen listening for more noise. We heard none.

"The atmosphere isn't as oppressive in here," Kayla said.

"I read somewhere that the kitchen is the most important room in the house," I said. "It's where families gather not just for nourishment but also for conversations, debates, arguments, and hugs."

The way both women ignored me, I had the distinct impression that my words would end up on the cutting room floor.

Oh, well.

After a few moments, Hannah directed us back into the living room.

"You can really tell the difference, can't you," Kayla said. "This room is so filled with negative energy."

"Can you still feel the old man?" Hannah asked.

"No."

"Neither can I."

Hannah reached into her bag and pulled out what looked like little more than a black box in the darkness.

"What's that?" I asked.

"It's a K2 EMF meter. It detects electromagnetic energy, which often indicates the presence of spirits."

"Does that really work?"

"Yes, although . . . not tonight." Hannah dropped the meter into her bag and turned toward me. I couldn't make out the expression on her face, yet I could feel her eyes. "You're on."

I stepped into the center of the room knowing that both Cameras B and C were pointed at me.

"Leland," I said. "Leland Hayes. We've never been properly introduced. My name is McKenzie. I'm the guy who shot you in the head."

I waited. I saw nothing, heard nothing, felt nothing. I decided to explain myself.

"You robbed an armored truck, stole over half a million dollars, and hid it somewhere," I said. "When we caught you, you decided to shoot it out. You decided it was better to kill a handful of police officers than surrender. I'm the one who shot you in self-defense. You know what? They gave me a commendation for it. What do you think of that?"

Are you talking to Leland or the cameras?

Both, I decided. I wanted to justify myself to the TV audience. I didn't want them to think I was a killer.

We waited in the darkness in silence.

"I'm not receiving anything," Hannah said.

"Neither am I," Kayla replied. "If anything, the air seems lighter, somehow."

"Let's try the cellar."

We moved back into the kitchen and found a narrow doorway that led to a wooden staircase to the basement. Once again a camera went ahead of us. I didn't know which one; I had lost track of who was who. This time I made to go first, but Hannah put a hand on my shoulder and held me back so that Kayla could descend the stairs in front of us. Hannah went second. Suddenly I felt better about myself for going third.

The cellar was completely empty. It had a cement floor, stone walls, and the floor above us for a ceiling. If there was any heat on in the house, it had been set only high enough to keep the water pipes from bursting. The temperature in the basement was particularly low, although I couldn't see my breath. I put my bare hands in my pockets to keep them warm, fingering my car keys in one and the EVP recorder in the other.

"I'm not feeling anything," Kayla said. "The air is even lighter than it was in the kitchen."

"I'm feeling something," Hannah said.

"What?"

"Cold. It's freezing down here. Holy mackerel, turn up the heat."

"Don't cold spots sometimes indicate the presence of a spirit?" Kayla asked.

"Yes. They also indicate that it's December in Minnesota and we're standing in a basement."

Kayla and the cameramen chuckled, and I thought, The woman has charisma, you have to give her that.

"McKenzie," Hannah said. "Try again."

"Hey, Leland, you worthless piece of dog excrement—"

Editing your language for the TV cameras, are you?

"I met some guys you knew the other day. I wouldn't call them friends, though. You didn't have any friends, did you, because you were such a miserable SOB. You know what they

(281)

did for your funeral? Nothing. No one cared about you. Not even your own kid. They cremated your body and dumped your ashes into a hole because that's what you deserved."

My words echoed in the empty cellar and faded to nothing. Again we waited in silence. Again nothing happened.

"Let's get out of here," Hannah said.

We climbed the stairs. As we climbed, Hannah whispered to me.

"Next time ask about the money," she said.

We went up to the ground level and hung around some more. Eventually Hannah decided we should climb the stairs to the second story. Once again a cameraman went first.

We crowded into the smaller of the two upstairs bedrooms. I assumed that it had been Ryan's.

"It's not nearly as bad in here," Hannah said. "The darkness. It's almost like—it's like a bubble of light."

"There's a woman," Kayla said. "She's very quiet, very timid; she's afraid."

"Can you see her?"

"No. I can't see her, I can't hear her, but I can feel her. This isn't how it's supposed to work."

"In the past, the spirits wanted to talk to you," Hannah said. "They wanted you to help them communicate with their loved ones. Tonight, they're hiding."

"Please," Kayla said. "We're not here to hurt you. We're here to help you. Please, talk to me. Please, tell me who you are."

Hannah had retrieved the K2 EMF meter from her bag and turned it on. The first three lights—green, light green, and yellow—were flashing.

"Keep talking," she said. "Ask what her name is."

"Who are you?" Kayla said. "Why are you here? Are you trapped in this house? Please, let us help you."

"Are you Judith?" Hannah asked. "People called you Judy?"

All five lights on Hannah's meter flared, including dark red, which indicated the highest concentration of electromagnetic radiation.

And then they went out.

Hannah actually shook the meter, but the lights would not go back on.

"Who's Judith?" Kayla asked.

"Leland's wife. She died of cancer years before Leland was killed."

"Then why is she here?"

One of the cameramen said, "Look at this."

We turned toward his voice. On the floor in the center of the bedroom across the hall was a light; we could see it flashing through the doorway.

"What is that?" I asked.

"It's an infrared motion detector," Hannah said. "Did anyone go into the bedroom? Anyone?"

There was no answer.

"C'mon," she said.

We piled into the empty room—the master bedroom, I decided—and circled the motion detector. It was encased in an off-white plastic container that was designed to hang on a wall, but it had been set on its back on the floor by a member of the production company's crew. Instead of a white light, it flashed bright orange-yellow, and I wondered if the color had been chosen by the special effects guy. No one attempted to turn it off.

"Oh my God." Kayla was clutching her temples with both hands. "Immediate headache in here. Horrible headache."

Hannah clutched her stomach and sank to her knees.

"Bad nausea," she said. "I feel vertigo. I feel dizzy. There's too much negative energy in here."

"The older man . . . Ohhh, this person is not stable."

"It's a trap," Hannah said. "He wanted us to come into this room. This is where he's strongest."

I felt none of the things that Hannah and Kayla were feeling, and hadn't since we entered the house, yet watching the young women being assaulted by a ghost . . .

Are you listening to yourself?

I was compelled to act.

"Hey, Leland, you gutless chickenshit," I said. "Is this all you've got? You're too cowardly to take on a man, so you attack a couple of girls? That's about your speed, isn't it? You're nothing but a coward. Even now that you're dead, you're too much of a pussy to take responsibility for your actions. You ruined your life and your ruined your son's life and now you're hiding in the dark—"

Kayla was on her knees and doubled over. I could see the anguish on her face in the flashing light.

"We need to get out of here," she said.

"No," Hannah said. "Not yet."

"Tell you what I'm going to do," I said. "I'm going to buy this worthless pile of crap you call a house, and after I search every square inch of it for the money you stole, I'm going to burn it to the fucking ground and then me and your kid are going to piss on the ashes. You can be the dumb ghost haunting an empty lot where the meth-heads go to shoot up."

The motion detector flew off the floor and hit me square in the chest.

It was like being hit with a slap shot except I wasn't wearing a chest protector.

The force of the blow pushed me backward against the wall; the motion detector clattered across the floor.

I clutched my chest because of the pain.

My first thought: Who did that? Was it a cameraman?

Then I felt it in my gut; it was like feeling the effects of being punched hard without actually feeling the blow itself.

I felt it again.

And again.

How is this possible?

I became nauseous; I began hacking as if I were about to vomit.

That felt a lot less agonizing than the searing pain vibrating in my head.

I fell to my knees.

"Stop it," Kayla screamed. "Stop it."

She moved to my side and cradled my shoulders in her arms, trying to protect me the way a mother might. She really was that caring. I immediately felt the pain and nausea leaving me—and entering Kayla.

This is crazy!

Kayla began hacking the way I had.

"What kind of man are you?" she shouted.

Leland answered by shoving her away. Kayla fell backward at least a half-dozen feet.

She landed on the floor.

I could hear her head bounce against the bare wood.

I could hear her gasping as if she suddenly couldn't breathe.

I knelt next to her. She was writhing in pain. I attempted to cradle her the same way she had embraced me.

"Stop it," I yelled. My head twisted back and forth as I searched for an adversary, someone I could hit. All I found was cameramen pointing their cameras at us, as impassive as furniture. "Leave her alone."

Hannah crossed the room and eased me out of the way like an EMT who was taking charge. She reached into her bag and pulled out what looked to me in the flashing orange-yellow light like a bundle of tobacco leaves held together with blue yarn. There was a cheap lighter in her hand, the kind you find on display at the checkout lines of gas stations. She set fire to the leaves, waited a moment, and then blew out the flame.

"What is that?" I asked.

"Sage."

The leaves began to glow like tobacco at the end of a lit cigar, the smoke creating a cloud above us. It had a kind of fragrant, woodsy scent like cedar.

Hannah slowly waved the smoldering sage above Kayla's writhing body.

"St. Michael," she said, "archangel, invincible in battle, be our guardian against the wickedness and the snares of the devil. Oh glorious prince of the heavenly armies, by the power of God, cast into hell Satan and all the evil spirits that wander the world."

Kayla's body slowly calmed. She rolled on her side. Her breathing became less erratic and raspy.

"Come to the assistance of those whom God has created in His likeness and whom He has redeemed at great price from the tyranny of the devil. Our protector, to you the Lord has entrusted the souls of the redeemed to be led into heaven. Crush Satan beneath our feet. Bind him and cast him into the bottomless pit that he may no longer seduce the nations."

Kayla rolled onto her back. She became still; her breathing was under control. She closed her eyes, opened them, took a deep breath, and spoke with the exhale.

"Smudge stick?" she asked.

"White sage. From my own garden."

With Hannah's help, Kayla sat up and massaged the back of her head.

"That hurt," she said.

"I can imagine."

Kayla gestured at the smoking bundle of sage in Hannah's hand.

"Do you have one for me?" she asked.

Hannah handed the smoldering stick to Kayla, reached back into her bag, and produced a second stick. She set it afire with the same cheap lighter, blew out the flame, and watched it smoke.

Hannah smiled at Kayla, Kayla smiled back, and I thought, They're sisters in battle.

"Let's go get him," Hannah said.

Hannah helped Kayla to her feet and began chanting.

"In the Name of Jesus Christ, our God and Lord, of blessed Michael the Archangel, God arises; Satan and his cohorts are scattered. As smoke is driven away . . ."

"As smoke is driven away . . ." Kayla repeated.

"So are they driven . . ."

"So are they driven . . ."

It reminded me of the call and response of the old blues songs that came out of the bayous of Louisiana.

"As wax melts before the fire . . ."

"As wax melts before the fire . . ."

"So the wicked perish at the presence of God."

"So the wicked perish at the presence of God."

Hannah and Kayla circled the room before moving into the hallway, their smudge sticks leading the way, and I realized, They're chasing the sonuvabitch.

"We drive you from us . . ." Hannah chanted.

"We drive you from us . . ." Kayla repeated.

"Unclean spirits, all satanic powers, all infernal invaders, all wicked legions . . ."

They went into the smaller bedroom, waved their smudge sticks some more, then headed down the staircase. Cameras A, B, and C did their best to keep up while trying to stay out of the way.

"Most cunning serpent, you shall no longer deceive the human race . . ."

Once downstairs, they circled first the living room, then the kitchen, then the living room again, Hannah leading the way, Kayla following behind while repeating every word that her mentor uttered.

"Be gone, Satan, inventor and master of all deceit, enemy of man's salvation . . ."

Together, the two women slowly pushed toward the front door.

"Tremble and flee when we invoke the holy and terrible name of Jesus . . ."

They stopped at the door.

"Lord, grant us Thy powerful protection and keep us safe and sound."

They stood looking at each other for a few beats.

"He's gone," Kayla said.

"I should hope so."

"I don't feel anything. The house is clear."

Hannah actually laughed a joyous, gleeful laugh like I've heard from athletes after they've won a close championship game.

"You have to admit, that was fun," she said.

"Are you crazy?" Kayla asked.

But I noticed that she was laughing, too.

"Will Leland return?" Kayla asked.

"He might. We'd have to do a full-blown cleansing, possibly even an exorcism, to finally send him to the other side. Or he may realize that there's nothing to gain by staying here and go to the other side on his own, finally taking responsibility for his actions."

"Wait. The woman. She's still here."

"Negative spirits will not stay when you stand up to them like we did," Hannah said. "It's like what they say about bullies—stand up to them and they'll back down; they lose their power if you don't cower before them, if you stay confident and strong. Good spirits, though, they're not threatened by us. They won't leave unless they want to."

"I can see her."

"Where?"

Kayla gestured toward the center of the living room.

"What do you see?" Hannah asked.

"She's very beautiful. And young. And . . . I can hear her. Her name is Judith. Judy. Yes, yes we will—she wants us to follow her. McKenzie, she wants you to follow her."

She does?

Kayla led us across the living room and into the kitchen. We went straight to the back door and opened it. Camera A tried to get in front of her, but Kayla was having none of it, so he had to film her from behind.

She paused outside the door and waited for Hannah and me and the camera guys to catch up. It was darker in the backyard than the front, yet there was still enough light to make out the spotty lawn, the cyclone fence, the garage, and the small, worn wooden shed that was leaning heavily against it.

"Oh," Hannah said. "It's very peaceful out here. Not like inside the house at all."

"Follow us," Kayla said.

Us?

She led us across the lawn, halting in front of the shed. She pointed at the door.

"In there, McKenzie," Kayla said.

I stared at her for a few beats. It was like my brain had turned off; I didn't understand what she wanted me to do.

"Judy wants you to open the door," Kayla said.

"McKenzie," Hannah said, "it's all right. I feel only lightness and warmth."

Cameras A and B positioned themselves so they could see me grab the latch and yank the door open. I looked inside the shed. It was empty. There weren't even any tools on the floor or hanging from the walls.

"I don't understand," I said.

"Judy says you've been kind to her son."

To Ryan?

"She says you deserve to know what happened. She wants you to know what happened."

"About the money?" I asked.

"Judy wants you to look beneath the floorboards."

For a moment, excitement thrilled through my body. I stared at the shed, then practically leapt toward it. I fell to my knees and began pulling at the boards even as my inner voice chanted, *The money, the money . . .*

The boards didn't budge, though. I felt along the edge of the floor and discovered that they had been nailed to a two-by-four. I was able to work my fingers underneath the two-by-four and lift. The entire floor came up like a trapdoor, and I rested it against the back of the shed. All I saw beneath the boards, though, was a black hole. I pulled my cell phone from my pocket, turned on the flashlight, and looked again. There was plenty of dirt. And nothing else.

"It's empty," I said.

Kayla started laughing. I glared up at her.

"I'm sorry," she said. "It's Judy."

"Tell her the money isn't here," I said.

"She knows. But she says it was there. She said this is where Leland hid it before he was killed. It's gone now."

"I can see that."

"Leland didn't know the money was gone, though. That's why he stayed in the house. He thought he was hoarding the money for himself."

"Ask Judy why she stayed," Hannah said.

"She didn't. Judy says she came from the other side when we—meaning you and me—connected Leland with her son. She wanted to help protect her son from Leland."

Kayla laughed some more.

"Yes," she said. "I'll tell him."

"Tell me what?" I asked.

"Judy says she knows you're upset about not finding the money. She says you want to know what happened to it."

"I really, really do."

"She says you're a smart fellow. She says to think about it; you'll figure it out."

Jodi, the director, the crew, both Hannah and Kayla, and even Esti were positively delighted by how everything had turned out. They were all convinced that they had just filmed the greatest paranormal TV show of all time. I personally didn't have much to compare it to, but what the hell. Maybe they were right.

They all wanted to retire somewhere, anywhere, and bask in the glory of it. I understood. Nearly every hockey game I ever played ended with me and the guys heading to a neighborhood pub to talk it over. Esti invited the production crew to her house. She didn't have much to drink, she said, only wine and hard ciders. A member of the crew said he'd stop to get some beer on the way over there. I thought Esti and Hannah would probably have a guaranteed thirteen-episode contract before the evening was concluded.

The company seemed genuinely disappointed when I

begged off; they figured that I was in a mood about not finding the money. The director shook my hand and said I was a helluva performer. Hannah, Kayla, and Jodi Steffen each hugged me in turn. Esti did, too, but I don't think her heart was in it.

I gave them all a wave, headed for my Mustang, and fired it up. I drove off. After a few turns, making sure that I was well out of the sight of Leland's house and the crew, which was now busy packing up its gear, I pulled over and parked.

I slipped the EVP recorder out of my pocket. I would have returned it to the production crew if someone had asked me to, but no one had.

It took a few moments before I was able to figure out the controls. Finally I rewound the recording until it was at the beginning of the ghost hunt and hit PLAY. And listened hard. Especially when the recording reached the part where Judy was supposed to be speaking to Kayla.

I didn't hear a damn thing except for—what did Jodi call it? Mushy static.

TWENTY-EIGHT

It was midmorning when I stepped inside Good Spirits. The store had just opened, and there were no customers. In fact, I couldn't detect any movement in the Witch District at all. If I had learned anything from my haunted house adventure, though, it was that witchcraft and ghost hunting are more or less nighttime pursuits.

I stood just inside the entrance and glanced around. A voice called to me.

"I'm back here, McKenzie," it said.

I moved toward the rear of the store. LaToya Cane was sitting at her desk and working with her laptop.

I wondered how she knew I was there.

Then I noticed all the small CCTV monitors stacked in front of her.

Well, duh.

"I don't know what to say to you," she told me.

"I'm not sure what to say to you either. Have you spoken with your son recently?"

"Yes."

I pulled his Smith and Wesson out of my pocket, along with a clear plastic sandwich bag filled with his bullets. I offered them to Toy.

"I don't want these," she said.

"Then toss them in the trash."

"McKenzie . . ."

"I promised Jackson that I would give his gun to you."

"He told me."

I waited for a few beats. Finally Toy took the gun and the bag from me and dropped them into the bottom drawer of her desk. She closed the drawer with a bang.

"What else did he tell you?" I asked.

"He said you were going to accuse him of all kinds of terrible things."

"No, I don't think so."

"Oh?"

"Toy, I think the kid's a little messed up, but it's nothing that can't be fixed by a long conversation with his mother."

"What would we talk about?"

"That's none of my business."

"Then why are you here?"

"The money," I said. "The $654,321 that Leland Hayes stole from the armored truck. And hid. The money he said he would pay to have me killed. It was all bullshit."

"I thought it might be."

"For one thing, he didn't have the money."

"No?"

"Someone else found it, God, twenty-some years ago. 'Course, Leland didn't know that. At least we don't think he knew that. That's why he was haunting the house where he lived all this time. Was haunting—past tense. Hannah Braaten and her associates went over there the other day and cleared the house, sent him on his way."

Toy didn't so much as raise an eyebrow. A house exorcism was apparently an everyday occurrence in her world.

"The money," she said.

"It was hidden beneath the floorboards of an old tool shed that was leaning against Leland's garage. It was the same shed where Ryan used to go to get away from his father, the shed where he kept a photograph of his mother. The only thing he had of her, he once told me. The photograph that he sent you to find, that you did find, that you brought to him before he was sent to federal prison in Kentucky."

Toy stared at me long enough for it to become uncomfortable.

She wants to know what you're going to do, my inner voice told me.

I'm not going to do anything.

Tell her.

"You did very well with the money." I gestured at my surroundings. "All of this. A kid in an expensive, top-ranked college. Way better than what most people would have done, I think."

Toy chuckled and sighed at the same time.

"It helped that I lived in Ventura Village," she said. "Minorities are more apt to deal in cash; we don't have the same access to credit cards and checking accounts as you do. I'd buy groceries, pay my rent, fix my car or buy a new one, and no one wondered where the money came from. It allowed me to save all of my paychecks, make investments even, and cash deposits, too. Never more than a couple hundred dollars a week. The bank tellers probably thought I was a whore, that I earned the money selling myself. I didn't care. I was saving and investing nearly $30,000 a year—after taxes."

"All of it right beneath FinCEN's nose," I said.

"There were a few setbacks, but I stayed patient. When

the time came, I moved out of Ventura Village into Standish-Ericsson. It was a much better neighborhood, more middle-class, yet not a place where I would stand out. I kept saving. I kept learning. Eventually I reached the point where I was able to open this store, and because of the store, I could pay $66,000 a year to send Jackson to Macalester College without anyone wondering how I managed it. The store's doing very well, too, by the way."

"Did Jackson know what you were doing?"

"No. It never occurred to him to wonder about it. He was a child, why would he? Now that he understands about economics, about how money works, he thinks I'm the smartest woman he knows. At least he did."

"What does he think now?"

"I don't know," Toy said. "The way he looks at me . . ."

"You might tell him the truth. I'm impressed. I'm sure he would be, too."

"Can I tell him one thing without telling him the rest?"

"You mean about his father?"

"Did Leland's spirit tell you about that, too?"

"I kinda guessed. Between what you told me and what Ryan told me—it's a very sweet story when you think about it, you and Ryan."

"I doubt Jackson would agree."

"It's a better story than the one he's living with."

"What story is that?"

You went too far.

"McKenzie?"

It's none of your business.

"McKenzie, tell me."

You might as well, now.

"Jackson thinks Leland is his father," I said. "He thinks Leland raped you."

Toy recoiled at the words and then slumped down in her chair to the point where I thought she might fall out of it. Her body shuddered. I rested a hand on her shoulder. Instead of giving her comfort, though, it sent an electric charge through her. She jolted upright and shrugged my hand away.

"This is what he meant by you saying terrible things," she said.

"Yeah."

"I'm glad you told me, though. I needed to know this."

"What are you going to do?"

"I can't tell Jackson the truth until after I've told Ryan. I called him, you know. Ryan. I talked to him at work. He seemed so happy to hear from me."

"You were one of the very few people in the entire world who was kind to him."

"Probably it would have been better if I hadn't been so kind," Toy said. "No. No. Without him I wouldn't have Jackson. It'll be all right. Ryan's coming for dinner tomorrow night; I still have no idea what I'm going to make. I'll decide what to tell him then."

"He seems like a nice guy," I said. "Young for his age."

"I got that impression, too, when I spoke with him." Toy gestured at her surroundings. "In a very real way, Ryan paid for all of this. I want to give him something in return; I need to give him something. I'm not sure a son is the right gift."

"A family?" I asked.

"That would be up to Jacks. Once I explain it all to him . . . Jacks is a good kid. No, he's a good man."

I started to move away from her.

"I wish you luck, Toy," I said. "I wish you nothing but good things."

"Wait," she said. "What now?"

"What do you mean?"

"About the money."

"Finders keepers, losers weepers. It's the law of the land. You can look it up."

"Are you trying to be funny, McKenzie? The FBI isn't going to forget about this."

"Actually, it already has."

"The bank . . ."

"It's not the bank's money. It's the insurance company's money, and they wrote it off twenty years ago. The only reason they're interested now is because of me, and telling them the true story—hell, even I don't believe it. Besides, it would only screw up their paperwork."

"I doubt it would bother them, though," Toy said.

"Don't worry about it. Your name won't be mentioned. I'll take care of it."

"Why would you do that?"

"Because I love happy endings. You're going to find a way to be happy, aren't you, Toy?"

"Lord above, I hope so."

The Meritage promoted itself as a chef-driven, award-winning French brasserie, which is why I wore a sports coat, slacks, and dress shoes when I went to meet Maryanne Altavilla there for lunch. She ordered oysters on the half shell to start and escargots à la Bourguignonne to finish.

"I could get used to this," Maryanne said.

I had a chicken salad croissant and said, "Meh."

"So to what do I owe the pleasure?" Maryanne asked.

"What do you mean?"

"You didn't bring me here because you enjoy my company."

"Actually, Maryanne, I enjoy your company very much."

"McKenzie . . ."

I reached into my pocket, found the flash drive she had given me, and set it next to her water glass.

"Are you trying to tell me something?" she asked.

"The money is gone."

"Define gone."

I curled all the fingers on my right hand, brought them to my lips, kissed the tips, and let fly.

"Poof," I said.

"All right, now define poof."

"Leland Hayes hid the money immediately after he stole it," I said. "He didn't plan on getting caught, but if he had been, he figured he could collect the cash after he got out of prison. 'Course, if he had done twenty-five years like his son that would have worked out to only $26,172.84 per year, but nobody said Leland was smart. Anyway, we know all this because he went to the East Side of St. Paul immediately after the robbery looking for a place to hide. His friend turned him down, and so on and so forth.

"Now, there weren't many places where he could have hidden the money, places that he trusted. There was his house, of course. But the FBI searched it pretty thoroughly."

I pointed at the flash drive.

"So did your SIU," I said. "But what they didn't search was the small tool shed that was leaning against his garage. Or, more to the point, they didn't search beneath the floorboards of the small tool shed that was leaning against his garage."

"You're saying that's where Leland hid the money?"

"It's no longer there, in case you're wondering. We believe that it was eventually discovered by one of the dozen or more families that lived in the house after Leland departed from this earth, or at least someone close to one of the families. Anyway, poof."

"We?" Maryanne asked.

"Me and the psychic mediums."

Maryanne looked as surprised as I had ever seen her. After a few beats she managed to say, "Ummm."

"You seem skeptical, Maryanne."

"Imagine that."

"The dozen families—the reason so many people moved into and then quickly moved out of Leland's house during the past twenty years is that it was haunted."

"Haunted?"

"By the ghost of Leland Hayes. I went over there the other day with a couple of psychic mediums. We made contact with Hayes, and after a lot of this and that, we figured out about the money. One of the psychics believes that Leland didn't actually know the money was missing; that's why he had been haunting the house all this time."

Maryanne took a long sip of her drink. I don't think she was thirsty so much as she wanted to avoid saying what was on her mind.

"Long story short, the psychic mediums sent Leland to the other side, so," I added, "case closed."

"How did they do that?"

"Do what?"

"Send Leland . . ."

"Oh. They waved some sage around and chanted a few prayers."

"Sage? Like what I use in my world-famous butternut squash and sage pierogi recipe?"

"Except they burned it."

"You're kidding, McKenzie. Right?"

"Maryanne, you're one of the smartest people I've ever met and you didn't know that they cleared haunted houses by burning sage? Huh."

"I don't believe it."

"Which part?"

"All of it."

"Well, it's going to be on TV, so you know it's true."

"What do you mean; it's going to be on TV?"

"There was a production crew filming it all for a show that they're going to call *Model Medium.* I told them they should call it *MILFs.* You know, *Mediums I'd Like To—*"

"I get it."

"But they won't listen to me. They're hoping to have it on a cable network by next fall."

Maryanne started drumming her fingers on the tablecloth, so I knew she was thinking.

"If they so much as mention the name Midwest Farmers Insurance Group we will sue you personally, the mediums, the production company, the network . . ."

"We'll all have it coming, too."

"I still don't believe it."

"Hell, Maryanne, I don't believe it either, and I was there."

Maryanne kept drumming her fingers.

"I cannot put this into a written report," she said.

"If you want me to explain it all to your supervisor in person—"

"Shhhhhhhh, McKenzie. Absolutely not."

A few moments passed, and Maryanne resumed eating her lunch. What else was she going to do? After a few bites, she began to chuckle.

"What?" I asked.

"*MILFs.* I'd watch a ghost show called *MILFs.*"

JUST SO YOU KNOW

The show wasn't called *MILFs*, of course, or even *Psychic Babes*. It was titled *Model Medium* and featured "supermodel" Hannah Braaten as she went about her daily life, which somehow consisted of equal parts celebrity sightings, photo shoots, ghostbusting, and readings with ordinary people who wept a lot. Most of the readings seemed to be spontaneous and involved random men and women Hannah met along the way, although how anyone could have a chance encounter with a psychic medium who has a full camera crew following her around remains a mystery to me.

The episodes that seemed to create the most buzz, however—and the most on-demand views—were those that featured "fledgling" psychic medium Kayla Janas, whose skills seemed to blossom under Hannah's watchful eye.

Unfortunately, there was a problem with the chemistry between the two women. In the beginning, it was fine. However, as the episodes mounted up, Hannah started coming off less like Kayla's friend and mentor and more like a jealous older sister. And as pretty as Kayla was, standing in the shadow of Hannah's otherworldly beauty gave her an accessible girl-next-door vibe that had the audience rooting for her—and against Hannah. They call it the underdog syndrome. Plus, it was obvious that Kayla was a straight-up better psychic medium than Hannah. As a result, Hannah's show lasted thirteen episodes, an inauspicious number, before it was replaced by *Medium for Hire*, which was all Kayla all the time. It's still on the air. You can look it up.

But that was way down the road. Before Kayla became a cable TV star, she made one last visit to the Dunston home.

We had a dusting of snow just before the holidays to make all those people hoping for a white Christmas happy. Afterward, it started snowing and kept snowing all the way until May. The Twin Cities were buried under seventy-seven inches; some places in Minnesota had as much as a dozen feet. Snowfall records fell that had stood for over a century. What's more, it got cold and stayed cold. We set a record—thirty-six consecutive days with temperatures below zero, so the snow didn't melt. It just kept piling up. The drifts and mounds became so high that strolling along a shoveled sidewalk was like walking through a trench.

It was near the beginning of this weather pattern that Nina and I went to visit the Dunstons. Kayla arrived soon after. Shelby had been expecting her, of course, but Bobby had not, and while he was polite, if not downright charming, I could tell that her presence made him anxious. I began to wonder if any unsolved homicides or kidnappings had occurred recently that I was unaware of.

Only Kayla didn't come to see Bobby. Or Shelby. Or me, either, for that matter. She was there to speak to Nina.

"Why?" Nina asked.

"I have a message for you."

"I don't want to hear it."

"Ms. Truhler—"

"Besides, I don't even know if I trust you."

"I appreciate that," Kayla said. "But I only need a few minutes of your time. You don't have to believe a word I say."

"Then why should I listen?"

"The message isn't so much for you to hear as it is for your mother to speak."

"What does that mean?"

"Our sins aren't just wiped away when we go to the other side. We have to suffer the way we made other people suffer. We have to feel the pain we caused and accept the full consequences of our past behavior. We need to take responsibility. And whenever possible, we have to make amends to the people we harmed. We have to make restitution. That's why I'm here. Your mother needs to confess her sins out loud to the person she's hurt the most."

"She needs—?" Nina said.

"Walking around with the weight of her crimes, that really sucks. Living with the guilt and shame of her past wrongdoings—it's preventing her from moving on."

"You're saying you came here to help my mother, not me."

"Nina, your mom can't move forward without your help."

"That's just too damn bad."

"You can't move forward without hers."

"Be very careful, little girl."

"Self-centeredness must be replaced with awareness of other people," Kayla said. "Where we were selfish, we must be selfless. Where we were angry, we must be forgiving. Instead of indifference, we must begin to care. Otherwise our misery just goes on and on and on."

"Well, we can't have that, can we? By all means, let's talk about human misery with my mother."

Kayla glanced around her. Nina did the same. They saw

Shelby, Bobby, and me watching them. I didn't turn around to look, but I was willing to bet that Victoria and Katie were standing at the top of the staircase listening, too.

"C'mon," Nina said.

She took Kayla's arm and propelled her toward the front door. Kayla was already dressed for winter, and Nina grabbed her coat on the way. Once outside, they walked across the porch to the sidewalk near the street.

I couldn't hear them, yet I stood at the window and listened carefully just the same.

The conversation seemed intense. No one was screaming; of course, Nina had never needed to raise her voice to express her anger.

Shelby stood next to me.

She stroked my arm.

"It's going to be fine," she said.

"If it isn't, I may never forgive you."

The exchange ended. Kayla turned and started walking down the sidewalk. Nina watched her go.

She called to her.

Kayla stopped.

Nina walked up to the young woman, wrapped her arms around her, and hugged her tight.

They hugged for a long time.

Finally they parted. Nina kept her hands on Kayla's shoulders. She leaned in until their foreheads nearly touched. Nina spoke slowly, carefully. Kayla nodded as if she were being told something that she was relieved to hear.

They hugged again and parted again.

It was Kayla who was crying, not Nina, when they separated and walked off in opposite directions.

I left the window and headed for the Dunstons' front door.

Shelby took my arm.

"Wait," she said.

I went back to the window.

Instead of coming back inside, Nina crossed the street and walked into Merriam Park. She climbed the small hill, her boots sinking into the snow as she went, and took refuge among the oak trees there.

I moved to the door again.

Again Shelby stopped me.

"Not yet," she said. "Rushmore, you must trust me on this."

I wasn't sure that I did, yet Shelby was the only person in the world who was allowed to call me by my first name, so . . .

I gave Nina time alone. A lot of it. The sun slowly arced across the sky and started setting behind us.

"Okay," Shelby said.

I grabbed my coat and started out the door. I zipped up and put on gloves as I crossed the street. My shoes were smothered by the snow, yet I didn't care.

"Hey," I said.

"Hey."

Nina had been crying, though her tears were dry by the time I reached her.

"Thank you for not rushing over the first chance you got to ask if I was all right," she said. "To see if you could make it better."

"I figured you needed some alone time."

I owe you, Shelby.

I pointed at an ancient oak tree.

"Did I ever tell you about the time that I kissed Mary Beth Rogers right over there?" I asked.

"You did. Whatever happened to her, anyway?"

"I have no idea. I don't really want to know. By not knowing, I can always remember her the way she was that night. The way I was."

"It's a pleasant memory. Your first kiss. Why change it? The bad ones, though—the bad memories you need to do something about."

"Is that what Kayla told you?"

"In her way."

"What did she say about your mother?"

"I might tell you someday, but not now," Nina said. "Is that okay?

"Sure."

"It's not a deep, dark secret. It's just . . . I haven't really got it figured out yet."

"I understand."

"You've always been kind to me in that way. Understanding, even when you didn't."

"Actually, I would say it was the other way around," I said. "You putting up with me all these years, with my investigations, with my constant intrusions into other people's lives."

"You've done a lot of good, McKenzie. So many favors for so many people. Will you do one for me?"

"Of course. Anything."

"Don't say that until you've heard the favor," Nina said.

"Anything," I repeated.

"Will you marry me?"